HICKVILLE CROSSROADS

Hickville High * Book 5

MARY KARLIK

GPK Publication LLC

Cover art by Rebecca Poole at Dreams2media, images used under license.
Copy edited and formatted by Moonshell Books, Inc.

Hickville Crossroads / Mary Karlik—1st ed.

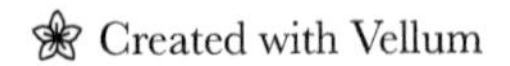

To Solveig and Carola MacCallum.
Thank you for helping me keep the Scottish bits authentic! (Anything that is not authentic is entirely my mistake.)

To Emily,
Thank you for joining me in the Fall Into a Book Giveaway!
I hope you enjoy Fraser's story as much I enjoyed writing it!
♡
Mary Karlik

Praise for Mary Karlik

"The ending. What can I say except I need to read the next book as soon as possible!"

Confessions of a YA Reader, on *Hickville Confessions*

"A really well done, engaging young adult romance with a mystery thrown in and I devoured it happily."

Wicked Reads on *Hickville Redemption*

In this series

HICKVILLE HIGH

Welcome to Hickville High
Hickville Confessions
Hickville Redemption
Hickville Confidential
Hickville Crossroads

Introduction

Frasier Anderson is one of the hottest teenage actors in the UK, but he's virtually unknown in the US. Now he's landed the leading role in a big-budget Hollywood film that could make him an international star.

So how do you prepare a Scot for a role as a Texas high school student? Embed him in a Texas high school. He only has to follow three rules:

No drama. No girls. And no telling who he really is.

Jenna Wiley is smart, funny, and has a few no-drama, no-dating rules of her own. Her friendship with new kid Ethan Smith is perfect and might even lead to something more. Except for a few things that don't add up. Like his mom being afraid to have company. Or their house, which is more staged than lived in. Or his sister, whom nobody talks about.

It all comes to a boil when Frasier's biggest secrets hit the tabloids and the paparazzi swarm Hillside with Jenna in their sights. Can Frasier convince Jenna that shy, goofy Ethan Smith is closer to real than the image the tabloids have created?

And can she ever forgive him for breaking the most important rule of all? Because for Jenna, when it comes to love and science, the truth is all that matters.

HICKVILLE CROSSROADS

1

Frasier Anderson

THE ODDS WERE AGAINST ME.

So how did a Scottish lad whose experience consisted of commercials and a four-year stint on a BBC period drama get the lead role in a major Hollywood film set in Texas? First, I nailed the American accent on my audition video. Second, I have mad horse-riding skills. I learnt to ride for my role on *Morlich Castle*—which doesn't exist, by the way—the castle, that is. And my skills? I can ride bareback at a full gallop shooting a rifle. Yes, the horses are very well trained, but it still takes skill, and I have a way with horses.

After *Morlich Castle* was abruptly canceled—long story—I thought my career was over. But then my agent came through with the audition and I got the part. I was virtually unknown outside the UK and this film—*Hashtag Cowboy*—had the potential to explode my career internationally.

I was excited about moving to the US for a few months. It would have been smashing to go alone, but I was seventeen and the film-industry laws stated I had to have a parent or guardian on set at all times. That would be Mum and Dad. Still, it was going to be crackin'.

I'd been to America before. L.A. New York. It was all fast and flashy. But Texas… do the girls really wear cowboy boots with those short little frocks? Or was it like kilts in Scotland? FYI, the only time kilts are actually worn is for formal occasions like weddings. Except for the tour guides. They always wear them. I think it must be a requirement.

I didn't have to be on set until mid-September, but I had to learn to calf-rope for my part and was scheduled to work with a trainer for a few weeks before filming. Mum and Dad wanted to see Texas before my schedule filled and I wanted to see girls in short dresses and cowboy boots, so we arrived in Austin in early August.

I knew Texas was hot, but stepping outside was like stepping into a sauna. The humidity made my shirt stick to my body and the heat pressed it there. It was feckin' thirty-seven degrees. Or in American terms, one hundred. Just saying *one hundred degrees* sounds like your skin should be melting.

We were booked at the Four Seasons near city center on the banks of Towne Lake—which looked more like a river than a lake. The first thing Mum did was to inquire about shops to buy cooler clothes. The first thing Dad did was retreat to the air-con in our hotel room. Me? I couldn't wait to explore the lake. Flip-flops, shorts, sunglasses, and I was ready to find those lasses. I made my way from the hotel to the path around the lake, but before my flops flipped, my mobile played Dad's ringtone.

"What's up?"

I got a sense before Dad spoke that he was in manager mode. His tone confirmed it. "I got a call from Peggy." Peggy Muller is one of the biggest agents in the UK. I had been lucky enough to snag her when I was six and doing porridge commercials. We've always gotten on well. She adores my parents and constantly reminds me how lucky I am to have "a decent set."

"And?"

"I need you back at the hotel. We're meeting with Michael and Dave in thirty."

Michael Ramos was the executive producer and well respected in the industry. The kind of man I did not want to disappoint. Dave Coleridge, the production manager, could have been a Red Bull superathlete for fast talking—if there was such a thing. The film was still in pre-production, so for them to call a meeting was a little unusual.

I watched two lassies in bikinis paddle-board past, and uneasiness rippled through me like the wake around their boards. "On my way."

By the time I'd changed and gone down to the cafe, my dad was already deep in conversation with them. They barely looked up when I approached the table.

Dad gestured for me to sit. "There's been a slight change in plans." Dad's expression was bland, which told me nothing.

"O-kay." I drew the word out and tried not to fiddle with the cutlery.

Dave leaned back in his chair and a salesman's smile formed on his lips. You know the kind—a little too wide—a little too fake. "It's good to see you again, Frasier. How's the accent coming?"

"I think okay." I used my newly acquired accent to show him.

"Nice. Our voice coach will work with you to make it Texan."

"I'm looking forward to it." I knew they hadn't called this meeting to talk about my accent. Eventually, Dave would get around to the real reason they wanted to have this wee chat. My job was to listen to what they had to say and dazzle them when I spoke. I relaxed back in my chair and fixed the look of confidence that I'd practiced over the years.

Dave rolled his gaze over me, sizing me up—or down. I

wasn't sure which. Either way, the look forced my vertebrae to click into place until I sat straight and tall. I may have towered over the man outwardly, but with each pulse beat that passed without words, I felt myself shrink on the inside.

He leaned forward with his elbows on the table and his index fingers steepled together. "It's been, what… four years since you've been in a real school?"

"Yes, sir. We had a tutor on the set of *Morlich Castle*." What was this about? Had he suddenly decided that at seventeen I was too old for the role? No. That was ridiculous. Besides, I had a contract. Contract or no, my nerves were a mess.

He nodded and pressed his index fingers into the center of his lips.

I tried to ignore the tension twisting inside me and shot a *What's this about?* glance at my dad. He answered with a slow nod, which didn't really help ease the knots in my gut.

Dave jerked his fingers away from his lips as if an idea had just occurred to him. "American high schools have a culture of their own. I think you need to spend time in one."

Relief untwisted those knots. This was good. This was exciting. "Aye. I'd love to visit an American high school."

"Good. Good." Michael bobbed his head up and down so fast it was as if the words were shaken from his lips. "But not just for a visit. The horse trainer, Bob Morgan, lives in a small town called Hillside. We thought it might be interesting for you to enroll in the high school while you're there."

Enrolling in school wasn't on my list of Top Ten Things to Do in Texas, but I'd swim up a longhorn's arse if Dave and Michael thought it would benefit the movie. Besides, during the *Morlich Castle* years, while my mates were going to parties, I was either studying or learning lines. This was a chance to experience at least a wee bit of what I'd missed. I fixed a Hollywood smile on my face and said, "Sounds smashing."

"Glad you're on board. But you can't go in as Frasier

Anderson." Michael's soft voice was such a sharp contrast to Dave's enthusiasm it was almost unsettling. "*Morlich Castle* was shown here. If you go in with a Scottish accent and your real name, people will recognize you."

"You want me to go undercover. Cool." And it was. I could create a character, be whoever I wanted to be.

"Yeah. American accent and all. At the end we'll do a big reveal." Dave fanned his fingers and waved his arms in front of us as if he were unveiling the big picture. Then he tilted his head and half-squinted at me. "I don't think we have to change a lot. Maybe cut your hair. It has to be short for the movie anyhow."

I tried not to react, but my fingers raked through my hair anyway. "Sounds good. When do I start?"

An apologetic expression crossed Michael's face. "I know you'd planned to sightsee while you're here, but your dad agreed that it would be to your benefit to start training with the horses early. School starts Monday here. It makes sense for you start with it."

"Monday. Perfect." Less than a week away. Still, I could practice my accent. Learn about life in Texas and train with horses. What could possibly go wrong?

Michael and Dave shook Dad's hand. Michael said, "We'll have a courier send over papers for you to sign."

When he shook my hand he said, "Thank you for being a team player. We'll see you in a couple of weeks."

As they walked away, Dad's shoulders relaxed, but his eyes held a trace of worry.

I gulped my water. "What is it, Dad? Do you think Mum will be okay with this? I can't imagine she'll be excited about moving to Hillside, Texas."

"She'll be okay. She's a wee bit worried about being out of the country for so long. If they find Fiona…"

"Dad, she's been gone for three years."

"Aye. That's why Mum agreed to come."

Fiona. My older sister. She ran away when she was sixteen, again when she was seventeen, again when she was seventeen and a half. You get the idea. And in between, she was in and out of rehab.

After she left the last time, I begged her to come home. Her reply could be summed up in two words. F-off. Or is that one? Then, she cut all ties with the family. And aye, I am bitter when I think about her and what she's done to Mum and Dad—so I don't.

Besides, I have a sweet life. I love acting. I'm good at it. I make my own money.

I looked over Dad's shoulder, beyond the patio where we sat, to the steps that led to the path to the lake. I thought about the paddle-board lassies. "When do we leave?"

"At the weekend. We'll drive to Hillside on Friday and settle in. Dave connected us with an estate agent who knows of a house to let. Apparently, it's a small town and there isn't much in the way of hotels."

MUM, Dad, and I worked with a voice coach for the next four days. On Friday, we loaded into the hired car and drove north on Interstate 35.

Well, Dad drove and Mum yelled every time he tried to overtake another vehicle. Driving on the right side of the road with the wheel on the left side of the car threw his perception completely off. He nearly clipped every car he overtook. Or at least that's what I gathered from Mum's screeches. I sat in the back with my eyes shut and tunes plugged into my ears.

We managed to get to Hillside in one piece and to the house on Maple Street. It was a modern detached brick and stone, with lush green grass and two spindly trees in the front garden. When Dad pulled into the drive, a man came out of the front door. He looked a few years older than my dad and wore blue trousers and a blue tee shirt with a red emblem on the left breast.

He stopped just short of opening Dad's door and waited with a wide grin on his face. He started talking before Dad was all the way out of the car. "Howdy, folks. Welcome to Hillside." He could not have sounded any more stereotypically Texan.

He shook Dad's hand. "I'm Al Miller. Most people just call me Chief." He pointed to the emblem on his chest. "Hillside Fire Chief."

"Gordon Anderson." Dad was trying his American accident. He pointed to Mum. "This is my wife, Sarah, and my son, Frasier."

The chief shook Mum's hand, then mine. "Pleased to meet y'all. When the feller at the studio contacted me, he told me about your secret. I promise it's safe with me. Your accent is pretty good. Does anybody at the school know?"

Dad nodded. "The headmaster, Mr. Bledsoe."

"Bill is a fine man." The chief cocked one eye. "But we don't have a headmaster. He's the principal."

"Principal, right. Thank you." Dad reverted to his normal accent. "There are some words that could trip me up."

Chief shook his head. "You're really going to hide that beautiful accent?"

"Aye." Mum smiled. "Well, they are. I can't do an American accent to save my life."

Chief rocked back on his heels. "Sooo. How's that going to work?"

Mum and looked at Dad and back at Chief. "We're only here for a fortnight. I plan to keep to myself."

Chief nodded. "We're a small town, but we're friendly. I don't reckon folks are going keep their noses out of your business."

Mum's face fell a wee bit. "I guess these two will have to do all the talking."

"Well, we're happy to have you. Accent or not." Chief handed dad the house keys. "It's completely furnished." He checked his watch. "I'll leave y'all to get settled."

"Before you go, can you direct us to the nearest Co-op?" Mum asked. "We need to pick up at least a few groceries."

"Co-op?"

"Grocery store," Dad translated.

"Ahh. We have a heck of a grocery store." He gave directions to Mum and Dad as I carried our bags in the front door.

Mum went bonkers over the massive kitchen. Dad was happy that there was enough room for each of them to have their own office. It was a three bedroom house, and each bedroom had its own en-suite. I was happy with that.

As soon as we dropped our bags, Mum was ready to go to the grocery. She refused to drive in the US, so we went as a family. Not my favorite place to go, but I figured it would be a good way to get the lay of the land. Besides, even though Dad's accent was better than Mum's, he couldn't quite keep it together and neither of them had a handle on American money. In the end, they paid with a card, which was probably how they should pay for everything.

I picked up a couple of wire-bound notebooks and unexpected anxiety rose in my gut. I hadn't been to a real school in four years. I had passed my A-Levels last year. But I knew first impressions would set the tone for the whole experience. It was two weeks. I had no reason to worry about making friends. But the real me, the one who wasn't an actor, was awkward, shy, and wanted to be accepted.

My hair had been cut short on the sides and back. What was left on the top wasn't much longer. As odd as it felt to have short hair, it was pretty standard for the lads around my age. As were jeans and T-shirts. But Mum wasn't having it—especially when it came to school dress.

"Mum, every teenager will be wearing jeans and a T-shirt."

"That's fine. But you won't be."

"This isn't real." I countered. "My character will be in jeans and T-shirts the whole movie."

"Well, you're not on set yet. You'll be wearing trousers and a shirt."

Then my dad stepped in. They double-teamed me. "Frasier, it's a fortnight. Let it go."

I knew when I was beaten and resigned myself to playing the part of the loser kid.

When Monday morning rolled around, my dad managed not to get us killed on the way to school, but Mum was still shaking when we were ushered into the principal's office.

Mr. Bledsoe shook our hands. "Please, have a seat." He bypassed Mum and Dad and spoke to me. "So, you're a teen idol in England."

He said *teen idol* like it was a disease. And the confidence that I'd walked into his office with turned to apprehension. "I don't know about idol, but I am an actor."

"A good one, from what I've heard." He blinked several times, like it was a tic or something. "Dave Coleridge made a substantial donation to the Arts Department, so I'm willing to play along with this little charade. Under one condition."

"Yes, sir."

He leaned forward across his desk. "You will be the model student. I don't want drama with the girls—or boys. You are here as an observer. Do I make myself clear?"

"Yes, sir."

Mum released the tight smile stretched across her face. "You'll have Frasier's full cooperation, I assure you."

Mr. Bledsoe relaxed and rocked back in his chair. "Welcome to Hillside High. I think you'll find it a great place to learn about rural Texas. I 'spect we'll see the Anderson family at the game Friday?"

"Aye," Dad said, "we'll be there, but remember we're the Smith family. Frasier is now Ethan."

Mr. Bledsoe stood. "Yessir." He looked at me and grinned. "All right, Ethan Smith, you can pick up your schedule from the secretary in the front office. I have some papers for your mom and dad to sign."

I thanked him and made my way to the front desk, fully intending to keep my promise to stay away from girls and drama. Really, I tried.

But the odds were against me.

2

Jenna Wiley

I JABBED the tip of my spoon into the blob of yogurt puddled over Mom's homemade granola and sighed.

Mom topped off Grandma's coffee with a frown. "What's got you so glum? You love the first day of school."

Yes. Nerdy as it is, I used to love the beginning of the school year. It wasn't just the new notebooks, pens, highlighters, and clothes. Okay, it was totally about new clothes. But also about possibilities. About moving one step closer to graduation and college.

"I dunno. I just can't get excited." Which made no sense. I was a senior. I had a newish maroon Ford F-150. A new laptop. A new phone. All the things that should have made me giddy.

Grandma patted my shoulder. "Are you worried about friends?"

I shrugged. "Maybe a little. Melanie Joy has been in New Mexico all summer. Bree works all the time. I feel like we've drifted."

"What about Kenzie?" Mom let the coffee carafe dangle from her hand. "Is everything okay between you two?"

Grandma swished her hand in the air dismissively. "I

wouldn't blame you if you had a falling out after what she did to you and that boy."

I rolled my eyes to Mom. It was a silent plea for her to step in, but she didn't get it. "Grandma, for the thousandth time, Travis and I would have broken up anyway. I don't like him in that way, and he and Kenzie are good together. If you'd give her a chance, you'd see that she's really a nice girl."

"Nice girls don't kiss other girls' boyfriends."

I stirred my yogurt. "Well, get used to her coming around. Since Travis is off at college, Kenzie and I can spend way more time together. It's what friends do."

Mom set the carafe on the table and took a seat. "So I'll ask again, what's got you so blue?"

"I dunno. It's just this town. Nothing ever happens here."

Grandma harrumphed. "Maybe you'll meet a handsome boy and show that Kenzie Quinn a thing or two."

"Oh my God. Grandma. It's been nearly a year since all that happened. Let it go. Besides, there are zero guys at this school I would ever be interested in."

Mom pressed her lips together and tucked her chin in a classic I'm-not-going-to-smile move. After a breath she said, very weakly, I might add, "Don't disrespect your grandmother."

"Sorry. Grandma. I didn't mean to disrespect you."

She nodded, but I could tell she was ruffled. "It's okay. But you need to adopt a more open attitude. Besides, who knows? Maybe a new boy will move to town."

Now it was my turn to press my lips flat. Not because I was trying not to laugh, but because I was getting tired of the *boys bring happiness* theme Grandma had going. "That is highly unlikely. And if it did happen, I wouldn't like him."

Grandma's eyes widened. "How can you say that? You haven't met him yet."

I pushed back from the table and stood. "Because I'm not

worried about dating or boys. I'm going to focus on STEM. I know it's hard to believe, but I want to be an engineer way more than a girlfriend."

We both looked at Mom. I'm sure Grandma was wondering where she'd gone wrong. But Mom was ignoring the look, her eyes on me. She let a smile escape along with a nod. "Then you'd better finish getting ready—" Her words were cut off by my ten-year-old twin brothers Josh and Andrew clomping into the kitchen. "Tell Abby to get a move on." Mom's words trailed me as I escaped to the bathroom to brush my teeth.

Abby passed me in the hall and rolled her fourteen-year-old's eyes. "I heard. I was helping Lucy with her shoes."

Lucy was the baby and spoiled. It was all of our faults. She was just too cute, with her big eyes and super curly blonde hair.

Mornings were always chaos in our house. But getting Grandma to stop going on about Kenzie was a definite win and by the time I got to school I was feeling better. Kenzie met me in the parking lot with swollen eyes and a blown-red nose.

"Did you and Travis have a fight?"

"No. He left for fish camp yesterday."

"And… you knew it was coming."

She sniffed. "I didn't think it would be so hard to say good-bye."

Seeing one of my best friends a complete disaster over her boyfriend going literally two hours away confirmed my pledge to focus on school and not dating. I hooked my arm in hers. "Come on. Let's get this year started."

We'd made it all the way to the courtyard by the cafeteria when I heard Melanie Joy scream, "Jenna!" Two seconds later I was body-slammed.

"You're back!" I screamed as I tried to keep from falling over.

"We got in late last night. We were supposed to be home Friday, but it took longer than expected to winterize the cabin."

Bree joined us and everybody squealed and hugged again.

First period was AP English, which I would have been excited about had I managed to score Mrs. White as my teacher, but no such luck. Everybody wanted Mrs. White for AP English. Unfortunately, half of us ended up with Mr. Shipley—a maniacal, power-hungry weirdo of a teacher. He was a short little man with a big handlebar mustache. He loved to pick on students, especially athletes. I wasn't an athlete, so I was spared the ridicule, but it was still painful to watch.

As soon as the bell rang, he started his list of rules. Most of them were reasonable. It was the delivery that made everyone squirm. Case in point: He stood in front of Jesse Alvarez's desk, bent over at the waist until he was eye-level with the football player. "I don't care what extracurricular activity you're in, I make no exceptions."

When Jesse didn't respond, he moved to Jamal Miller's desk and assumed the same position. "It is your responsibility to get your assignments in by the due date." Jamal nodded.

Shipley straightened and moved to the front of the room. He was about to go on to the next rule when a kid sitting to the left of me raised his hand.

A new kid. And by the looks of him, Mr. Shipley would have him in tears by the end of the week. Not that he didn't have cute-boy potential. His dark brown hair was cut short on the sides but just long enough on the top for his bangs to tip over on to his forehead and just messy enough to make it interesting. And there was an adorable sprinkling of freckles across his nose and cheeks. But as much as his face had the potential to sell the cute-guy look, his clothes most definitely did not. Khaki pants pressed crisper than Uncle Joe's Marine Corps uniform. Ten to one when he stood up, those suckers would be high-waisted, too. To top off the look, he wore a tucked-in—yes, folks—*tucked-in* white button-down shirt.

Really?

So nerdy new boy raised his hand. Mr. Shipley hesitated before he called on the poor kid. Probably preparing to fire something from his long list of insults. "You have a question?" My stomach clutched in anticipation of Mr. Shipley's abuse. Judging by his tone, this was going to be bad.

Mr. Shipley raised his eyebrows and motioned for the kid to continue.

"Well, sir, what if the day we're absent is the day an assignment is due?"

The rest of us held our breaths. Mr. Shipley's mustache twitched. "I have been assured that all people who might miss my class because of an inane activity will know ahead of time. Now, how do you think you should resolve that problem?"

"Turn in the assignment early, sir."

Shipley looked like he was trying to decide if nerd-boy was a smartass or sincere with his questions and *sirs*. I was sure he was going to hurl some sort of insult at the kid, but he didn't. He snapped, "Correct," and returned to the front of the room to finish his list.

That was nice, for Shipley.

Then he started on the roll call. A chance to find out who this new kid was. Unfortunately, I had to wait until near the end of the list. Ethan Smith. I was kind of hoping for something more exotic. I mean, really, other than the hair, and the sort of cute face, he needed all the help he could get.

"Ethan Smith." Shipley couldn't let it go with just saying his name. "My notes tell me you're a transfer student from Minnesota. Well, Minnesota, tell us about yourself." He dragged out the middle part of the word *Minnesota* because that was just the kind of jerk he was.

Ethan Smith smiled at him. And I had to admit, it was sort

of dazzling. "As you said, I moved here from Minnesota. Both of my parents work from home. I don't have any brothers or sisters."

"And do you play sports?"

"Yessir. Soccer."

"Fascinating." Shipley might as well have said, "I don't care," because that's the tone the word held. Then, true to form, he turned his back on Ethan Smith and grabbed a stack of papers from his desk.

Class seemed to last forever, but I think it was because I was dying to talk to the girls about the new boy. No. Actually I was dying to talk to the new boy. Somebody needed to warn him about Shipley.

When the bell rang, Kat Morrison and Sophie Hudson swooped in on him.

Kat slung her backpack over one shoulder. "Hi! I'm Kat Morrison. Don't let Mr. Shipley scare you. It's just the way he is."

Ethan nodded. "He's seems decent enough."

Sophie almost pushed Kat out of the way. "I'm Sophie Hudson. How long have you been here?"

"We moved in on Friday."

Sophie wormed her way next to him. "Then you need someone to show you around. Kat and I will be happy to. Where is your next class?"

Ethan looked overwhelmed, but handed Kat the printout of his schedule.

I wandered out of the room and found Kenzie. "We got a new kid."

"And?"

"I don't know. Weird. He seems kind of formal. I half expected him to stand beside his desk when he asked questions."

Kenzie watched as Kat and Sophie ushered him down the hall. "That him?"

"Yeah. Kind of almost cute, right?"

"A little too clean for my taste."

"Yeah. Underneath the starched kakis there is sort of a military-academy-kid look." I nodded. "And he is a little pasty. I wonder if he was incarcerated."

"Incarcerated? Really?"

"How else do you explain his behavior?"

Kenzie rolled her eyes. "I don't know, but I seriously doubt he served time. He doesn't even have a tat."

"That you can see." We both laughed.

Kenzie said, "Don't go spreading that rumor. I gotta go. I'll see you later."

I turned and made my way to Chemistry. As fun as it was to have a new kid in school, Kat and Sophie could have him. I had bigger plans than worrying about the new kid in town. There were five kids in my family and if I was going to get an engineering degree from Texas A&M, I needed scholarships. Which meant I needed to be valedictorian. No boy was worth sidetracking me from my goal. Not even a cute, nerdy weirdo who might or might not have been incarcerated.

I took a seat at an empty lab table in the back of the room. Not that I minded sitting with other people, it's just that other people hadn't made it to class yet. Okay, a few had, but their table was full. But as people made their way into the room, nobody even came close to my table. Apprehension snaked through me. Had I done something wrong? I wasn't popular by any means, but I wasn't a reject either. I watched a couple of girls hesitate before sitting at the table next to mine. Had I become a reject? My skin felt hot and prickly and my insides began to fold in on themselves.

The five-minute bell rang and still nobody had ventured to the table in the back of the room where I sat. I knew what was happening. One person at a table was the sign of a loser. Nobody wanted to make the move to sit with them and risk being a loser by association.

Why had I sat in the back, by myself? I should have stood around until I saw a friendly face I could join. That was what normal people did.

Mrs. Sanchez stood in the doorway with her hand on the door handle. She was halfway to closing it when Ethan Smith slipped into the classroom. "Sorry, ma'am. I got lost."

"Well, you're here now." She nodded in my direction. "Take the empty seat in the back."

Great. Not only was I now a loser, I was a loser with the weirdo new kid. Yes, I had said that I wanted to talk to him. But that didn't mean I wanted to get stuck with nerd boy as my chem lab partner for the entire semester.

He sat next to me and stuck out his hand. "Ethan Smith. I'm new."

I shook his hand even though the gesture was old school and creepy. "Jenna Wiley. We have AP English together too."

"Oh. I wish I'd known. I could have followed you here."

"I thought Kat and Sophie were showing you around."

"They did. Just not in the direction I needed." He smiled, and suddenly he wasn't nerd boy. He was hot guy with beautiful, sparkly green eyes. Eyes I knew I should stop looking into, but somehow couldn't quite pull away from because he was looking into mine. And then my chest got all tight and tingly.

The bell sounded and the spell or whatever it was ended. I turned to focus on the front of the room and pretend the whole eye-gazing incident hadn't just happened. I was doing a pretty good job too.

Then a whole new embarrassment heated my skin when Ethan said, "Wow. How do you do that?"

"What?" But I knew what. My index finger twirled a lock

of hair to my scalp and back down. Over and over. Faster and faster.

I stopped and lowered my hand to my lap. I needed to cut my hair. A pixie was the only way I was ever going to break the habit.

He looked around the room like he wished he hadn't said anything. Thank God Mrs. Sanchez chose that moment to call roll.

We spent the rest of the class going over rules, regulations, and safety in the lab. We were seniors. We'd all had lab before, but we still had to take a test on lab safety.

When class ended, Ethan pulled out his schedule and flattened it on the table in front of me. "Can you get me to my next class?"

As it turned out, our schedules matched except that he had gym when I had Calculus. I didn't mind getting him from class to class, but tour guide was the extent of my charity. Because no matter how much his green eyes sparkled, or how sexy his smile was, this girl didn't do crushes anymore.

3

Frasier

I SHOULD NOT HAVE FLIRTED with her. The girl in Chemistry—Jenna. It was a total reflex to connect gazes. I didn't mean anything by it. So, maybe I wanted to see if she'd blush. She blushed. And then I got sucked in.

But I liked the way her brown hair framed her face. She was pretty. Not overdone makeup pretty. Just natural. And she seemed shy and curious—which made me curious.

And then she did this thing. She twirled her hair. It was crazy. Up and down. Faster and faster. Obviously a nervous habit, but it was kind of cute too. Until I embarrassed her by mentioning it. Oops. I wasn't sure if I ought to apologize or ignore it.

I had settled on apologize when Mrs. Sanchez called my name from the register. I wasn't used to my fake name and she had to call it twice, which made everybody laugh. My face heated and I reminded myself I was playing a role. Except these kids weren't actors and their reactions were real.

Jenna Wiley. I decided I wanted to know her. I was treading on thin ice, asking her to help me get to the rest of my classes. Mr. Bledsoe had lectured me on girls. Dave and

Michael had lectured me on girls. My dad had lectured me on girls.

No girls. No dating. It was a non-negotiable edict—especially after Cara Gentry. The fact that she'd ripped my heart out wasn't their concern. The social media storm that followed was. I had to give her credit, though—she was creative with her lies.

It was nice to be a normal lad, in a normal school, asking a normal girl to help me out. She didn't know who I was and by the time she found out, I'd be long gone.

We worked through the lab safety exercises together, but it was all business. She was completely focused on getting things correct down to the last detail. There was no small talk—until I asked her to help me find the rest of my classes. Genius on my part.

As soon as we stepped into the crowded hallway, she looked up at me under long dark lashes… that weren't covered in mascara, by the way. "What do you think of Texas so far?"

"It's hot."

She nodded. "People say you get used to it. I've lived here my whole life and I've never gotten used to it. It is cooler here than Brenham, though."

"Brenham?"

"It's about three hours south of here. It's where I moved from. Think a hundred and five degrees and a hundred percent humidity."

"We were in Austin last week. I kind of hoped it would be cooler here, but I guess when it gets over a hundred it's just unbearable no matter what." My American accent wavered a bit but she didn't seem to notice.

"Pretty much. What brought y'all here?"

A simple question. I should have had a ready answer, but I couldn't remember the exact words of my cover story. I should have listened better. My gut tensed and I went with the truth—

or close to it. "Work, and I guess a chance to experience rural Texas."

"Oh." The word came out a little weak, although she nodded like it was a reasonable explanation. Then things got weird and quiet as her gaze drifted down the hall. Her face got an uncomfortable look, as though she wished she were walking with someone else. And I knew this because—yeah—I was staring at her. Not creepy at all. *Eyes forward, not at Jenna.*

I struggled to find clever words to fill the gap. But let's face it, I was a natural at the awkward new guy role and I came up empty.

Seconds passed that felt like long minutes. At an intersection, I half expected her to peel off and leave me behind. Instead, she grinned and waved at a lass with blonde hair. As soon as the girl was close, Jenna said, "This is Kenzie Quinn." She looked at Kenzie and pointed to me. "Ethan Smith. He moved here from Minnesota."

"Good to meet you." Was that right? Was that what Americans said? They didn't look at me oddly, so I reckoned it was close enough.

Then Kenzie asked the dreaded question that I was soon to discover everybody wanted to know. "What brought y'all to Hillside?"

Jenna answered for me. "His dad's work."

Kenzie pulled on her rucksack's straps. "Oh. What does your dad do?"

I felt my face heat as plausible answers sailed through my mind. "He works remotely. Um, but he wanted to experience rural Texas."

Kinzie raised her eyebrows. She wasn't buying it. "That's sort of a random reason to move here, but okay."

Jenna turned back to me. "Siblings?"

"No." The lie fell from my lips easily enough, but it left a hollow feeling in my chest. What would happen if I'd said yes, and that she was a drug addict and nobody knew if she was even still alive? I'd never shared that information with anybody. I couldn't imagine trusting anybody enough to talk about it. That's the kind of juicy stuff that would go viral. The potential for it to affect my career in a bad way was too great to risk talking about it with anyone.

Jenna kept talking as though she hadn't really heard my answer. "I have four siblings. I'm the oldest. I have two sisters and twin brothers. My youngest sister just turned five. My house is crowded. Mom, Dad, five kids, and Grandma."

"It sounds nice."

"It's loud. That's why I hang out at my friends' houses. Kenzie has two sisters, but her house is big and in the country. The voices don't quite echo like in my tiny house."

Kenzie shrugged. "True. Plus, my oldest sister is at college. Ryan is working all the time or doing her art thang. It's mostly me and the chickens."

"The chickens, the pig, the horses. We spent all summer riding." Jenna's gaze shifted to me. God, those eyes. They were like magnets for mine.

"Sounds crackin'."

Smiles lit both their faces. Jenna said, "Crackin'. I like that word."

I winced. "It's a Minnesota thing."

In an obvious change of subject, Kenzie smacked Jenna's upper arm with the back of her hand. "Hey, what lunch do y'all have?"

Jenna pulled out her mobile and tapped on her schedule. "Third." She looked over my shoulder at my printout. "You have the same."

Kenzie groaned. "I have fourth." She looked at Jenna. "If you'd go out for cross-country, we'd have the same lunch. You run anyway. You might as well get credit for it."

"I don't have time for sports. You know, grades."

"You have the grades." Kenzie rolled her gaze to me. "She's going to be valedictorian."

"Not if I don't beat out Melanie Joy."

"Melanie Joy? Kat introduced me." Tall. Slender, with long white hair and porcelain skin. She looked like a model. "She's your rival?"

"Sort of. She's one of my best friends, so I'm not sure it's much of a rivalry."

Kenzie jutted her chin at Jenna. "She's on the cross-country team."

"Yeah, but she's wicked smart." Jenna huffed. "There's something wrong with the universe. I mean, it's unfair enough that she's smart, athletic, and beautiful. Does she have to be nice too?"

"She *is* nice. Volunteers at the food pantry on weekends." Kenzie's tone fell somewhere between admiration and frustration.

"Saint Melanie Joy." I said it jokingly but both girls just nodded.

We came to a large intersection near the office and Kenzie said, "Here's where I split off. Nice to meet you, Ethan."

"You too." With Kenzie gone, I was afraid things might get awkward again, but I was ready. "I get a sense that not joining cross-country is more than just because of your grades."

She shrugged. "I'm not into competition."

"Except where grades count."

"Except that. Honestly, as much as I hate to admit it, I kind of agree with Mr. Shipley. Too much emphasis is placed on school sports. I don't know about football in Minnesota, but in Texas, it rules. It's sort of a requirement that everybody go to the Friday night games."

Remembering Mr. Bledsoe's comment about the game, I nodded. "I'm looking forward to seeing a real Texas high school game."

"Well, don't get your hopes up. Three of our best players graduated last year, so who knows how we'll do this year. You're welcome to go with Kenzie, Melanie Joy, Bree, and me."

"What, no dates?"

"Kenzie's boyfriend is one of the players who graduated. The rest of us are single, so it's just us girls." She raised her eyebrows to emphasize the statement.

Going with Jenna as a date was out of the question, but as a group it was safe. Right? "Sounds like fun."

Jenna led me into the classroom. "Cool."

As the day went on, I grew more and more interested in getting to know Jenna. In the classroom she was all business—a total contrast to the girl who became bubbly and talkative as soon as we stepped into the hallway. Our conversations flowed easily without pauses or gaps.

We saw Kenzie a couple of times during the day. She was nice and cute and totally into some guy called Travis. Melanie Joy and Bree were in several of our classes. Both were pretty, but my chest didn't get that tingly feeling when I looked at them.

It wasn't until what I called football and they called soccer that I really talked to any lads. It took the length of the entire class to get our lockers and uniforms issued.

I was shoving my stuff in my locker when a lad opened the door next to mine. "So, you're from Minnesota?"

"Yes."

"What position did you play?"

"Mid-fielder."

He nodded. "Any good?"

"I can handle the ball."

He closed his locker door. "I'm Jason Wright. Striker." He pointed to a blond lad sitting on a bench. "This here is our best sweeper, Walker Stewart."

Walker Stewart tipped his chin. "S'up?"

He pointed to the lad next to Walker. "Meet our goalie, Chris Gomez."

I nodded. "Ethan Smith."

Chris looked at me like he'd smelled something rank and shook his head. "Ethan Smith, mid-fielder. Dude, I don't know how they do things in Minnesota, but this…" He waved his hand up and down, indicating my look. "This is not cool. Dude, at least untuck it. You look like you're going to church."

Mum and I had argued about tucking in the shirt. I gave in when Dad reminded me that the point was not to look cool. Heat filled my face and neck as I pulled out my shirttail. "I went to a private school."

Jason said, "Man, I'd melt if I had to wear khakis. Shorts are pretty much all I wear."

I'd noticed that almost everybody wore shorts, which made total sense. Hillside was evidently situated in the belly of hell.

The bell rang and the lads grabbed their rucksacks—er, backpacks.

Walker tipped his chin again. "Later, dudes."

While most of the other students made their way to the car park, I went to the bus line. I got a definite loser vibe standing there and reminded myself for the millionth time it was only for a fortnight.

As soon as I came through the front door of our temporary home, Mum and Dad attacked. Mum ushered me into the kitchen and poured me a cup of tea. "How was it?"

"Good. But everybody wears shorts. I'm not wearing trousers again."

"Shorts!" Mum's eyes widened. "Really?"

"Aye. I'm in shorts or jeans from here out."

Mum pulled one of those faces only mums can pull, but I was ready. Fortunately, Dad stepped in with a focus shift. "How were your classes?"

"Hard to tell. We didn't do much today. First day and all. Things are very casual here."

Mum nodded. "Apparently. Shorts?"

"Did you make friends?" Dad asked.

I thought of Jenna and tried unsuccessfully to hide my smile. "Yeah. I did. I'm going to the football game Friday night with some of them."

Dad nodded. "Good. All part of the experience."

"Yeah. It should be fun." And they didn't need to know the group was all girls.

"What about the footballers?" Dad shook his head. "I mean soccer team?"

"I met a couple of lads. Seemed nice enough." I grabbed a biscuit from the tin. Time for a subject change. "How did you two fill your day?"

Dad blew out a sigh. "After signing papers for Mr. Bledsoe, we made a generous donation to the parents' organization."

Mum slid a folded T-shirt off the counter and held it up. "And we got these." She widened her smile, but there was sarcasm all over her face. "Apparently, it's what we're meant to wear to the football game."

It was solid black with a yellow hornet in the center, and the words FEAR THE STING above the insect.

"Really?" I covered my smile with my hand and shook my head.

"Don't look so pleased. You have one too." Mum folded the shirt and set it on the counter.

I dropped my hand. "Me? What do I need with a Fear the Sting T-shirt?"

"According to Mr. Bledsoe, everybody wears them. It's called *blacking out the stands*." Dad overenunciated *blacking out*, making it sound ridiculous.

Mum and I both laughed and I felt a little guilty for mocking my new school.

Dad said, "We're embracing the experience."

I stared at the shirt. "To be sure."

Mum elbowed Dad. "Don't you have something for Frasier?"

Dad hurried to the laundry room. He came back bouncing a basketball. "I thought we'd make use of the hoop at the end of the driveway. What do you think?"

"Crackin'." I started for my bedroom. "I'll be out as soon as I change."

We hadn't played more than five minutes before Chris Gomez came out the front door of the house across the street. He jogged over. "Mind if I join in?"

I tossed him the ball.

He killed us. We played until Mum appeared on the edge of the drive. She didn't say a word, but Dad got the gist that it was time for tea. In his best American accent, he said, "I think dinner is ready."

Chris tossed the ball back to me. "Good game, but I hope you play soccer better than you play basketball."

"Way better."

"Cool. See ya tomorrow." He jogged across the street.

Dad leaned on my shoulder. "I'm getting too old to play like that."

"Isn't this just smashing." Mum's face was tense. "One of your classmates lives right across the street. How are we going to keep him from hearing me? You know I can't do an American accent."

"Maybe you just shouldn't talk at all."

Dad gave me a look.

"I didn't mean it like that."

Mum pressed her hands to her cheeks. "I'm going to have to be shut away. I can't go out."

"Can't Mum be Scottish?" I suggested. "Americans do marry Scottish people."

Mum shook her head. "If anybody is slightly suspicious about who you are, having a Scottish mum would lead them straight to you."

"But you can't not go out. Could you have laryngitis or something?"

Dad said, "I think Frasier is right. You need to develop a chronic case of laryngitis, at least until you can get the accent a little better."

Mum pointed her index finger into my chest. "I hope you remember this little sacrifice when I'm old and decrepit."

I hugged her. "I'll take care of you. Don't worry. I'll find the best pensioners' home possible."

Mum shoved me away and smiled. "Come on, let's get inside and have our tea."

4

Jenna

"I CAN'T BELIEVE I asked him to go to the game with us without asking y'all first," I said to Bree and Melanie Joy. "I'm sorry, y'all."

"It's fine. Who better to introduce him to the Hillside football frenzy than us?" Melanie Joy stretched her long legs across the powder blue rug that covered the floor of Bree's room. We usually hung out in Bree's den after school, but her twelve-year-old sister was driving us nuts, so we'd retreated to the bedroom. The three of us sat on the floor munching popcorn and doing homework—just like we'd done almost every day after school for the past two years.

"You know…" Bree tilted her head and got that I'm-about-to-be-philosophical-y'all look. "Ethan Smith moving to town has changed the dating pool dynamics. Every girl with a working set of eyes and half a brain will be wanting a piece of him. Having him with us at the game not only increases our odds, it protects him from the hordes."

"Hordes or whores?" I giggled at my joke, but I didn't even get a groan from the girls. I barely got an eyeroll. So I covered. "Well, maybe it increases the dating odds for you two. I'm not dating." And then, as if my heart were shaking a finger in my face, the memory of his eyes and his smile flashed in my mind and I wasn't sure I wanted Bree or Melanie Joy to have the better odds.

Bree grabbed a handful of popcorn. "He does have a beautiful face."

Melanie Joy sighed like a Disney princess. "And don't let his clothes fool you. There is a fit body under all of that."

I grabbed some popcorn too. "I know. I saw his sternocleidomastoid."

Both Melanie Joy and Bree stared at me like I'd grown an extra head. Bree said, "Sterno what?"

"You know, this muscle." I dragged my index finger down the muscle that extended from my ear to my collar bone. "Tell me the definition in that muscle and the bulging neck veins isn't hot."

Melanie Joy smiled. "Yeah. I thought you weren't noticing those things anymore."

"I may not be dating, but I'm not dead. I'm shallow enough to notice his eyes too. The green is so green."

Bree raised her brows. "I didn't notice his eyes or his neck. Hmm, I think you like our new boy."

"I don't even know him." I looked at Melanie Joy. "You had to have noticed his eyes."

"Nope."

I adjusted my Literature book on my lap. "It doesn't matter. I've placed him in the friend zone with no way out."

"We'll see." Bree threw a popcorn kernel at me.

It landed in the center of my book and I popped it in my mouth. "Y'all can keep dreaming about Ethan Smith. Some of us have to study." But my mind kept wandering to that moment in Chemistry when our gazes caught, and I wondered if his heart had sped up too. Had he felt the same tingles?

Just thinking about it brought the feeling back. And I

couldn't stop thinking about it, which is how I'd gone from "tour guide only" to "wanna go to the game?" I didn't even care about the game. Football was not my jam. Yes, I went to the games, but only because it was better than sitting home alone on a Friday night because everybody in town—including my entire family—would be in the stands screaming their heads off.

Anyway, I was glad we were going as a group. He would mix right in and sit in the midst of Melanie Joy, Bree, and Kenzie. Then I wouldn't have to resist those eyes or his smile or the dimple in his left cheek. Yes. I noticed. It was subtle but it was there.

Bree drummed the end of her pen against her notebook. "You know, though, as cute as he is, he is a little weird."

"Weird how?" And why did I feel slightly offended on his behalf?

"Okay, I know he's from Minnesota, but his accent is—I don't know—different. It's like it's exaggerated."

I shrugged like I didn't care. "I guess I didn't talk to him enough to notice." But I did kind of notice. I liked the way he said *crackin'*. It wasn't a word I'd heard before and the way he sort of rolled the *r* and dropped the *g* made it cool.

Melanie Joy shook her head. "It's a Minnesota accent. He just doesn't have a twang." She winked at me. "Jenna can fix that."

"Jenna is not going to be around him enough to fix that. And right now, Jenna is going to study." I looked down at the open pages in my lap and tried.

My phone dinged before I managed to get through a single page. I looked at the screen and my heart did a little shuffle. It was from Ethan. I didn't want the girls to see, so I held my phone close to my face.

Sorry to bother. You're the only number I have.

No worries. What's up?

Did we have Lit homework?

Yep.

Forgot my book.

I'm almost finished. I can bring mine by in about twenty.

Thanks.

He typed in his address and I set my phone screen-side-down on the carpet.

Bree cocked her head at me. "What was that about?"

"What do you mean?"

"You're grinning like it was a special text."

Melanie Joy grabbed my phone before the screen went dark. "You were texting *Ethan*."

"What? He left his Lit book at school. He just wants to borrow mine. It's no big deal. I'm the only number he has." Oh, that did not sound good. "Do y'all want to come with me?"

They both shook their heads.

Bree grinned. "Of the three of us, you're the only one even close to getting some guy action. I'm not going to get in the way of that."

"I'm not getting guy action. I'm loaning a friend a book. Stop talking so I can finish this."

My eyes went over the words on the pages. But my brain was not engaged. I didn't want to be excited to see him, but I was. How stupid was I? I couldn't control it. As soon as my eyes hit the last letter of the last word, I closed my book and loaded my backpack. I was going to take Ethan my book and look up the reading on Sparknotes.

Oh, how low I had sunk.

But when I pulled into his driveway, my excitement turned to nerves. What was I doing? I was not the kind of girl who ditched studying for a guy. But that's what I was doing, wasn't it? Could I change my mind now? Maybe I should read the section again before I gave it to him. Or wait for him to read it and take it back with me.

I was about to text him when he came through the front door and jogged to my truck. He'd changed into shorts and a T-shirt. I'm not gonna lie, I noticed the definition in his quads. He was definitely fit beneath those clothes.

I rolled the window down, fully intending to hand him the book and leave.

He opened my door. "Come in."

I couldn't be rude. I grabbed my purse and the book and followed him into the house. It was a new house and smelled of fresh paint. He led me down a short entry hall to the den. The den opened into the kitchen and dining area. The walls and cabinets were painted blue-gray, and the granite countertops were a gray-white mix. It was all very homey—except it wasn't.

I couldn't figure it out at first. Then it hit me. It didn't look lived in. Not just that it wasn't messy. There was nothing personal in the house. No pictures, no books on the shelves, no canisters on the counter. No boxes indicating they'd just moved in.

I told myself the boxes had to be in the garage, but that didn't put the uneasy feeling out of my head. Something was just *off*.

"Can I get you something to drink?" His voice was a little shaky, as though he was nervous, and he swept his arm toward the kitchen in an exaggerated way.

"No, thank you." I held out the book. "You wanted to borrow this?"

"Yes." He took it and set it on the counter. "I didn't ask you if you'd already read it."

"I have." *Sort of.* "You can bring it to me tomorrow."

"Yes. I will. For sure." His face blushed bright red and I felt kind of sorry for him. He was so nervous. Like he'd never talked to a girl before.

"Melanie Joy said she saw you in the bus line."

"Yeah. I don't have a car." He cringed as he said it.

"I can give you a ride. You're not that far from my house."

His whole face lit up. "That would be great." He reached behind him like he was going to lean on the counter and knocked the book to the floor. It hit the tile with an echoing *pop*. He bent to pick it up and when he rose, he smacked his back against the underside of the counter.

"Whoa. Careful there." I didn't think a human could turn as red as he did in that moment. I found it kind of cute. He was a welcome relief from the guys who acted like they were some sort of celebrity.

Ethan Smith was as plain and ordinary as his name. I got the feeling that with him, what I saw was what I got, and that made me smile.

I had to put him at ease. "Um, I think I would like some water."

"We have Coke too if you'd rather."

"Sure."

He grabbed a couple of cans from the fridge and handed me one. The two of us stood between the kitchen and den drinking our cokes in silence. Trying to put him at ease was one thing, but this was painful. I tried to think of something to say—anything—but the only thought that ran through my head was how uncomfortable I felt.

A man I assumed was his dad came into the room from the other side of the den. "Who's your guest?"

"Dad, this is Jenna Wiley. I left my Literature book at school and she's loaning me hers."

Ethan was almost a dead ringer for his dad. They were the same height, had the same eyes, same left-cheek dimple, and same dark hair with the same haircut—except Mr. Smith's hair was super curly on top and Ethan's was straight.

I smiled at Mr. Smith. "It's nice to meet you."

"Thank you." He looked at Ethan. "Well, now that you have your book, you can start studying."

And the discomfort level just ballooned. Definitely my cue to leave. I set the can on the counter. "Thanks for the coke. I'll pick you up at seven thirty." To Mr. Smith I said, "Welcome to Hillside."

Ethan flashed a look at his dad and back at me. "I'll walk you out."

As soon as the door closed behind us, he said, "Sorry about my dad. New school and all, he's a little tense, but it was nothing against you."

"Don't worry about it. He was fine."

Ethan stood by my truck while I climbed into the cab and buckled my seatbelt. I rolled down the window to say good-bye and he stepped close to the door. "Thanks again for loaning me your book." Then, oh Lordy, he smiled at me. That single dimple flashed my way and his eyes looked into mine and I couldn't think, much less breathe.

I managed to nod, but I think I was staring at him when I pushed the start button. I had to have looked like a loon.

I don't remember what happened next, but he must have stepped back, because I didn't run over his feet. I must have put my truck in gear, because I did make it home safely. It's just that my mind was stuck on the tingles I got when he looked in my eyes and smiled at me.

5

Frasier

AS SOON AS Jenna was gone, I jogged back to the house. My dad was waiting on the other side of the door. "Homework? Do you remember why you're here?"

I knew what he was going on about and I knew he was right, but I didn't want to admit it. And I was angry that I couldn't just have a few days of normal life. "Aye. I forgot my book."

"Forgot your book?" His eyebrows arched. "You do realize you're not really in school."

"I'm supposed to experience the American high school life. That's what I'm doing."

Then his brows narrowed in an unspoken accusation. "Did I hear her say she's picking you up tomorrow?"

"Aye. Don't make this something it's not. She's just being nice."

"Just don't forget who you are and why you're here."

"Leave it, Dad." I decided now was the time for a subject change. "Where's Mum?"

"Upstairs. Watching one of her crime shows."

I made my way up the steps to the lounge where the television was. She was curled in an overstuffed chair sipping from a mug of tea. She barely looked up as I came into the room. "Have you figured out who did it?"

"The girlfriend. It's always the lover. What was Dad going on about?"

"One of my friends from school dropped off a book." I tried to sound casual but apparently failed, because Mum turned to me full-face. "A book? Who and why?"

"Jenna Wiley. I left my Literature book at school." I waited for an overreaction and I wasn't disappointed.

"You invited a girl. Over here?" She set her tea on the table next to the chair.

"It's just a book for an assignment. That's all. Besides, even if I did want to hook up, she is too into school to date."

"You're sure."

"Aye." I sat on the edge of the couch. "She's going to give me a ride to school tomorrow. Please don't make it something it's not."

She turned back to her show. "Just be sure it stays not something."

"I know. I know. I hear the message."

Mum shook her head. "This whole scheme makes me uncomfortable." She grasped the handle of her mug but didn't pick it up. "We're trying to fool a whole village. I think you could have got the experience you needed without lying to the community."

"I don't know." Dad spoke from the doorway. "I think the reveal will be well received."

Mum looked up at him. "Really?"

"Sure. There's going to be a big production around the reveal. It'll be good press for Hillside as well as for the film."

Mum tracked Dad as he moved into the room. "That sounds like Dave Coleridge speaking."

"It's his idea. He wants to bring some of the cast in to visit the school. Make a major donation to the community."

I liked the idea. "See, Mum? It's not like we're fooling the people and then sneaking out at night. It'll be fun."

"I still think we should keep to ourselves. And you, laddie…" She pointed her cup at me. "You need to keep away from the girls. We don't need to leave broken hearts in our wake."

"I can't immerse myself in the culture without becoming friends with a few people. Jenna's friends are the first ones who reached out. Jenna's picking me up to go the game with them on Friday."

"Great. Here we go." Mum rolled her eyes at me. "You couldn't go with the boy across the street?"

"Chris didn't ask." I stood and stretched. "It'll be fine. It's not a date. I'm going with a group of girls."

Mum shook her head. "You be careful, Frasier Anderson. This whole scheme is liable to backfire on you. You don't need any more rude pictures getting out there."

"You make it sound like it was my fault. Cara broke up with me. And I wouldn't call them rude. Mostly they were just her yelling at me."

"It was the captions and the comments on Twitter that were rude," Mum said.

"It's in the past, Mum. I'm not going hook up with anyone. It's just me going to a football game with a group of girls."

Dad plopped on the sofa. "See that it stays that way."

"Honestly, how much trouble do you think I could manage to get into in two weeks?"

Mum sipped her tea. "Be sure the answer is none."

"Mum, it's not a date. My life has been crazy for the past five years. Let me enjoy this wee bit of time out of the spotlight."

Mum's face reddened. "You can step away from acting any

time you wish. There's more than one Uni who'd be glad to have you."

"I don't want to stop acting. I just want to be normal for a few days."

"And pretending to be someone you're not, speaking with a fake accent, is being normal?" Mum's tone was ripe with her feelings over the scheme.

"You know what I mean." I started for the stairs. "This may be a fake week, but Mr. Shipley will expect me to have read a real assignment. I'll be in my room."

I WAS UP EARLY the next morning. I'd thought about what Mum had said about lying to the whole village. There was a huge potential for this to backfire, but I wanted to believe that Dad was right too. If things worked out, this scheme could be good PR for the film and there would be no hard feelings when we were gone. But a little worry took root in my conscience.

As I made my way to breakfast, I braced for another stay-away-from-Jenna-Wiley lecture, but it didn't come.

Mum's eyes were red and swollen and Dad didn't look much better. Usually that was a sign that there'd been news about Fiona. It'd been at least a year since that had happened, so I doubted that was the case. The next obvious scenario was that they were fighting about me. I didn't want to be responsible for Mum's swollen eyes or Dad's irritable mood, so I grabbed a protein bar and waited outside for Jenna.

When she pulled up in front of the house, I could hear the bass pounding in her truck from where I stood on the porch. Pure joy lit her face as she danced behind the wheel and sang along to the music.

I didn't want to spoil the moment. Besides, watching her made me forget the stress inside my house.

It was only a few seconds before she waved me to the truck. I jogged to the passenger side with a grin stuck on my face almost as big as the one she wore.

"Good morning." She sang the words and my chest lightened.

"Good morning. You're in a good mood."

"I'm in a great mood. It's my senior year. I have the *best* friends and now a new one." She pointed to me. "Had a great run this morning and my siblings didn't make me late. It's the little things, baby." She said the word "baby" like she was squishing the letters together and it made me laugh.

"It is the little things."

GOING through the motions of school would have been boring if Jenna hadn't been in my classes. We fell into an easy routine. Walk to class together. Sit next to each other. Walk to the next class. It was casual and comfortable.

I didn't want comfortable.

I wanted her to look at me again with those amazing eyes. I wanted her to feel the same chemistry I felt when we walked so close our arms nearly brushed.

She'd made it clear that this was not what she wanted. She had closed herself to the idea. I felt it. She was firmly in no lads, STEM-only mode. Charm wasn't going to work on her. I had to figure another way to get her to look at me as more than a just a friend.

We met up with Kenzie, Bree, and Melanie Joy after Chem class. Chris and Gage joined us. Chris couldn't keep his eyes off Melanie Joy and she was totally clueless.

In the dressing room before *soccer* practice, Chris sat on the bench and looked up at me. "Dude, I've been trying to talk to

Melanie Joy since seventh grade. Second day here and you're hanging out with her."

Jason shook his head at him. "It's new guy syndrome. She's known you too long. She remembers what a loser you were in seventh grade."

I shrugged. "You're talking to her now. Don't waste it."

Chris said, "What does that mean?"

"It means don't be a loser." Jason shut his locker door. "Come on."

We ran drills in practice, but we also got to play a bit. It felt good to kick the ball around again.

After school, Jenna and I walked side by side to her truck. Almost like a couple. Almost. When we reached it, she looked over the bonnet at me. "Do you mind if we drop by my house before I take you home? I promised Bree I'd loan her a book and I need to pick it up."

"Sure." Anything to spend more time with her.

It was supposed to be a quick trip to her house, but her brothers talked me into playing basketball while I waited for Jenna to find the book. I assumed it would be five minutes tops. Twenty minutes later, she came out of the house carrying the book and a bottle of water.

"Sorry it took so long. I couldn't find it." She thrust the water at me. "Peace offering?"

"I don't need a peace offering, but I'll take the water."

I sucked down the water as soon as I was in the truck. That's when I noticed her grinning at me. "What?"

She gave a tiny shrug that I found really sexy. "I don't know. Just… thank you for playing with my brothers. You didn't have to do that."

"They're great." Did I just detect a slip in her no-dating rule? The thought was thrilling even though I knew my parents would gut me if I broke the rule.

And speaking of my parents, I dreaded coming home to

the tension I'd left. But whatever had been going on in the morning must have been resolved. We had a great evening. Even played *Settlers of Catan*.

When Jenna picked me up the next morning, it was my turn to be in a super great mood. I'd planned to ask her if we could do something together after school, but I didn't get the chance. She'd barely pulled out of the drive before she asked, "Hey, do you want to play basketball after school today?"

"Sure. I just need to text my parents."

She flashed a sideways smile. "Great."

So, imagine my disappointment and complete surprise when she pulled alongside her house and stopped before turning into the drive. "I should be back in a couple of hours to take you home."

"Be back? You're not playing?"

"No. I always study with Bree and Melanie Joy after school. Don't worry, I'll be back in time to get you home for dinner."

I hesitated with my hand on the door handle.

She tipped her head toward the house. "The boys are waiting."

I almost said something before climbing out of the truck. But I didn't. She'd totally played me. But I wasn't a quitter and getting to her family just might get me the leg up I needed.

6

Jenna

I FELT KIND OF MEAN for tricking Ethan into spending time with my brothers, but it was a fair trade. They'd agreed to do my chores for a whole week. That left time for me to do things like run before school. I figured I'd make up for my deception with Ethan—in a non-dating way of course. Otherwise, he might never forgive me for leaving him with the twin terrors.

But when I came home from Bree's, the house was scary quiet. Mom was working on dinner. Lucy was coloring at the table and Abby was doing homework. "Where's Grandma?"

"Bunco. She won't be home for dinner."

That explained the order in the house. "Where are the boys?" I tried to ask nonchalantly, but let's face it, I wanted to see Ethan and it was written all over my voice.

Mom raised her brows at me. "The twins—or the boy you pawned off on them?"

I replied with my best *whatever* expression.

Mom indicated the direction with a head jerk. "Den."

I hung my backpack on the hook by the door. "I guess I'll rescue Ethan."

Only no rescuing was needed. The three of them sat on the

sofa, headsets on, game controllers in hand. Ethan's eyes cut to me and back to the TV. "Oh, hi, Jenna."

I sat in Dad's recliner and reached for the fourth controller and headset. "Can I play the next game?"

Andrew shook his head. "No. Not part of the deal."

Josh nodded. "You playing isn't keeping Ethan out of your hair."

I wanted to die and kill him at the same time. "I never said that."

Ethan kept focused on the game, but I saw the corner of his mouth turn up.

Andrew said, "Well not exactly, but you said—"

"I know what I said. The deal was that I'd get Ethan over here if you took my chores for a week."

Ethan's guy got killed and I was pretty sure he let it happen. He removed the headset, and placed it and the controller on the coffee table. "So, I'm a bargaining chip."

"Yes. But I did not tell them to keep you out of my hair." I was blushing, and judging by his smile, he was enjoying it. I stood. "Come on. I'll take you home."

As he unfolded himself from the couch, I tried not to notice the definition in the muscles in his legs. But he was wearing shorts and his legs were right there. How could I not notice?

I snapped around so fast my feet tangled and I stumbled into the hall leading to the kitchen. *Could the floor swallow me up now, please?*

There was no way he hadn't seen that, but he followed without a word. Thank God.

As soon as we entered the kitchen, Mom smiled like an eighties fangirl at a boyband concert. "Well Ethan Smith, did the boys beat you again?"

"Yes, ma'am."

Then Mom giggled. Yes, *giggled*. "I told you they were ruthless."

Ethan walked over to Abby. "How's the maths going?"

Maths? Did I hear that right?

"Good, now that I understand it." She gazed up at him in full hero-worship mode.

He smiled. "Well done."

Lucy turned her coloring book around. "Do you want to color another picture with me?"

"Next time. Jenna's taking me home."

"Can't you stay for dinner?" Lucy batted her eyes at him. She's only five and she batted her eyes!

Mom said, "We have plenty. You're welcome to stay."

Ethan looked at his phone. "I should check in first."

I wasn't sure if I was irritated or thrilled that he'd made friends with my family, but I was leaning toward irritated. I mean, it was one thing to tolerate him or even like him, but in a matter of a couple of hours my family had fallen in love with him. Mom had *giggled*.

Oh no, we were not having that.

I grabbed Ethan by the arm. "Come on." I wasn't allowed to have boys in my room, so the only two alternatives were the back patio or the den. Since it was a million degrees outside, I dragged him back to the den. My brothers were about to start another game. "Don't you guys have homework?"

Josh barely looked up. "We can do it after dinner."

"Nope. You have to do dishes. Remember our deal."

He dropped the controller on the coffee table. "Fine."

Andrew jerked off his headset. "Worst deal ever."

I sat on the end of the sofa opposite Ethan. "You made fast friends with my family."

"I like your family. It's pretty boring around my house. A lot of reading and little TV." He stretched his arm across the back of the sofa and his shirt went tight across his torso. I hadn't meant to notice that the rest of him was as defined as his legs and neck, but I had, and suddenly the room was a little too hot and the air a little too thick to breathe.

If he noticed, he didn't show it. He kept right on talking. "I expected it to be chaos, but it wasn't at all. It was fun getting to know everybody. I was nervous about being dropped off to fend for myself, but I'm glad it worked out that way."

"Cool." But it wasn't. Now that Mom obviously loved him, I was sure she would enlist Grandma on a full-scale boyfriend campaign and my siblings would be their allies.

And what was up with dinner? Dad got home just in time to slide into his chair. There wasn't even the obligatory grilling of the potential boyfriend. And the rest of my family acted like we were some kind of uber-normal TV family. Not once did Mom have to yell at the twins to put their cellphones down. Lucy didn't spill her drink and Abby didn't complain that her mashed potatoes were too lumpy.

It was horrifying.

Ethan helped my brothers clear the table. *They* were supposed to take care of it. That was the deal. And Mom kept thanking him for his help. Please. He was my friend first.

He probably would have offered to do the dishes for my brothers if I hadn't stepped in. "Okay, y'all have had Ethan long enough."

Andrew batted devil eyes at me. "You abandoned him."

Ethan tried to stop a smile, but I saw it sneak onto his mouth.

Mom said, "He has a point."

"No. I made a *deal* with the twins."

Ethan shrugged. "I should probably get home anyway."

Thank God. I don't think I could have taken any more Ethan worship.

As soon as we got into the truck the apology spewed forth. "I'm sorry. I shouldn't have left you there."

"It was cool. I like your family."

"We can be too much. I mean, that's a lot of people in that little space."

"It was fine." Then he looked at me with those eyes and my pulse revved. "Do you want to do something else? My house is too quiet."

"It's only seven thirty. We could get some coffee on the square. My treat for leaving you with my family."

"You don't have to do that."

"You say that now, but you have no idea how this is going to snowball."

"So tell me."

"My family has decided you are going to be everybody's new best friend. You can never visit my house again." I was joking, but there was an underlying seriousness in my statement.

"That doesn't seem fair." He laughed and his gaze cut to me. "Why must I stop hanging around people who like me?"

"Because they'll get too attached." I blurted out the words before I thought about what I was saying.

"Whoa." He held his hands up and everything turned dark and heavy and serious. "What's this about?"

I stopped at a red light and my finger twirled my hair and I didn't even care. "My family drives me crazy. But part of what makes me crazy is the way they cling to my friends. I should never have agreed to the whole basketball bargain."

"I had a great time."

"Now. But what happens if you get a girlfriend or move again? They'll take it harder than they should. My grandma has never gotten over my last boyfriend cheating on me." And when Ethan decided that there were more interesting girls out there—and he would—it wouldn't be just me he left hurting. It would be my entire family.

"Have you? Got over it?"

"What? Of course. The girl he cheated with is one of my best friends."

"Wow, that's generous of you." The words were sarcastic, but I don't think he meant it like that. He was tone was too sincere.

"Not really." I made my way to the square and parked in front of the coffee shop. "I'd had a crush on Travis for a long time, but I knew he really liked Kenzie. So it's not like he hurt me." But he had hurt me, badly. I'd never let anybody know that, though. I'd made a fool out of myself going after him. So I decided not to care that he hadn't. Somehow that took the sting out of it.

As we walked into the coffee shop, Ethan placed his hand on my back just below my neck and I didn't mind. He leaned in and said, "He sounds like a jerk."

"No. He's not. There's a lot to the story. We all make mistakes. Isn't that what kids our age are supposed to do?"

"I guess so. Although I'm not sure my parents would allow me to make mistakes." I sensed a heavy load of frustration in his tone.

We got our drinks and found a small table in the back corner. We ended up sitting next to each other and the air between us danced with electrons or pheromones or whatever reaction was happening that made my skin tingle. I sipped a breath of that charged air and hoped my voice didn't reflect the quivering I felt inside. "Are your parents hard on you about your grades?"

He stared into his frappuccino. "They're hard on me about everything."

"Maybe because you're an only child."

He flicked his gaze to me. "I'm not an only child."

"I thought you said—"

"I did. I have a sister. She ran away and we haven't seen

her in three years. My dad has a guy looking for her, but…" He looked away. "It's just easier to say I'm an only child."

My chest squeezed. "I'm so sorry. I can't even imagine what that's like."

"I hope you never know." He cleared his throat a couple of times and rubbed his palms against his thighs. "I've never told anybody before. It's a family secret. Mom would kill me."

"I won't tell." I wanted to reach out and take his hand, but I didn't. But because I am incredibly shallow, I became very aware that the sides of his sneakers were touching the sides of mine.

His shy smile made my heart flip. "Thanks. So anyway…." He rolled his eyes up to as if looking for the next topic on the ceiling.

"Parents." I finished for him. "Yours are too controlling. Mine are too… everything else."

"But they made us who we are." His gaze caught mine and tingles spread from the wrinkles in my brain to the tips of my toes.

"They did. And we're pretty good." I almost didn't sound breathless. Go me.

He tapped my foot with his. "Except you."

"Me?" I said in mock surprise.

"Yeah, you. That was a dirty trick you played on me." He hooked my foot with his and pulled it toward him, then reached under the table and tickled my knee.

I jumped and pushed his hand away in a giggling fit. "You said it was fine."

A man working on a laptop glared at us from beneath tangled eyebrows.

I stifled my giggles and tried to gesture toward the man with my eyes, but Ethan didn't get the message.

"Oh, yeah. Once I got over the fear of knocking on your door and asking your ten-year-old brothers to play."

"Mom knew you were coming."

"It's a good thing too. Since you left me." He reached under the table again, but I grabbed his hands before they found my knee. We giggled and wrestled until we nearly upended the tiny table.

We were both laughing and breathing hard when he pulled his hands away and raised them in surrender. "Okay. I give up."

Eyebrow man glared again.

I lifted my drink. "Come on, let's walk around the square."

He grabbed his drink and we beelined out the door.

"Did you have a lot of friends in Minnesota?" I sipped on my straw as I waited for an answer.

"No. I had almost no friends. I was working, so I didn't really have time."

"Yeah. A lot of kids here work like that too. Mom says it's the rural work ethic."

"I guess."

We took our time walking past the shops that lined the perimeter of the square. It was so relaxed it was almost magical. We were becoming friends.

When we circled the square, he took my hand and pulled me across the street to the wall in front of the courthouse. We dropped our empty cups in the trash and perched on the wall.

He bumped his shoulder against mine. "Thanks for today. It's been great."

"It turned out pretty good, didn't it? My family really surprised me."

"Because they were nice?"

"No. Because they were normal. They didn't interrogate you."

"Well, that had already happened while you were away at Bree's."

"Oh, my God. I'm so sorry."

He laughed and bumped my shoulder again. "It wasn't bad. They just asked the usual. Who my parents were, how much money Dad made—"

"They didn't!" I was horrified until I saw the laughter in his eyes.

"Of course not." His expression turned serious. "Your family is really cool. You do know that."

"They drive me crazy, but I wouldn't trade them." I wagged my index finger between us. "But you haven't met my grandma. She's amazing, but she's also… well, let's just say there is no filter between her brain and her mouth."

Ethan's phone rang. He pulled it from his pocket and looked at the screen.

I didn't mean to look at his screen, but it was right there. And it was impossible to miss the word written below the picture of the woman that popped up.

Mum.

7

Frasier

I STOOD and walked away from Jenna to keep her from hearing Mum's accent through the phone. "Hello."

"Hi, Frasier. Any idea when you might be home?" Her tone was so light she practically sang the words over the phone. At the same time, it was strained, as though she was struggling to keep it together.

"We're about to leave. Is everything okay?"

"Sure. I was curious." There it was. A little hitch in her voice.

"I'll come home now."

"Thank you." She breathed the words and I could almost see her close her eyes and let out a long, slow sigh.

I ended the call and turned to Jenna. "Mom wants me to come home." To hide the anxiety over what was waiting for me, I flashed an emoji full-teeth grin. "See? Overprotective."

Jenna looked up at me from the wall with her head cocked and a suspicious smile on her lips.

"What?"

She shook her head. "I think it's sweet that you have your mom labeled as *Mum*."

My insides curled inward a bit. "Do I?"

"What do you mean, *do I?* You don't know what you put on your phone?"

"I guess I just never thought about it." I needed to derail this topic. Now. I reached out and she let me pull her to stand.

That wee bit of skin contact between us was glorious. Everything inside me felt charged and I wanted to wrap my arm around her, or at least hold her hand. But she'd dropped mine and stepped away as soon as she was on two feet. My heart sank a wee bit. Ethan Smith couldn't get a pretty girl to hold his hand.

Would things be different if she knew I was really Frasier Anderson? But I couldn't tell her and wasn't sure I'd want to. Ethan was more me than Frasier was.

Frasier was my real name, but it was also a platform carefully crafted by the people who handled me. Confident, smart, charming, athletic. I could never show the insecure, shy lad who sometimes wanted to hide from the world.

I reminded myself that Frasier Anderson had got me to America, to Hillside, to the pretty girl standing in front of me smiling. I wanted to look into her eyes forever. There was something about her gaze that pulled me in and made my head spin and my heart dance.

Totally uncool. I had to stop staring.

I looked away and faked an uncomfortable laugh. "I guess it's kind of lame to call her Mum."

She wrapped both hands around my bicep and leaned in. "Don't be embarrassed. It's sweet." We started across the street to her truck and she didn't let go. "Is there anybody English in your family?"

"English?" I sounded incapable of comprehending words —which to be honest, was kind of true since my heart was doing a celebratory dance that she was still hanging on to my arm.

"The whole *mum* thing. And sometimes… I don't know how to explain it, but some of the words you say are kind of accenty."

"Accenty? Is Miss Y'all making fun of my accent?"

"I have a Texas accent. I can even hear the twang. But your accent is different. Not bad. It's just some words. It's kind of cute."

At her truck she dropped my arm and flattened her back against her door. I wanted to stand in front of her and lean in for a kiss. Instead, I hitched my shoulder against the door frame. "Like what words?"

"Hmm. I can't think of specifics. I think it's mostly words with *r*'s. You put a little roll on them."

"I'll work on it." Oh, this was an acting job, to be sure. I poured sarcastic humor into my tone and casually pushed off the door frame. But on the inside, I was freaking out.

"No. Don't change. It's what makes you unique." She climbed into her seat as I rounded the bonnet. "Like the way you say 'at the weekend.'"

What did Americans say? Panic was pretty much raging through me at this point. I thought I'd nailed the accent. Thought I knew the little nuances of American language. Two days in Hillside and I was on the verge of being outed. There was no way I was going to last two weeks.

As I buckled in, Jenna looked at me and placed her palm on my arm. "I didn't mean to insult you. I really do think it's cute. I don't think anybody else even notices."

I covered her hand with my mine and my gaze found hers. "You didn't insult me." The words came out almost as a squeak.

She slid her hand away. It was a smooth move, not a reflex jerk in any way, but she might as well have punched me in the heart.

It should have been a Hollywood moment. My voice

should have been husky, not prepubescent teen. Tension should have built in the truck and all of the touches and long gazes should have led to a kiss.

But that would have broken the no-dating rule. The more I was around Jenna, the more I was coming to hate that rule.

Jenna put the truck in gear and backed out. "When we first moved here, I hated Hillside."

I turned in my seat toward her. "Really?"

"Yeah. Dad teaches at the community college in Spring Creek. But he used to teach at a college a few hours south of here. It was tied to A&M. I loved it. I loved the excitement of being close to a major university and I've always wanted to be an Aggie."

I had no idea what A&M was, or an Aggie, but it was obvious I should have. "What changed your mind?"

"Friends like Melanie Joy and Bree. But more than that, this town. The way everybody supports everybody."

"You mean like the way the whole town shows up for the football on Fridays."

"Yeah. But it's not just that. Hillside has a history of tragedy and scandal. I don't know if that's made everybody closer, but we definitely watch each other's backs."

I liked the idea that people in the town took care of each other. My village in Scotland was the same. But it also worried me about how this whole deception would go over. Guilt dug into my gut. If I could tell one person—if I could tell Jenna—I'd feel better.

She pulled up alongside my house and stopped. "We're here." She smiled at me and God, I wanted to kiss her. But there was no *kiss me* signal in her face.

"Thanks. I had a great time."

"Me too."

I reached into backseat. "I'll just get my backpack."

And then the atmosphere got really wonky. There was a lot

of residual chemistry floating around in that truck, which added to the awkwardness between us.

"I'll pick you up at the same time tomorrow."

"I'll be ready." I opened the door and executed a perfect pratfall out of the truck. I thought it would be hilarious, but the way Jenna screamed suggested otherwise.

I popped up and waved. "I'm good. I'll see you tomorrow."

"Thank goodness. Be careful."

"I will." I closed the door and made my way up to the house with the knowledge that Jenna now thought I was a complete nub.

THE HOUSE WAS SURPRISINGLY QUIET. Mum and Dad were upstairs watching television.

Dad barely looked up when I entered the lounge. "How was your day with Jenna?"

"Good." I sat in the chair opposite the sofa. "Why are you being so calm about me spending time with her?"

Mum shook her head. "I've given up. You're seventeen. You have a career. You make your own money. You can make your own decisions."

"No. Something's not right. Just ten minutes ago you asked when I was coming home. You are the poster parents for helicopter parenting."

Mum clicked off the television. "We failed Fiona. We don't want to fail you too."

I'd just been gutted. "Mum, you didn't fail Fiona. And you haven't failed me."

"I think Fiona would disagree." I saw a crumpled tissue in her fist and knew what this was all about. From time to time Mum gets emotional about Fiona. Usually after Dad has talked to the PI looking for her.

I sat forward in my chair. "Have you heard from Billy?"

Dad nodded. "He thought he had a lead in Paisley, but it turned out to be a dead end."

Mum dabbed her eyes with a tissue. "If I could change the clock, things would be so different."

"Dad, are you sure this guy is any good? You've paid him a fortune for little return."

"He's supposed to be the best."

Mum reached toward me and I moved next to her on the couch. "I need you close right now."

"I'm not going anywhere." I wrapped her hand between both of mine. "Can I hire a second investigator?"

"You don't need to do that." I'd asked the question a million times. Dad always said no, but this time his voice wasn't as stern, so I pressed.

"I have plenty of money saved. Let me do something to help. Maybe two investigators will be better than the one."

"I don't know. There's so much ground that's been covered. Does it make sense to go back over it?"

"Dad, it's been three years. Whatever Billy Bynum has uncovered is redundant at this point. He has you by the ballocks. If you release him, you'll lose the information he may or may not have. I get that. Let me hire a different investigator."

Mum turned to Dad. "Frasier's right. He's held us hostage long enough."

Dad ran his hand through his hair and stood. "More than you know." He paced around the lounge. "When I got the call today, I threatened to discharge him. He said he'd go straight to the tabloids. In a single day, the whole world would know Frasier Anderson's sister is a runaway drug addict."

The bastard was threatening my dad with my career? "Good. Let him. Maybe then we'd find her."

Mum leaned close to me. "Think about what you're saying.

You know the tabloids will twist it. They'll make you the villain in all of this. It wouldn't be the first time."

"I know what I'm saying. I don't care what the tabloids write. If there's a chance we can find Fiona, we have to take it. I'll announce that we're looking for her before he has a chance to get to the papers."

Mum shook her head. "If you do that, you're liable to expose that you have the role in *Hashtag Cowboy*. It could be a breach of contract and that would wreck your career."

Dad perched on the arm of the chair. "Let's get through this movie before we make any decision about discharging Billy. He did come highly recommended. He may not have scruples, but he has managed to find her before."

"Then let's at least hire a second. We can do it anonymously or use a pseudonym. Please, let me help."

Dad looked at Mum. "What do you think?"

"Aye. Let's do it. I need to know if she's dead or alive. I can't give up on finding her." Mum turned a weak smile toward me. "So, how was your day with Jenna?"

I echoed her smile. "I didn't see her until dinner."

"What? I thought you were going to play basketball."

"Aye. I did. With her ten-year-old twin brothers. She wasn't even home."

"Did you know you were going to be left with the lads?" Mum was indignant.

"No. But I figured it out as soon as she drove away." I knew this wouldn't go down well with Mum, so I laughed to make light of it.

Still, she was not pleased. "She did what?"

"It's fine, Mum. Really. I had a good time. I like her family."

Dad laughed. "Frasier Anderson ditched by a lassie. That hasn't happened before. Good for her. It's good for you to have the ego deflated now and then."

Mum stiffened. "Well, I don't like it. It's one thing if you knew what you were getting into…"

"Mum, it's fine. And anyway, she came back for dinner and I think she was sorry she missed the fun."

"She should be sorry," Mum said with a little pout.

"We went for a coffee after dinner. She's a nice girl."

Dad went into manager mode. "Just don't forget this is temporary."

"I won't." But I also wasn't willing to stay away from Jenna. There was obvious chemistry between us and I really wanted to kiss her, but if she was determined to stick to her no-dating rule, that was okay too. I hadn't had a friend in a long time. As badly as I wanted to kiss Jenna, being her friend was way more important.

The rest of the week went smoothly. Jenna and I talked a lot between classes. But it wasn't deep or world-changing, it was just nice. She told me about growing up with a house full of siblings and I told her about the good memories I had of my sister. I had kept Fiona a secret for so long it was refreshing to be able to talk about her. To be able to remember the happy times.

After school Jenna studied with her friends and I trained with Bob Morgan. He was amazing. The first thing I had to learn was to lasso a plastic calf's head. Way harder than I thought. When I finally got it, we moved on to the real thing, which took my riding to a whole new level. It was wild and exciting and I wished I could share the experience with Jenna.

Professionally, I was chuffed about how the week had gone. I had a good sense of American high school life and my accent was getting more natural every day.

Personally, I was a wreck.

As my friendship with Jenna grew, so did my feelings for her. I think she was keen on me too. But it was all built on lies. One slip of the truth would bring it all crashing down.

8

Jenna

I HAD PLANNED to drive to the game.

I figured it was the one sure-fire way to keep Grandma from meeting Ethan, from assuming we were dating, and from making embarrassing comments. I'd told Mom, Grandma, the whole fam that I was going with the girls and that it was my turn to drive.

Except that wasn't what happened.

Melanie Joy scored her mom's brand-new BMW SUV and wanted to drive. It was a nice ride. Heated and cooled steering wheel. Heated and cooled cup holders. Heated and cooled seats. You get the idea. I told her to please pick me up first. I didn't want anybody associated with the Wiley family to know Ethan Smith was going with us.

Did she listen? No. When Melanie Joy arrived at my house, Bree was riding shotgun and Ethan was in the backseat.

A normal family would have said good-bye before I left the house. Not mine. Oh no. The whole freaking crew came out to see the BMW. Dad. Mom. Grandma. The twins and my sisters. Eight freaking Wileys staring through the rolled-down windows. Eight freaking Wileys staring at Ethan Smith in the backseat.

And yes, all but Grandma knew him, but they hadn't known he was going to the game with us. And, the only seat available for me was in the back. With him.

I sat on the opposite side of the car. The *way* opposite side —the hugging the door side. But did that stop speculation? Oh, no.

Grandma: Who's the new boy, Jenna.?

Me: Ethan Smith. Ethan, this is my Grandma. Okay, Melanie Joy, let's get going.

Grandma: Ethan Smith. Are you new?

Ethan freaking-talks-too-much Smith: Yes. We moved here on Friday. Reaches across me to shake Grandma's hand.

My five-year-old big-mouth sister: He's Jenna's new boyfriend.

Oh-hell-to-the-no-you-did-not-say-that Ethan: Well, I'm a boy and I'm her friend. So, in a way that makes me her boyfriend.

Grandma: Not as good lookin' as Travis. Kind of pale if you ask me. But if he doesn't kiss another girl I s'pose he'll be okay.

What in the name of big nosey families just happened here?

I flashed them all a stay-out-of-my-business smile, reached across Ethan, and pulled back on the little black button that raised that precious tinted, shatter-proof glass between me and the crazies.

"Bye. Have fun."

When the window slid into the little groove at the top of the door and stopped, I said to Melanie Joy, "Drive." To Ethan I said, "Sorry."

He smiled. "It's fine."

"My Grandma, though…"

Bree looked over the front seat at me. "I can't believe she mentioned the whole Travis thing. That was like forever ago."

I was ready to drop it, but Ethan squinted at me. "This is your ex who is currently dating Kenzie?"

Melanie Joy said, "So you know about it?"

"Sort of." Ethan looked at me and cringed in a kind of apologetic way.

Bree said, "Last year Travis and Jenna were dating."

"It should never have happened," I interrupted. After all, it was my story to tell. "He and Kenzie were always together as *friends*." I did little air quotes to make the point. "She started dating another guy and Travis asked me out. We didn't last long."

"Because you caught him kissing Kenzie." Bree said it like I'd forgotten.

"Technically, almost kissing Kenzie." I said to Ethan, "Mom, Grandma, and I were coming out of the Pizza House and saw Travis's lips moving toward Kenzie's. I was pissed at first. But to be honest, they are much better together than we were." I flicked my hand in the air as if dismissing the situation. "Anyway, I don't have time for a boyfriend." I pressed my head into the headrest. "I just wish Grandma would get it. The thing is, she's not against me going into biomedical engineering, she just thinks I should have a boyfriend along the way."

Ethan turned to me. "Why?"

"Mom says it's because she's a romantic."

He smiled. "That's… different. "

"That's my family. Different."

"Different is good." He looked directly into my eyes and his smile turned sexy.

I hated that smile. I hated the way I felt when he looked at me. I wasn't the kind of girl guys got goggle-eyed over. But his gaze drilled right past my defenses straight to something that stirred in my chest.

It had started on the first day of school. There was electricity between us that sent messages to my arrector pili, making my arm hairs stand straight and tall. And whatever electrons were floating between us had made the air feel heavy.

Just like now. The heavy air, and the electricity on my skin, and the buzzing in my chest sent questions swirling in my brain. Was there a scientific theory for what actually happens when the air between two people charges? Was it real? Was my body having a chemical reaction? Was his?

And—oh God—am I still staring into those unbelievable green eyes?

I snapped my gaze away from his. "Are we picking up Kenzie?"

"She's riding with Ryan," Bree answered.

"Ryan? Should I know that name?" Ethan was still looking at me as he asked the question.

I wasn't going to fall for those tractor-beam eyes again. I stared straight ahead. "Kenzie's sister. Their dad owns the feed store. They work all the time."

I shifted my eyes enough to see him still looking at me.

"Oh, yeah. Kenzie mentioned her." He looked away.

And I kind of wanted him to keep looking at me.

Melanie Joy glanced in the rear view at Ethan. "We go to Pepperonis after the game. Can you come with us?"

He pulled his phone from his pocket. "Sure. I'll just text my dad."

"Are they going to be at the game? My mom would love to meet your mom." Melanie Joy's tone was hopeful, like maybe their moms could be friends and then she could spend more time with him.

Wait. Shut up, brain. You don't care. And even if I did, I could never compete with Melanie Joy.

But then Ethan got a panicked look on his face and said, "My mom is really shy. She hardly talks—even at home."

Melanie Joy laughed. "My mom will not let your mom be shy, believe me."

Bree said, "She'll do all the talking."

Melanie Joy nodded. "True story. She can hold a conversation with a brick wall."

"Just tell her not to be offended if my mom declines." Ethan said it nonchalantly, but there was a wave of nerves in that tone.

"It must have been hard for her to move here. Did she have many friends in Minnesota?" I was just trying to make conversation, so why did I turn to look at him?

He'd turned the tractor beams off, but then I noticed his face. It was beautiful. No. It was hot on a whole new level of hotness. I think my face must have registered some sort of reaction to this revelation, because he blushed and his gaze flicked to the back of Bree's headrest. "My mom works from home. I don't think she really has friends. I've never thought about it before."

Melanie Joy said, "Then we definitely need to introduce her to my mom."

It shouldn't have bothered me that she was so insistent, but it did. As much as I reminded myself that I was not interested, it crawled all over me that Melanie Joy was doing something nice. Which made even less sense. Melanie Joy would have done it even if Ethan Smith had looked like a toad.

Ethan's thumbs raced across his phone as he texted.

"Do you miss your friends?" Bree asked.

He looked up. "No. I never really had time to make friends."

Melanie Joy asked, "Because of soccer?"

"No. I… worked a lot."

"We get it," Bree said. "Most of us have jobs. This is not a town of millionaires. We do what we have to do."

Melanie Joy laughed. "In the movies you always see

teenagers throwing a rager in some rich kid's house. Can you imagine that happening in Hillside? First of all, there are no rich kids. Secondly, our parents would kill us."

Bree shook her head. "Brice Morgan threw that pasture party. Remember?" She turned to me. "It was before you moved here. We were in eighth grade."

"What happened?" *Yes, let's move the conversation away from Ethan.*

"Brice's brother bought a keg," Bree said. "Justin Hardy and Anthony Marak were too drunk to close the pasture gate. The cows got out on the road. The cops were called and practically the whole football team was busted for underage drinking."

"The whole team? Wouldn't that put an end to their season?" How had I not heard this story before?

"It was post season. The ones who played other sports got off because it didn't happen on school property. Mr. Morgan was nice about it, though."

Ethan jerked his attention from his phone like he'd been stung.

"You okay?" I almost reached across to touch him, but resisted. Go me.

He nodded in a kind of spastic way. "Yeah. Yeah. I just wondered… What about the cows? Were any of them hurt?"

Okay, that should not have warmed my heart, but who can resist a guy who's worried about the animals? Maybe it was overreacting a little, but still…

Bree answered, "Fortunately, it was a farm-to-market road, so the only traffic was people coming and going from the party. Brice's dad wrangled them back into the pasture. He's like some sort of expert horse trainer. People come from all over to train with him. He even has a show on some farming channel."

Melanie Joy slid her gaze to Bree. "How do you know all this?"

"My brother was friends with Brice and he was at the party. Brice's dad made them come back at six in the morning and clean up the pasture. My parents were *so* pissed. If Jason hadn't gone off to college, he'd still be grounded. When they started giving him his life back, Mom obsessed over making sure she knew where he was at all times."

"I'm guessing he doesn't have the Find My Friends app," Ethan said.

"If he does, it doesn't include Mom or Dad."

"It was a pretty harsh punishment. I mean, it was one time." Not that I condoned the pasture party, but it did seem over the top.

Bree shook her head. "He was horrible for those two years. Always in a bad mood. Four years later, he's graduating, has a job lined up, and getting married."

Ethan looked up from his phone at Bree. "There hasn't been a big party since?"

"Maybe not as epic as the whole football team getting busted, but I'm sure they're happening."

Bree contorted her body around her seat to get a full view of Ethan. "What about you? Did you go to ragers in Minnesota?"

"No. My parents keep a noose around me. They don't follow me on their phones, but they don't have to. They never let me out of their sight."

"What are you going to do when you graduate?" It was a simple question that everybody gets asked, but he looked like he'd never thought about it before.

"I—I don't know. Something in the arts."

In the arts? What did that even mean?

Melanie Joy and Bree exchanged a look. Then Bree asked, "Like what?"

"I'm interested in the film industry."

"You want to be an actor?" I tried not to stare as I sized up his movie-star potential. He was hot, but movie-star hot?

His face turned red and he gave an embarrassed laugh. "No. I could never… I'm thinking more behind the scenes."

"Nice." All three of us said the word. Bree untwisted herself and awkward silence filled the SUV. But really, this was the real world. In the real world, people from Hillside, Texas, didn't make it in the movie industry. But hey, we all have dreams, right?

9

Frasier

MELANIE JOY CIRCLED the car park looking for a space wide enough to pull into and my thoughts circled back to the conversation. Had I said too much? I'd freaked out when the Morgan ranch was mentioned, which was a total overreaction. There was no way they were going to find out I was training with Bob Morgan. And to cover, I'd said I was worried about the cows? And why did I tell them I wanted to be in the film industry? The plan was to not reveal anything even remotely close to my career. Judging by their looks of disbelief, it was probably not something I needed to worry about—which, ouch, stung a bit. I had to be more careful—couldn't have my lies slipping.

As I got out of the SUV, I forgot all about lies and the sting of their skepticism. I was too busy looking at the stadium. Of course I'd seen it from the road, but walking toward it I realized how truly massive it was. It was almost as big as Pittodrie Stadium in Aberdeen.

Kenzie waited outside the gate and waved her mobile at us as we walked up. "What took you so long? You texted like ten minutes ago that you were here."

Jenna raised her eyebrows at Melanie Joy. "We parked in New Mexico and walked."

"It wasn't that far." Melanie Joy flapped the front of her T-shirt to let some air in. "But I need a coke."

I took in the enormity of the place as we made our way to concessions. "Is this just for high school football?"

Jenna answered. "Mostly, but it's also used for soccer and track. Your games will be played here."

My games. It would be sweet to play on that pitch. But I'd be long gone by the time the first game rolled around.

We got our drinks and made our way to the stands.

Jenna elbowed me. "Ethan, they're yelling for you." She pointed to where Chris and the lads were sitting.

I jogged up to say hello. I hadn't expected the girls to follow, but they did. And it was a good thing too, because the girls watched about five minutes of the game before they took off to see who was around. It didn't take long for me to realize that for them, it wasn't about the game at all. It was about socializing. They came back periodically. But I'm not sure they actually saw a single play.

I was left to save their seats. But I didn't mind. It was good to be with the lads.

I'd seen American football a few times. There are a handful of teams in Scotland and I'd seen the Dallas Cowboys on television. This was the first time I'd seen it in person.

The stadium was full and everything was so big and so in your face it was fantastic. It was truly as if the whole town came to watch high school football. I will admit there were a lot of starts and stops on the field, which was a bit frustrating—especially since I didn't really have a grasp of the rules. At halftime the band marched and there were dancers on the field and some impressive flag drills.

The Hornets lost by ten points. There were a few

comments and shakes of the head as we headed toward the exit, but nobody seemed broken up about it.

I saw my parents just outside the stadium. "Dad. Mom."

They turned toward me. Mum smiled, but the look in her eyes said she didn't want to hang around not talking.

I introduced them to the girls. My dad nodded and smiled. "Good to meet you. Did you enjoy the game?"

Melanie Joy answered, "It would have been better if we'd won, but we always have fun. How about you? How did you enjoy your first Hornet game?"

Dad said, "It was good." But the word came out *gooot* and my head snapped toward him. He coughed and tried again. "Good."

I backed away from them. "Well, I guess we're off to the pizza place. What's it called?"

Jenna answered, "Pepperonis." She looked at Mum. "Are y'all coming? A lot of parents go. It's sort of a thing."

Mum softened her smile and shook her head.

Dad answered, "Sarah's throat is a little rough. Another time."

We walked four across down toward the car. As soon as we were out of earshot of my parents, Jenna said, "Your mom really *is* shy."

I nodded and had a feeling this was going somewhere that it didn't need to go.

Melanie Joy looked across me to Bree. "Maybe our moms can have a welcome coffee."

"No." That came out a little strong and all three girls stared at me in surprise. "I mean, I think she needs time to settle in first."

Bree did a little half shake of her head. "I don't think she meant tomorrow."

"Sorry." I flapped the collar of my shirt. "This move has

been hard on Mom. New people. New place." *Scottish accent.* "Give her a couple of weeks to adjust." *And we'll be gone.*

"Sure." Jenna placed her hand on my arm. "It was brave of her to come to the game. It's such a crowded place."

"Yeah." That was all I said. One word. But that was all it took for things to spin out of control. To be fair, Jenna's hand was on my arm and I was wearing short sleeves. But I could have been wearing a wool jumper and still tingles would have shot straight through me, muddling my thinking. I looked at her pretty eyes, and the way her hair curled in a perfect S across her shoulders, and the way her full lips moved when she spoke. The problem was, I didn't hear the words.

Until I heard Bree say, "Jamie B's cousin's friend's aunt has agoraphobia. We should talk to her."

"Wait. What?" *Agoraphobia?*

She waved her hand in front of her face as if that half explained what she meant. "I just thought if we talked to Jamie, she might have some insight on how to help your mom."

"Help my mom?" Great. How had they got the idea Mum had agoraphobia?

Melanie Joy shook her head at Bree. "Jamie B is not going to know how to help just because her cousin's friend's aunt has it."

At least someone seemed to be thinking straight.

Then Melanie Joy pulled her mobile from her hip pocket. "We can do our own research."

By the time we were buckled into Melanie Joy's mum's fancy SUV— seat coolers turned on—she explained that according to Google, agoraphobia is an anxiety disorder in which a person avoids places or situations that may cause anxiety attacks.

She gave me a sad but comforting look. "I'm sorry, Ethan. It says it can't be cured."

I dug into my actor's kit of reactions and managed a straight face. "I don't think she has agoraphobia."

Melanie Joy handed her mobile over the seat to Jenna and put the SUV in reverse. "Show him."

Jenna leaned across the car as far as the seatbelt would allow. I leaned toward her and we met in the middle with our shoulders in each other's space but not touching. She held the screen so I could read the symptoms. "Feelings of panic, entrapment, helplessness, or embarrassment."

Jenna turned those big eyes toward me. "Does that sound like your mom?"

I thought about my answer before I spoke. We were going to be in Hillside for one more week. Mum didn't want to go out in public where she might have to talk, and she did have a panicked look on her face when the girls introduced themselves. She would be cured as soon as her accent wasn't an issue, but it was weird how she fit all of the other symptoms.

"Yes. It does sound like my mom." The sadness in my voice was freaking first-class acting.

"I'm sorry." Jenna handed me the phone. "Here, you can read the rest."

I pretended to concentrate on the words on the screen but she was still leaning in, and I was still leaning in, and the bumpy roads caused our shoulders to touch, and we just sort of left them that way, and all I could think about was how badly I wanted to kiss this girl.

Melanie Joy stopped at a red light—maybe the only one in town—and flung her hand over the back seat for her mobile. "What did you think?"

I placed the phone in her palm and sat back. Jenna had already retreated to her corner. "It sounds like her. You can see how having your moms reach out wouldn't be the best idea right now. We need to get her help first."

My gut tightened. *Get her help?* It was a perfect way to keep her from talking, but I had a feeling she wasn't going to be happy about her Google diagnosis. Common sense told me to shut it down. But how? The ball was already rolling. I reckoned the best I could do was keep it from wobbling out of control.

"It's not like she can't go outside. She does it all the time." All three girls nodded as I spoke. Jenna added sympathetic eyes with the nod. I started talking faster and making less sense. "She just doesn't talk in public or go out alone. She's really funny when you get to know her. Like you know, when she's inside…" My words trailed off and I leaned my head into the leather covered head rest and closed my eyes. *She's going to kill me. Then Dad's going to kill me.*

Jenna's soft voice wafted across the car. "It's going to be okay, Ethan. There is help out there. And no matter how hard things get, we're here for you."

I opened my eyes and managed a smile. "Thanks." But I knew that when this lie was out in the open, it was not going to be pretty. I needed to talk to my parents like yesterday. This great high school adventure was headed off the rails, fast.

WE WALKED into a mass of people at Pepperonis. Melanie Joy led the way through the crowd to a picnic table. She introduced me to Kenzie's sister Ryan. I saw the resemblance between the sisters. But unlike the rest of the girls I'd seen in Hillside, she had super short hair. It was different and cute. She grinned as she said hello, but her face told me she'd seen sadness in her life too.

No, I'm not psychic. I'd seen it before. A lot of people in the industry have that look.

I sat across from Kenzie and Ryan, a little deflated when Jenna sat next to Kenzie. Bree sat on my right and Melanie Joy on the left.

Bree flapped her hand in front of her face, fanning herself. "Don't expect much. The pizza isn't great, but it's all we have. On game nights it's buffet only. The waitress will bring plates and get our drink order."

No sooner had she spoken than one appeared. As soon as we ordered, I grabbed my plate and followed the girls to the buffet line.

We were in line behind Walker Stewart. He had his arm slung around a girl wearing band uniform trousers and a T-shirt. He tipped his head. "Smith."

I returned the gesture. "Hey."

The girl looked up at me. "You're the new boy."

"Yeah. Ethan Smith."

"I'm Haley Robinson. My mom met your parents in the stands."

"Oh, nice." I didn't mean to sound shocked but that's the way it came out.

Bree jumped into the conversation. "His mom is super shy."

Thank God the conversation didn't go further, although I did notice a look pass between Haley and Bree. I shrugged it off as paranoia and loaded my plate. I thought they were ahead of me, but when I returned to the table, Ryan was the only one there.

She took a bite of the pizza and pushed it away. "I can't do it. Not tonight." She looked at me. "What do you think so far?"

"Greasy, but I've had worse."

She laughed. "No, of Hillside."

I smiled. "I know." I let the end of my slice dangle toward the plate and tried not to notice the grease pooling in the pepperoni slices. "Everybody is really nice here. I like it."

"Everybody is really nosy here, but you'll get used to it."

"Did you—get used to it?"

"No. But I've come to terms with it. My boyfriend's

stepdad owns the Early Bird Café. He's sort of a cowboy philosopher. He says if you don't keep secrets, then there's nothing for anybody to gossip about."

"I guess that's one way to look at it." I hoped the topic of gossip wasn't going to be my mum's newfound anxiety disorder. And where were the girls, anyway? I looked around, but couldn't see them in the crowd.

Ryan gave me a suspicious look. "How did you wind up sitting with Kenzie's friends?"

"Jenna asked me." I half stood and saw them standing in a circle talking to Haley and some other girls. The concerned looks on their faces filled me with feelings of panic, entrapment, and helplessness. I was pretty sure I'd just acquired Mum's fake anxiety disorder.

"She's nice. And smart. Did she tell you Kenzie's boyfriend used to date her?"

"What?" I sat back down. "Oh, yeah. And so has everyone else." I rolled my eyes. "I guess that's small-town gossip."

Jenna spoke from behind me. "What's small-town gossip?" She sat next to me. And as if she were my first crush, I got nervous and excited on the inside.

Ryan shrugged. "The scandal with Travis, you, and Kenzie."

The others came back and sat down. Kenzie shook her head. "It's really not a scandal. We're fine. It's the rest of the school who won't let it go."

Ryan smiled. "Yeah. But until we have something new to talk about, you know that won't happen."

I wondered how much of a not-scandal it was. Jenna had said Kenzie was one of her best friends, but there was something in her face that told me that there was still a little sting left.

Jenna stared into her pizza. "My grandmother has this idea that I need a boyfriend to be happy. I'm not opposed to having a boyfriend, but can't it be okay that I want to focus on my education and career first?"

"Have you ever not known exactly what you wanted to do in life?" I took another bite of pizza.

"No. Even before I knew what to call it, I wanted to be a biomedical engineer."

"That's... impressive. Why that route?" I pushed my plate away. I had two more slices of pizza but there was no way I could manage to choke down that much grease—and I'm Scottish.

"I've always wanted to be an engineer. I love math. But I love science too. I can combine both and help people." Her eyes lit up and she leaned into the table as she talked. "Did you know A&M is doing research on a light that can detect early cancer cells in the mouth? Imagine if we could catch cancer early without invasive testing."

"That's awesome!" I may have been a little overenthusiastic, but that no-boyfriend comment had been harsh. And no, I hadn't forgotten about the no-girls edict. I was just starting not to care.

Bree pointed at me but looked at Kenzie and Ryan. "Ethan wants to do something in film."

Kenzie looked mildly impressed. "Really? As in acting?"

"No," I lied. Again. "Something behind the scenes."

Melanie Joy looked around Jenna at me. "Where are you going to college?"

"I don't know. I'm going to work until I figure it out." The working part was the truth.

University had never been a part of my big plan. I'd scored well enough on my A-Levels to go, but—acting. I loved acting. I was never going to change the world—I pretended to be someone else for a living. I read other people's words for a living. And I was good at it. I was happy with it.

Everybody sort of shifted in a universal sign that they had

no idea how to respond to such an absurd scheme. I felt the word *loser* hovering over my head. The girls exchanged looks and Jenna sort of blurted, "So what's everybody doing this weekend?"

Kenzie half-raised her hand. "Working."

Melanie Joy said, "Same."

Bree echoed Melanie Joy.

Jenna shook her head. "I have to get out of the house."

I didn't have training Saturday because Mr. Morgan was shooting a clinic. This was my chance for some alone time with Jenna. "You could show me around. I'd even pitch in for your petrol."

Oops—wrong. I hoped they wouldn't notice the slip-up. But they had.

Bree sat up extra tall, straightened an invisible necktie, and in a tragic British accent said, "Oh I say, yes, you must pay for her petrol."

We all laughed. I cringed on the inside.

Jenna tried her British accent. "Only if you take me for fish and chips too."

And I could've played along. I could've responded with a bad version of an English accent. But I went the other way. I bowed my head and said, "As you wish."

That sucked the laughter from the table. Kenzie wiggled her eyebrows at Jenna. "Princess Buttercup."

"There is no Princess Buttercup here." The words came out sharp and fast and slapped my ego flat.

Wooo rose around the table. And Melanie Joy said, "Harsh."

I slapped my hands over my heart and fell back in my chair. "I'm wounded."

Then Jenna leaned her shoulder against mine, tilted her head in a flirty way, and said, "But Jenna, the not interested in dating, soon to be biomed engineering student, would be happy to show you around."

And my ego crawled to its knees. But then *ahh* rose from the crowd. Not the *I've just seen a cute puppy* kind. More the *sorry mate, she's not interested* kind.

And my ego fell flat again.

Trying to revive what was left of said ego, I looked around the table. "Anybody else want to come?"

Ryan smiled, "We're all working, dude."

"Of course. You all said that." At which point my ego flat-lined.

10

Jenna

I LOOKED IN THE MIRROR, changed my top for the hundredth time, and scolded myself for caring. But dressing for this tour-o-town was a delicate situation. I wanted to look nice but not too nice. Was a sleeveless blouse with shorts too much? Was a T-shirt and shorts too casual?

I started to text a picture to the girls, but that would raise things to a whole new level. It would put weight into the time I spent getting ready and meaning into the time I spent with him. I pulled on a copper V-neck tee. Was it too long?

"You look nice." Mom's voice came from the doorway as she stepped into my room. "What do you have going today?"

Heat crawled up my face. "Come in and close the door."

Mom closed the door and sat on the edge of my bed. "What's going on?"

"I'm going to show Ethan Smith around town, but it's not a date. The only reason I'm doing it is because everybody else is working."

"Okay. Why the secrecy?"

I gave her a wide-eyed-head-tilted-duh look. "Grandma."

"She just wants to make sure you're happy."

"But I don't need a boyfriend to be happy."

"Of course you don't." She patted the mattress.

I sat next to her. "Mom, I love Grandma. But she's just too much sometimes."

"You know she has your best interests at heart."

"Do you even remember the whole episode when Melanie Joy picked us up for the game? She humiliated me. Why would she say those things?"

Mom put her arm around my shoulders. "I don't know. Sometimes I think she does it to get a reaction out of you."

"Please don't tell her where I'm going today. She'll make a big deal out of it. Ethan is a nice guy, but we're just friends."

Mom gave me a squeeze. "I won't say a word."

"Thanks. It's just—there's so much pressure to date. That's all anybody talks about. Can't it be okay for me not to?"

"It's absolutely okay. I think Grandma is a little sore about what happened between you and Travis. She hates to see you hurt—and to tell you the truth, I think she was a little hurt too."

"Why was she hurt? She wasn't the one who was cheated on."

"No, but she loves you. It's hard to see someone you care about hurting. And she liked having Travis around. She'd never admit it, but in a way, when he hurt you, she felt a little betrayed too."

That made no sense. "Mom, Travis and I were a mistake. He is still a nice guy."

"I'm sure he is." She gave me another sideways hug. "You have a great time with Ethan—as friends. I'll make sure Grandma stays off your back."

"Thank you."

She stood and started toward the door.

"Mom, don't read anything into this, but… T-shirt or blouse?"

"Blouse. T-shirts are for ball games and picnics."

I'm not sure where she got that bit of etiquette from, but I changed into the first blouse I'd put on—a sleeveless, dark blue print.

I grabbed my purse and had almost made it to the door before Grandma stopped me. "Where are you off to?"

"Just hanging out with friends."

"Just a minute." Grandma made her way to the kitchen while I stood near the front door twirling my hair. Whatever Grandma was up to, I was sure I wasn't going to like it.

She came back and held out a twenty. "Here. Have a good time with your friends."

"I can't take this."

She pulled my hand from my hair, placed the folded bill in my palm, and curled my fingers over it. "Yes, you can. When girls get together, they usually shop. You never ask for anything. This won't get you a dress from Neiman Marcus, but it might get you something from the sale rack at TJ Maxx."

I gave her a tight hug. "Thanks, Grandma." I released her and shoved the twenty into my purse. "We're actually not going shopping, but it could buy us lunch."

She backed away and smiled. "You just have fun."

"Thanks." I practically skipped to the truck. I didn't know if Mom had said something to Grandma or if Grandma was trying to make up for embarrassing me, but either way, I was happy.

When I got to Ethan's, I was relieved to see him coming out of the house before I had a chance to get out of my truck. Not that I minded walking to the door, but with his mom's agoraphobia I wasn't sure if it would create anxiety.

But as he walked toward my truck, I was the one feeling anxious. He wore cargo shorts and a short sleeve, solid yellow button-down shirt. Not a T-shirt. God, he was hot. And I was not interested. Remember?

He slid into the passenger seat. "You look nice."

"Thanks. Are you ready for the tour?" I was proud of myself. My hand didn't even come close to twirling my hair and I didn't sound out of breath, although my insides were a swirling mess of hormones. If I could just control the stupid grin that stretched across my face, it would be great.

"Yes. I want to see everything."

"That will take about fifteen minutes." The grin stayed on my lips as I spoke and I'm pretty sure I looked like a female version of the Joker.

"Then drive slow." He smiled and winked and my hand went straight to my hair. I didn't even try to stop it from spinning up and down. There was so much nervous energy racing around inside me, there was no telling where it would have gone if it hadn't been directed at my hair.

I managed to put the truck in gear. "Where do you want to start? The square or the cemetery?"

"The cemetery?"

"The park goes through the cemetery. It's kind of cool. We could go there before it gets too hot. Then head to the square and get lunch. I scored a twenty from Grandma."

"Perfect. But you're my tour guide, so lunch is on me. No arguments."

"This time." I pulled into the street and blew out a slow breath. I decided right then that as soon as I could, I'd ask Google what really happens when there is chemistry between people. Knowledge was power, and if I knew the physiological response, I was sure I could figure out how to control it. Meanwhile, my truck cab was full of it. At least on my end. I had no idea what he felt.

On the way to the park, I mentioned a few landmarks, but other than that, conversation wasn't happening. So I tried another tack. "Tell me about life in Minnesota."

He took his time answering. Was it a touchy topic?

"There isn't really a lot to say. It's cold in the winter and has giant mosquitoes in the summer."

The conversation ended there. How had I not realized he was shy? I scrambled for something to say to fill the void in the truck, but came up with nothing. Everything inside me tensed. My face was on fire.

"Are you okay over there?"

"What?" I almost barked the word. When had I lost control of my volume?

He wagged his finger at me. "It's just that you're doing that thing with your hair. You tend to do that when you're nervous."

I forced my hand to the steering wheel. "I'm good." I didn't think my face could feel hotter, but my autonomic nervous system managed it. And as a bonus, sweat peppered my hairline and my voice cracked too. Yay! Go me!

"I think it's kind of cute, but… did I do something wrong?"

"No. Of course not." I squeezed the steering wheel a little tighter. "I'm kind of known for talking a lot. Dad says I can talk to a post. I don't mean to."

"And I'm not a post?"

"It's just… shy people make me a little nervous. It's nothing personal. Kenzie is shy."

"Okay, first, I've never been called shy before. Second, why do shy people bother you?"

"It's not that they bother me. They make me nervous. Shy people are watchers and listeners. I know half the stuff I say is probably stupid and unimportant. But it fills the quiet gap. If I'm talking to someone who is also a talker, I know they're only partially listening because they're waiting for their turn to talk. But when I'm talking to a shy person, like Kenzie, they're really listening. They're thinking about the words and the context and my secret is out."

He shifted to angle toward me. Yeah, he was really listening. "What secret?"

"That I'm not smart." The words fell out of my mouth without a second thought and my heart did a little why'd-you-tell-him-that dance.

"Your grades say you are."

"No. My grades say I study hard."

"You're right. I guess it is pretty weak to have to memorize all those facts to make good grades. If you were smart, they would just appear in your brain."

For two beats or maybe three, my heart hopped like it had been kicked.

"I'm joking." There was a little laugh in his voice that made my heart do a different dance. "Think about it. Knowledge doesn't just fall into your brain. You have to have an interest, for one, and then you have to be able to understand and learn."

He was right, of course. But calling me out on my secret fear didn't help and I had no idea how to respond to his words. Nobody should have to comfort me. I was strong. I didn't need it. But I couldn't leave what he'd said hanging. I managed a weak thank you and worked to drive the conversation almost anywhere else.

I pulled in at the entrance to the park. "Here we are." I pointed across the playground. "That's the walking trail that cuts right through the cemetery."

The day was already heating up, but the playground and picnic tables were filled with moms and kids. I snagged the last empty parking place.

Ethan got out first and waited for me on the path. "Does everybody in Hillside have a truck?"

I looked around the parking lot. "I guess so. All my friends do—at least in their family." I scrunched my nose. "Is that weird?"

"I think maybe it's Texas. There are a lot of trucks in Minnesota, but not like here."

We started down the path toward the cemetery. "What was your school like there? What were your friends like?"

"I went to a small school. My friends were like the guys here, I guess."

"Did you have a best friend?"

A half smile made its way to his lips. "Yeah. James. We played football together."

"You played football? I thought you were more of a soccer guy."

"Oh… I meant when I was younger. He was probably the funniest person I've ever met."

"Was?"

"Is. I haven't seen him in a couple of years." He pointed ahead. "Is that the cemetery?"

"Yeah. I guess some people might think it's creepy having the path skirt the edge of the cemetery, but I think it's kind of cool."

A whizzing sound came from behind us. I turned in time to see two bicyclists heading toward us, with three more behind them. I grabbed Ethan's arm and pulled him off the path into the grass.

In all, about eight bikes zipped past. "Jeez. That was crazy. I run this trail all the time. I've never had that happen. Most cyclists are really cool about warning when they're about to pass."

Ethan looked down the path after them. "Are you okay?"

"Yeah. I saved you, remember?"

He smiled and I was a little grateful that I couldn't see his eyes behind the dark lenses of his sunglasses. But tractor-beam eyes or not, something was happening between us. His hands reached out like he was going to touch my arms. My whole body tingled with anticipation of his touch. But then he let his hands drop to his sides. "Think it's safe enough to walk to the cemetery?"

"I'll take my chances." We walked side by side, arms swinging, not touching but wanting to. At least, I think he wanted to touch mine. Mine sure wanted to touch his. I had to stop this nonsense.

The path widened to a road at the cemetery. "What is it about graveyards that makes them fascinating?" Good for me. There was nothing romantic about a cemetery.

He stopped walking and faced the line of headstones. "I don't know. There's history there. I'm always curious about what kind of life people had, what their family was like. It's like old homes. Wouldn't it be cool to be able to peek back in time and see what they were like when they were new?"

I shook my head. "I've thought the same thing. Especially the really old homes. A hundred years ago, what were they like?"

He cocked his head. "A hundred years ago. In other parts of the world, that would be considered new."

"True, but I've never been to other parts of the world, so a hundred years seems ancient. Have you been overseas?"

"Yes."

"Really? What part?"

"Scotland and England mostly."

"That's so cool. I want to travel overseas. I think it'll be the first thing I do after college. What's your favorite country?"

"Scotland, without a doubt."

"Why Scotland?"

His face went into full smile mode. "It's a beautiful country."

"Doesn't it rain like every day?"

"That's why it's so beautiful."

"To be honest, I don't know much about it. I've heard of

the Isle of Skye and Edinburgh and Glasgow, but that's about it. Do men really wear kilts?"

He shook his head. "Other than the tour guides? No. If they do, it's mostly for special occasions."

"What's your favorite city?"

"City would have to be Edinburgh. But my favorite town is a little village called Alford. It's in the northeast."

"What makes Alford special?"

He rubbed the back of his neck. "I don't know. I guess because it was the first village we visited."

"First village?"

"My parents really like Scotland." He smiled, but there was a change in the atmosphere between us—almost as if he'd shared something he hadn't meant to. "How about showing me the rest of your town?"

"Sure." We turned down the path back to my truck and I tried to squelch the feeling that he regretted our conversation about Scotland. But why? And who was this guy who apparently jet-setted across the ocean all the time?

11

Frasier

WHAT WAS I THINKING? I told her I'd been to Scotland. I even mentioned Alford. I might as well have told her that I was Scottish and a liar and this whole thing was just research. And what was that moment after the bicycles nearly flattened us? I'd come so close to running my hands down her arms. I wanted to feel her skin beneath my touch. I wanted to kiss her.

Dave's words rang in my head. *No girls. No dating.*

But she was so real and she didn't know who I was. Aye, hardly anybody in the US knew who I was and aye, I had chosen to be an actor. No, I wasn't sorry. But truth—I had seen fans struggle to be normal around me or my castmates enough to know that people were different when you were a celebrity.

Celebrity. Such an odd concept.

I was just a lad who happened to be really good at pretending to be someone else. It's kind of creepy when you think about it. When fans were nervous around me, I would try to put them at ease. Usually I'd end up doing or saying something ridiculous. It was refreshing to take this little hiatus from celebrity life.

Jenna and I were becoming friends and there was chemistry between us that could take things beyond friends. Except everything about me was a lie.

We buckled into the truck and I smiled at her. "Tell me something interesting about Hillside."

"There's nothing interesting about Hillside. It's just a typical quirky small town."

"Okay, tell me something quirky about Hillside."

"Hmm. Our courthouse is quirky and kind of cool."

"How so?"

"First, it's got gargoyles, which is not common for Texas courthouses. But mostly it's the faces carved in the stone."

"Faces?"

"There's some story about the stone mason falling in love with a girl. He carved her beautiful image into the stone, but she rejected him. To get his revenge, he carved versions of her face getting uglier and uglier until she was hideous."

"That's tragic."

"Yeah, nothing like unrequited love." She looked at the time on her mobile. "Are you hungry?"

"I could eat."

She glanced at me and back to the road. "Have you been to the Early Bird Café?"

"No. We don't eat out much."

Her mouth fell open and she reached across the truck and squeezed my arm. "I'm so sorry. I forgot about your mom."

So did I. "It's okay. Don't worry about it. It's not like she never goes out. She'll get out when she feels more settled." *And the lies just keep coming.*

She released my arm almost as fast as she'd squeezed it, but her energy still buzzed where she'd touched my skin. I needed to think about something else. "What's good at the Early Bird?"

"Everything. And they have everything. Hamburgers. Chicken fried steak. Fried catfish."

I'd never had catfish or chicken fried steak. I had never even heard of chicken fried steak. Should I have? Was this an American staple, like haggis or black pudding is for us? And before you turn green, they're both amazing. It all depends on the spices.

Jenna parked in front of the courthouse, a looming, pink granite building. There were turrets on each corner and gargoyles everywhere. How had I not noticed it when we'd gone for coffee? Oh yeah, I'd been with a beautiful girl.

We got out of her truck and stood side by side gazing up at the structure. She shielded her eyes against the sun with her hand. "What do you think?"

"Beautiful. It's completely out of place compared to the other buildings, but at the same time, it fits right in." I scanned the building. "Where are the faces?"

She pointed to the arched entrance on the corner. "See the pillars beneath the arches? They're around them. Come on. I'll show you."

Each of the four corners of the building had arched entrances. Granite pillars held up the arches and at the top of each pillar was a carving of the face of a woman. The beautiful faces looked cherubic. But the faces morphed into various stages until monstrous versions of the woman were revealed. "We think revenge on social media is bad," I said. "This is etched in stone for all time."

Jenna laughed, "Yeah. At least if someone spills tea on Twitter, it only matters until the next big thing happens."

Unless you're Frasier Anderson, in which case it almost costs you an acting gig. Old hurt and anger threatened to get into my head. Not today. Not worth it.

I put my hand on my stomach. "I'm starving. Are you ready for lunch?"

"Sure." She led me across the street to the Early Bird Café. It was a classic American diner with old-school aluminum tables. Framed American football jerseys on the wall accompanied by newspaper clippings. A short counter at the back with four barstools.

Only a few tables were occupied, but Jenna seemed to know everybody. A group of women kitted out in horse-riding gear sat at a table next to the one we chose. A lady wearing an orange shirt turned to Jenna. "Hello, Miss Jenna. Is this the new boy?"

"Yes, ma'am. This is Ethan Smith." She waved a hand between me and the lady in orange. "This is Melanie Joy's mom, Mrs. Stapleton."

"Pleased to meet you, Ethan. Melanie Joy has told me all about you."

I never know how to respond to that, so I just nodded and said, "Nice to meet you."

She leaned closer to our table and spoke in a quiet voice. "Do you think your mother would mind if one or two of us dropped by? We'd like to make her feel welcome in the community. We wouldn't stay. Just drop off a cake, that's all."

My mind raced for an answer that wouldn't drag me deeper into the tangle of lies I'd already told. If Dad were home, then he could intervene. Fortunately, Dad was almost always home. "Sure."

Mrs. Stapleton placed a hand on my shoulder. "Melanie Joy told me about the..." She mouthed the word *agoraphobia* with exaggerated mouth movements. "Should we call ahead to give her warning?"

"Probably."

She picked up her phone and I gave her Mum's mobile number. A little pinch of guilt and anxiety nipped at my insides. Actor Frasier Anderson would never give personal information to a stranger. But liar Ethan Smith had gone off the rails and given out two private numbers.

Mrs. Stapleton smiled and set her phone aside. "Thank

you. Y'all enjoy your lunch." She turned back to the ladies. I tried to focus on Jenna and not the fact that I'd probably just set Mum up for disaster.

A lady wearing jeans and a blue Early Bird Café T-shirt brought us menus. "Hello. Who's your friend?" She spoke to Jenna but eyed me.

"This is Ethan Smith. He just moved here from Minnesota."

"Well, welcome to Hillside. What would y'all like to drink?"

I ordered Coke and Jenna ordered a Dr. Pepper. I had no idea what a Dr. Pepper was but figured any American would know, so I kept my mouth shut.

After the woman left, I opened the plastic menu. "Any suggestions?"

"If you're starving, I'd suggest the chicken fried steak. It's huge. Or there's the special burger."

I looked down the menu until I found the burger section. "You mean the one with grilled onions and Muenster cheese on Texas toast?"

"Yep. That's the one. Loaded with calories but worth it. It's what I'm getting."

"Well, I've had plenty of burgers, but you've mentioned the chicken fried steak twice."

The chicken fried steak was huge and delicious and about two thousand calories. Not on the approved diet of the stars list —if there were such a thing. I tried not to think about what it was doing to my body as I forked up the last piece of breaded beef covered in thick white gravy. "Didn't Kenzie say you liked to run?"

"I do, but I'm not trying out for cross-country."

"Grades." I nodded. "After this meal, I feel like I need to step up my running. Would you like to go for a run tomorrow?"

She hesitated and I could almost see the struggle between her no-dating policy and wanting to say yes.

"Maybe Kenzie could join us." Then it wouldn't be a date.

She smiled. "That's a great idea. We'd have to run early, before it gets too hot, and before church. Would six work?"

"Perfect." I winced. "I don't have my license. If you don't want to drive, I can have my dad take us."

"I knew you didn't have a car, but you don't have your license?"

"I just never got around to it." Technically not a lie. The driving age is seventeen in Scotland, but my schedule was too full to add learning to drive to the mix.

"I don't mind driving. I'll text Kenzie."

Jenna didn't get a reply from her text until we were walking out of the café. She looked up. "She's in, but she'll meet us at the park trail."

"I haven't run since we moved here. I can't guarantee I can keep up. This could be humiliating."

"I'm not fast. Kenzie could leave me in the dust, but when we run together, she runs with me."

"Nice." We headed toward her truck and I had to resist taking her hand. Our conversations were becoming natural and easy and I felt like I'd known her forever. All she knew about me were fabrications. A paper life that didn't exist.

When we got to the truck, she looked over the bonnet at me and smiled. It was sweet and innocent and went straight to my soul. I almost confessed there and then.

But I had an agreement. The first thing I was going to do when this farce ended was tell Jenna the truth and hope she forgave me. For now, I was going to enjoy the anonymity of Ethan Smith and cherish my time with her.

We buckled ourselves in and Jenna said, "That's all there is to Hillside. Is there anything else you want to do?"

"Do you have any suggestions?" *Because I'm not ready to say good-bye.*

"Not really. We could hang out at my house, but I don't

think you really want me to put you through that. My grandma can be a bit much. And if I haven't said it, I'm really sorry about Friday night."

"She's just looking out for you."

"I guess, but it's also really annoying. That's kind of how it is with my family. We're big and loud and crazy and close. When Travis dated me, it was like he dated my family." She backed out of her parking space.

"I've never been around a big, loud family. It's very quiet in my house. Mom and Dad both work from home. Most of mom's work is in the UK and they're six hours ahead, so her hours are insane." That statement was completely true and it felt good.

"Is that why you've been over there so much? Because of your mom's job?"

"Yeah." Why hadn't I thought of that?

"What do your parents do?"

"Mom works for a finance company and Dad… Dad manages people."

"Manages people virtually?"

"Yeah. I don't get it either." Time to change the subject before I got my lies mixed up. "Do you want to hang out at my house for a while?"

She looked at me and back through the windscreen and I was sure I was about to feel the sting of rejection.

"We could do homework together. It would be quiet—that I can guarantee."

She smiled. "You had me at *quiet*. But I have to run by my house and pick up my books. It won't be quiet—that I can guarantee."

No dating. The words snaked across my mind, bringing a load of anxiety with them. But this wasn't a date. This was homework. My dad hadn't been happy about my going with

Jenna this morning. I'd had to remind him that I was supposed to be a normal American teenager.

"Hey, are you okay?"

I turned to Jenna. "Yes, why?"

"You looked lost. Is your mom going to be okay with me coming over?"

"Yes. Don't be afraid of her. She's nice—just an extreme homebody."

"I'm sorry. I didn't mean to sound like I thought that she wasn't."

"No. It's okay. I understand." I hoped Mum would too. I really needed to tell my parents that my new friends had decided she had agoraphobia.

Jenna parked on the street in front of her house because her brothers were playing basketball in the drive. The plan was for her to run in and grab her rucksack. But before she got out of the truck, her brothers were at my door.

One of the twins pulled it open.

"Hey, buddy."

"Do you want to play basketball with us?"

Jenna answered for me. "No. He does not. We're not staying. We're going to study at Ethan's house."

The other brother dropped his shoulders. "Oh, man."

I looked at Jenna. "How about if I play until you gather your things?"

Jenna rolled her eyes. "See why your house sounds perfect?"

"It's fine. Take your time."

We played for fifteen or twenty minutes before Jenna came out carrying her rucksack. I may have been playing with ten-year-olds, but they were good and I was dripping with sweat.

"Sorry guys. Gotta go." I tossed the ball to Josh.

He caught the ball. "Oh man. Will you play with us again?"

Andrew teased, "We might let you win."

"Sure." Once I was in the truck with the aircon on max and the vents turned toward me, I leaned forward and wiped my forehead with my shirttail. "That was fun."

Jenna shook her head at me. "Did they really beat you?"

"Yeah. But it was two against one."

"You do realize the hoop was lowered for them, which should have made it easier for you."

"To be fair, I suck at basketball."

She giggled. "To be fair, they're ten and you are at least a foot taller."

And then it happened. Her eyes. As soon as her gaze hit mine, I was caught. I couldn't look away and I didn't want to. Seconds passed and heat built between us and the air grew heavy and awkward. I tried to think of something to say, but my mind was white noise and there were no memorized lines ready for me to say.

She gave a clumsy chuckle-cough and turned back to the windscreen. "Buckle up, Buttercup. Time to study." She blushed and then squeezed her eyes shut long enough to shake her head and whisper something to herself. And I wished I'd laughed at the Buttercup comment.

The atmosphere in the cab was quiet and sort of chaotic, like we were both struggling for words. At least I was. But I was working without a script. There were no words or actions spelled out for me, and I had the feeling that if I screwed this up, there weren't going to be retakes.

She maneuvered through the streets without looking at me, without saying a word. I was no better. The whole way, she twirled her hair. I tried to look away, but it was mesmerizing to watch.

She parked on the street in front of my house and neither of us moved. I watched her bite her bottom lip and my breath caught.

She slid her gaze to me. "Maybe this isn't a good idea."

Desperation kicked my mouth into gear. "Don't say that." I reached across the cab and dragged my fingers along her arm without touching her skin. I covered her hand with my palm. "I want to spend time with you, but I know how important your grades are. I promise I won't cross the friend line unless you ask me to."

She didn't say a word. Just pulled her hand from under mine and turned off the ignition.

When I opened the door, it was if a pressure valve had been released. The air seemed lighter and normal. Only it wasn't normal. I was about to bring her into my temporary home where I lived with somebody else's furniture, where my parents were faking it as much as I was. Where everything was a lie.

She deserved better. I knew it, but I couldn't stop.

12

Jenna

I WAS A MESS. Worse than a mess. All my plans to stay away from boys and dating were crumbling and I was on the verge of not caring. When I'd seen Ethan playing basketball with my brothers, something had tugged inside me. Not to compare Ethan to Travis, but Travis was always kind of freaked out by my family.

Ethan seemed to take everything in stride. Even my crazy grandma. He wanted to spend time with me. And not because I was second best, but because he liked me, Jenna Wiley. The best part was that he was willing to do it on my terms.

No games, no lies, no hidden agenda.

My heart lightened as we made our way up the walk to his door, my no-dating armor beginning to crack. When we got to the door, I hesitated. "Did you warn your parents I was coming over?"

"Yeah. I texted. It's cool." He guided me through the door and led me down the entry hall to the kitchen.

Mr. Smith sat at the bar staring into the screen of his laptop. He looked up and smiled. "Hello, Jenna."

I smiled back and said hello and wondered if Mrs. Smith was hiding somewhere.

Ethan looked around, "Where's Mom?"

Mr. Smith raised his eyes to the ceiling. "Watching some romcom upstairs. I'm afraid you'll have to study down here."

Ethan gave an easy shrug and turned to me. "Can I get you something to drink?"

"Water is fine."

Mr. Smith pointed to the dining area. "You can spread your books on the table."

Ethan handed me a glass of ice water. "I'm going grab a quick shower." He looked at his dad and added, "Her ten-year old brothers gutted me in basketball."

Mr. Smith laughed, "I'm not surprised. I've played you. Go on. I'll entertain your guest."

Yes. There was a chink or maybe a split in my no-dating armor, but this felt too familiar, too much like girlfriend territory. His dad did not need to entertain me.

I pulled my books from my backpack and stacked them on the table.

Mr. Smith closed his laptop and turned to me. "Ethan said you showed him around town. Anything we need to revisit?"

"There isn't much to see, really. We went to the Early Bird for lunch. That's probably the highlight."

"Sarah and I have been meaning to check it out."

"You have?"

"Yeah. I've heard the food is great."

"Oh. Yes. It's very good so it's almost always busy… I just thought you should know and all…." My words sort of drifted away. I wasn't supposed to know about Mrs. Smith's problem and shouldn't have said that last part. But I had, and I couldn't just pull those words back in. Instead, I kept talking. "Not that busy is bad, though. It's just crowded. With lots of people. And if someone didn't feel comfortable around lots of people… it could be difficult." *Oh jeez, why can't the words stop coming? And now I'm twirling my hair.*

Mr. Smith sat back and folded his arms across his chest and looked at me with such concern there was a deep vertical line trenching its way right between his eyes. "Are you okay?"

"Fine. I'm fine." I puffed up my cheeks and released the air like a dying balloon. "Loook at all these books. Lots of homework."

"I'll leave you to it, then." He grabbed his laptop. "I'll just be upstairs if you need anything."

"Uh-huh." My head bobbled weirdly on my neck and I wanted to disappear.

I tried to read the Chemistry assignment, but I couldn't concentrate. I'd looked like a complete loon in front of Mr. Smith. I mean, the man was so uncomfortable he'd left the room. Not that I minded that part. It was a relief not to have the parent around, but I felt like I'd scared him away.

After my hundredth attempt at trying to read the same paragraph, Ethan returned carrying a pile of books. "You started without me?"

"Hardly. I can't seem to focus."

He stacked his books on the table and sat sideways in the chair next to me, facing me. "Everything okay?"

"Huh. Your dad just asked the same thing." My voice went into this weird high pitch at the end of that sentence. I had to get ahold of my nerves. I swung my legs around to face him. Our knees almost touched and that did *not* help me get ahold of my nerves. Oh no. Quite the opposite. Electrons bounced between our patellas and up and down my skin. And all of that made my heart race. Or maybe it was because of what I was about to confess. "I have this thing about being truthful. So, I hope what I'm about to say doesn't upset you."

His eyes widened until he had an almost panicked look. "Okay."

I squeezed my hands together to keep from twirling my hair. "It's not bad. I don't think. But I said something to your dad that I shouldn't have."

"My dad? What did you say?"

"Well, he asked me about the Early Bird and I thought about how crowded it was, and your mom, and then my mouth went out of control…"

He sat back and gave me serious side eye. "What exactly did you say?"

I took a deep breath. "That there were a lot of people and I thought he should know in case crowds made someone uncomfortable."

He tucked his lips like he was trying to hide an expression. Which was awful. I wasn't sure if he was angry, or frustrated, or amused.

"I'm sorry. When I get nervous my mouth takes over."

He reached across and covered my hands. "I'm sure it's fine."

Oh, boy. Tha-aa-t definitely did not help the nerves situation. What was this feeling? Heat. Yeah. Heat traveled from his hands through me, and my thoughts were kind of muddled and I was trying not to look in his eyes because… Well, we all know what happens then.

Somehow, I managed to form words. "I'm not supposed to know about your mom."

"If he says anything, I'll tell him the truth. You and the girls figured it out." He smiled, but I saw worry in his eyes and as if I needed more sensations going on inside me, my stomach tightened.

Must get control of my emotions. I pulled away and swung my legs under the table and tried not to sound like I'd just run a marathon. "Good. The truth is always right." *Great. That came out a little breathy.*

He straightened in his chair too. "Yeah." His voice was

raspy—almost a whisper and I had the feeling it wasn't as okay as he said.

Our "study time" was pretty much a disaster. My mind was playing a loop of what I had said to his dad and Ethan's reaction and my reaction to Ethan's reaction. And how much I wanted to feel his hands on my mine again. And what it would be like to hug him—to kiss him. I tried to make my logical brain argue with my heart that I did not need a distraction from my grades.

Five days into senior year and I was so distracted I was losing my mind.

Losing my heart.

After enduring an hour of mind looping and daydreaming and arguing with myself, I closed my book. "I'm sorry. I'm not into it today."

He nodded. "Me either. Do you want to watch a movie?"

"Do you think we should? I think I upset your dad."

He took my hand in both of his and ran his thumbs over my knuckles. *Oh yes. That's nice.* "You haven't done anything wrong. I want to hang out with you. It doesn't matter if we study or watch TV or stare at the wall. I like being around you."

And those chemistry-making microparticles shredded my no-dating armor. The energy between us made it hard to breathe, much less speak. And then there were his eyes. Yeah, I was lost. Couldn't look away. Didn't want to. It almost hurt, the way our gazes connected.

He squeezed my hand. "Say something before I pass out."

"I like spending time with you too. But I'm scared."

He reached toward my face and I held my breath. With his fingertips, he glided my hair away from my face and my lips fell open. My pulse thrummed in my neck and I wondered if he was going to kiss me.

"Finished studying?" Mr. Smith held his laptop under his arm and distrust in his voice.

Without missing a beat, Ethan released me and said, "Yep. We thought we'd join you and Mom and watch a movie."

Mr. Smith raised a brow. "You know how Mom is about her romances."

Ethan smiled. "I do. She's always asking me to join her." He took my hand. "Come on. They're usually pretty sappy."

"I love sappy." And I loved and hated that we weren't going to be alone.

Mrs. Smith was curled in an overstuffed chair, wrapped in a blanket, with a box of tissue and a glass of wine next to her.

"Hello, Mrs. Smith." I felt a little like an intruder, but she gave me an easy smile and friendly nod before turning back to her movie.

Ethan and I sat on the sofa. We weren't cuddled or super close. He didn't hold my hand, but it was still tense. I kept my eyes on the couple arguing on screen while Mrs. Smith's gaze bounced between us and the TV.

Then she took her glass of wine and got up.

Ethan reached for the remote. "Do you want me to pause it?"

She flashed a fake smile, shook her head, and headed downstairs.

I worked on not crying. Ethan took my hand. "Don't you dare let that get to you. It has nothing to do with you."

"I get the feeling your parents don't approve of me." I pulled my hand from his and stood. "I think I'd better go."

He stood and smoothed his palms down my arms to my hands. He laced his fingers with mine and squeezed. "There's a… thing… going on in my family that I can't talk about. Not yet. Just know that it's not that they don't approve of you. It's this crazy situation going on."

I nodded and tried not to take anything personally. But my eyes stung anyway.

He released my hand and tipped up my chin to look at him. "Hey. It's okay." His gaze dug into me, all the way to my heart. That gaze was stealing it and I didn't want it to stop.

"I want to kiss you, but I won't break my promise," he whispered.

"Cross the zone." The words rushed from my lips and somewhere in the deepest part of my mind I hoped I wouldn't regret them. But in that moment, all I could think about was what was happening between us.

He moved closer and breathed, "You're sure."

My lips burned to feel his, but I couldn't speak so I just nodded.

His lips barely touched mine but energy, chemistry, electrons, atoms, whatever, spread from the point of contact to every part of me.

My arms went around his neck and his circled my waist and we kissed again. Full body contact. He held me tight against him and it was a good thing—I don't think I could've stayed standing otherwise.

One would think an explosive kiss like that would release some of the energy in the room, but that's not what happened. The longer we kissed, the more the electrons danced around us as if they were pushing us together… or maybe keeping us together. Whatever. I just know it was glorious.

When we pulled away, we were both breathless.

"I was going to stay away from boys this year."

He smiled at me. "I'm glad I'm the boy you broke your promise with."

Just don't make me regret it.

All my insecurities—that I wasn't worthy, the memory of seeing Travis and Kenzie the moment before they kissed—

flooded back into my mind. The hurt of Travis's lies threatened to rise to the surface.

Then Ethan cupped my face and ran his thumb down my cheek. "I'm really glad I came here." He touched his lips to mine again. It was a mind-blowing kiss, but calmer and sweeter.

And that kiss seemed to wipe away the insecurity and the hurt of the past. I didn't belong there anymore. I wanted to be right where I was. In the arms of Ethan Smith.

When the kiss ended, he said, "Do you want to watch a movie from the beginning?"

"Yeah, I think I'm over my need to leave."

We sat on the couch once more and he grabbed the remote. This time his arm was across my shoulders and I was nestled into his side. We settled on *The Princess Bride* and were just at the part where Westley was declared mostly dead when Mr. Smith's voice rang up the steps.

"Ethan, could you come down, please?"

He threw his head back and paused the movie. "What now?" He pressed a quick kiss to my temple and said, "I'll be right back."

His *right back* seemed to take forever and although I couldn't hear words, it sounded like a heated discussion was happening downstairs.

When he finally came back, he flopped on to the couch next to me. "I am so sorry. There's been a situation with this family thing I can't tell you about." He pressed his head back into the sofa. "This is a nightmare."

I knocked my shoulder with his. "Hey. It's okay. Whatever it is, it's important. I need to study anyway."

"I'm sorry I can't talk about it."

"When you're ready, I'm here. For now, do what you have to do."

He kissed me again and I felt it all the way to my toes. I pulled away. "I'd better get going."

Go me. I sounded so sure of myself, so mature. But I was so *not* mature. First, I was dying to know what the big family drama was and second, I knew that as soon as I got into the truck, I was going to call Melanie Joy, then Bree, then Kenzie, and spill.

13

Frasier

I KISSED Jenna before we walked downstairs, again on the porch as soon as we were out of the house, and maybe a couple of quick ones as we walked to her truck. I couldn't help it. The girl got to me. Being with her was real and normal and reminded me of who I was.

At her truck, she leaned against the door and smiled up at me. "This was not in my senior year plan."

I rested my hands on her shoulders and studied her face. "Are you happy with the change in plans?"

She grinned. "Yes." Her arms went around my waist and I pulled her close. We stood there with her cheek pressed against my chest and my arms tight around her back, just rocking back and forth.

I wanted to tell her the truth right then, but I couldn't wreck what we'd found. Not yet.

She loosened her hold and leaned back enough to look at me. "I need to go."

"I know." I kissed her again before she climbed in the truck and resisted the urge to beg her to take me with her.

When she drove away, I turned toward the house and

braced myself for what I had to face when I walked through the door.

The assault began with Mum. *"Friseal!"* Most kids get the full name call when their mum is angry. We got the Gaelic version of our names. Neither of my parents spoke fluent Gaelic—just a phrase here or there—but they were experts at the pronunciation of our names—especially when they were angry. And Mum was angry. "What are you playing at, bringing her here?"

I didn't even get a chance to open my mouth before Dad fired a round. "What happened to the no-dating rule?"

"First, I'm supposed to be a normal high school kid. That means studying. Her house is too crowded, so I asked her to come here." The anger that infused my voice wasn't enough to support my flimsy counter. I hadn't just ignored the no-girls rule, I was in their face about it.

"Studying? Have you forgotten that you're not really in school?" Dad's voice was so loaded with anger that the pitch climbed with every word.

Mum shook her head. "He remembers. This was not about studying or being a normal high schooler. This was about spending time with the little lass."

"Her name is Jenna and she is a nice girl," I fired back.

"Aye, she is. But you're being cruel." Mum did not mince words.

They pierced me. I took a step back. "Cruel?"

"None of this is real." She swept her arms around her. "Not this house. Not us. Not you. How do you think she's going to feel when she finds out that you've been lying to her?"

Disappointment clouded Dad's face. "Frasier, this film is a huge opportunity for you and you committed to it when you signed the contract. If you want to be a normal seventeen-year-old, by all means, you've earned it. But meet your obligations first."

My mouth fell open, but no sound came out. Every word they'd spoken was dead on. I took a deep breath to sort my thoughts.

I loved acting. I worked hard for my career. I couldn't throw it away. "Okay." I fell against the wall and released a deep sigh.

Mum's expression softened. "Look. If you really want to date Jenna, you're seventeen, it's your choice. But be fair about it. Wait until the reveal. She needs to know who you are and all the things that come along with your career."

Mum was right. And maybe things with Jenna would work out. But I knew they wouldn't. I also knew I wouldn't wait to tell her who I was.

Dad put his hand on my shoulder. "Come on. Let's have some tea."

We'd started down the corridor to the lounge when the doorbell rang. We froze as if we were somewhere we weren't supposed to be.

I looked at my parents. "I'll get it. Jenna probably forgot something." When I pulled the door open, it wasn't Jenna standing on the porch. A woman wearing a blinding yellow frock and holding a cellophane-covered cake smiled at me. "Welcome to Hillside."

As soon as she spoke, I realized it was Melanie Joy's mum. Behind her were two other women. A short, dark-haired one wearing a green dress, and a ginger wearing shorts and a sleeveless blouse. Mrs. Stapleton held out the cake. "We brought you my special chocolate cake."

And you were supposed to call first.

I stepped back and ushered them in with a sweep of my arm. "Ladies."

Dad and Mum stood at the end of the corridor with freaked-out smiles stuck to their faces.

"We haven't met. I'm Charity Stapleton. My daughter

Melanie Joy goes to school with Ethan." Mrs. Stapleton held out the cake to Mum. "This is for your little family. A welcome to Hillside."

Mum touched her throat and shook her head.

Dad placed an arm around Mum's shoulders. "I'm afraid Sarah has laryngitis."

Mum, with the fake smile still on her face, nodded and mouthed, "Thank you."

Mrs. Stapleton said, "It's nothing, really." She introduced the short lady as Raeanne Kennedy. The ginger was called Mary Beth Nelson.

Mum took the plate to the kitchen and motioned me after her. She turned her back on the ladies and whispered, "I'll put the kettle on. You offer them cake."

I whispered back. "They're American. They'll want coffee."

"Then offer them coffee," she whisper-shouted. She turned back to the ladies with a smile and tipped her hand to me.

"Mom says thank you. She'll cut the cake. Would you like some coffee?"

Mrs. Stapleton smiled. "That would be nice."

Dad nodded toward the lounge. "Have a seat."

The sofa faced the fireplace. At a right angle to the sofa were two chairs. A coffee table was positioned in front of the sofa and the ladies did a little shuffle between it and the sofa before finding their seats.

Mum was busy making coffee and cutting cake, but she didn't miss a chance to shoot daggers at me with her eyes.

Dad took the chair closest to the three women perched on the sofa. Everyone smiled, but nobody talked.

I pulled a dining chair into the lounge. "How are you ladies today?"

Raeanne blushed. "Just peachy." She looked at my dad. "I hope you don't mind us dropping by. Let me tell you, Charity's chocolate cake is the best I have ever had. When she said she'd made one for your little family, I just had to come. Oh, but it's not just about the cake. I wanted to meet you too." Her words sort of quietly drifted into the atmosphere and she looked down at her hands.

After a few seconds of silence, Mary Beth took up where Raeanne had left off. "That's small-town Texas for you. Somebody's always got a cake ready in case someone is sick or dies." She looked around the room.

Charity twisted her hands in her lap. "We're happy that it was neither of those things. It's so much better to welcome neighbors."

Dad nodded. "I'm glad none of us are dead. We wouldn't want to miss this cake."

The ladies nodded almost in unison. We all sort of rolled our gazes around the room trying to think of conversation.

Mary Beth's gaze settled on me. "You know, I have strangest feeling I've seen you before."

My muscles tensed. "Me? Maybe at school?"

"No. That's not it." She shook her head. "I know I've seen you. I'll think of it in a minute."

My heart rate kicked up a notch. Surely she hadn't seen me in *Morlich Castle*?

My dad and I exchanged glances. I was sure he had the same thought.

Mum saved the day by passing coffee and cake to everybody. I brought cream and sugar to the coffee table, but Mum was the only one who used it. The atmosphere eased as soon as everybody had a plate of cake balanced on their lap and a coffee in front of them.

I had to admit it *was* the best chocolate cake I'd ever tasted.

Mum was in not-speaking-sore-throat mode, but that didn't keep her from moaning—which she did loudly, with big eyes. I thought she sounded like she was dying, but Mrs. Stapleton got the message. She grinned and said, "I'm glad you like my little cake. It's won the blue ribbon at the county fair three years in a row."

Raeanne aimed her fork at Mrs. Stapleton. "You know, Charity, you really should retire your cake from competition. How many blue ribbons do you need, anyway? Let someone else have a chance."

Mrs. Stapleton shrugged. "I know you're right, but Bill insists every year."

"Duncan Ross!" I stopped breathing. We all turned to Mary Beth. She sat a little taller with her back straight. "You look just like that boy on that show on PBS."

Mum choked on her cake and went into a coughing fit. Dad patted her on the back and fake-chuckled. "I guess it's true, what they say. We all have a lookalike."

My throat was bone dry. "Wh—what show?"

She looked at the other two women. "You know, the one about the castle in Scotland."

Raeanne narrowed her eyes at me. "No. I don't see it. That boy is broader in the shoulders and Ethan here is more handsome."

Mrs. Stapleton shook her head. "I see it. He does look like Duncan Ross."

My dad pulled the top of his ear. "Who's Duncan Ross?" His voice squeaked and there was a little of his natural accent in it.

Mary Beth set her plate on the coffee table. "It's a period drama. Well, there's a lot of humor too. Duncan Ross is the hot son of the laird." She slapped a hand over her mouth and looked at me with wide eyes. She dropped her hand and said, "I didn't mean to say you were hot. You look like him and all, but I'd never call a kid hot." She rolled her gaze toward the ceiling. "Oh Lordy. My mouth does get me into trouble."

It wasn't the first time I'd heard a grown woman call me hot. It sort of goes with being an actor.

Raeanne swallowed a sip of her coffee. "Have you ever heard that before? That you look like that Duncan Ross fellow?"

"No. Maybe I need to check out this show."

"It's not on anymore. I'm sure PBS will re-run it. But it ended last year," Mrs. Stapleton answered.

"Shame." My dad stood and started to gather the empty plates.

It was a clear sign that the afternoon visit should end, but the ladies didn't quite take the hint. They were stuck on talking about *Morlich Castle.*

Raeanne pressed her hand to her heart. "Do you remember the episode when Duncan finally kissed Gillian McAlpine?"

Oh, God. My first on-screen kiss. It had been a nightmare. Rachael Gordon aka Gillian McAlpine was a year older and knew I had a crush on her. I was nervous about the kiss. She'd eaten a smoked salmon sandwich before the big moment. On-screen kisses don't involve tongues, but the taste was still there. Oh, and in case you're wondering, she knew exactly what she was doing. She's a funny one, that Rachael.

The ladies on the couch almost swooned about the scene. Mary Beth confided to my mum, "We'd all waited for that moment. When it finally happened… it was so romantic."

Mum smiled and nodded. She looked at my dad fumbling in the kitchen. I was pretty sure she was sending him *get them out of the house* messages. But if Dad received them, he ignored them.

Raeanne said, "I wonder if those two actors were a thing in real life. They just seemed so right for each other."

Mum rubbed her throat. Most likely to keep her from

choking one of the ladies, but they took it as if she was feeling bad.

Mrs. Stapleton was the first to stand. "Well, I think we have intruded on your day long enough. Enjoy the cake. I'll pick up the plate later."

Raeanne and Mary Beth stood. Mary Beth smiled down at Mum. "It was such a pleasure meeting you. We're just as pleased as punch that you've come to our little community."

Mum mouthed, "Thank you," and I saw the ladies outside.

As soon as they were safely away, my dad and I started laughing. Mum not so much. She smacked Dad's arm with the back of her hand. "Stop it, you two. It's not funny." But as angry and stern as she wanted to be, she broke.

We caught our breaths and Mum said, "God, the way she talked about your being hot… she'd be mortified if she knew you really were Duncan Ross." She made air quotes when she said my character's name and we all went into a second laughing fit.

When we could finally breathe again, Dad got serious. "I need to call Dave. He needs to know this whole scheme is going sideways fast. I think you've had enough high school."

"Aye. I think you're right." I took the opportunity to retreat to my room. I wasn't going back to school—not as a student, anyway. I would turn in my books Monday and focus on lines and horse training until the reveal.

Which meant that tonight, I needed to see Jenna. Even if I had to sneak out, I was going to tell her, face to face.

I pulled up her number and was about to hit Call when Mum and Dad came into my room. They were both pale and Mum had tears in her eyes. What could possibly have happened in the thirty seconds since I'd left them?

My breath stalled. "What is it?"

"Fiona has been found." My dad's voice was strained. "She was badly beaten. The police found her unconscious, lying in a fountain. She—" He swallowed hard and blinked a few times. "She… um… overdosed on heroin."

The air whooshed from my lungs and I collapsed onto the edge of the bed. "Is she—" I couldn't say the word. "Okay?"

Mum sat next to me and grabbed my hand. "They got to her in time to reverse the drugs. She's in hospital in Aberdeen."

My chest was so tight I could hardly breathe. Questions and scenarios—none of them good—swirled in my mind. "We have to go. We can be there tomorrow."

Dad nodded. "As soon as we're packed, we'll drive to Dallas. I'll call Avery and have her book our flights." He took a steadying breath. "Gather everything. We won't be coming back."

14

Jenna

I CALLED MELANIE JOY FIRST, but she insisted I wait until I got to her house so she could give the situation the full attention it deserved. But those kissed-up electrons were still dancing in and around me and I needed to tell someone. Now.

Unfortunately, Bree and Kenzie were both still working so *now* didn't come until I was at Melanie Joy's. Those few minutes to her house seemed like an eternity.

I parked in front of her *Southern Living*–worthy home and practically ran toward it. She must have been watching for me, because she ran out of the door and met me halfway up the walk. We grabbed each other's hands and jumped up and down and squealed.

When we finally stopped, Melanie Joy stepped back. "Oh my God, Jenna. We just became those girls we make fun of."

I pressed my hands to my cheeks. "And… over a boy." The science-minded part of me poked my heart and whispered, *What about school?* "I'm a little scared, Melanie Joy."

"It's not a bad thing." She turned toward the house. "Come on, let's get some sweet tea. I want to hear every detail."

Melanie Joy's mom always had a pitcher of sweet tea in the fridge. And not just premade stuff in a plastic jug. This was homemade and had lemon slices floating in it.

We each got a glass and took off for the patio. And by patio, I mean it was an outdoor kitchen complete with a grill and pizza oven. Next to the kitchen was an L-shaped sofa and a couple of chairs. It was hot outside, but the whole area was covered and a fan whirled overhead. See? *Southern Living*.

We nestled into opposite corners of the sofa and Melanie Joy said, "Okay. I want to hear every detail, starting with when you picked him up. What was he wearing?"

"Khaki cargo shorts, a yellow short-sleeved shirt, and flops. When I saw him that first day of school, I thought he was a total nerd. Tucked-in shirt and chinos to school. Really? Now I like the way he dresses. It's nice to see a guy in something other than jeans and T-shirts."

Melanie Joy smiled. "I never thought he was a nerd. But it was obvious he liked you from the start. So tell me, Miss I-don't-date, where'd you go first?"

"I took him to the park. We walked to the cemetery and back. Then to the courthouse and lunch at the Early Bird."

"Mom said she saw y'all there. She and Raeanne and Mary Beth are on their way to the Smiths' now with cake in hand."

"Really?" My face must have shown my concern.

"Why? What's wrong?"

"I left because there was some family drama happening."

Melanie Joy set her tea on the coffee table. "Okay, back way up. Don't get ahead of the story. You went to lunch, ran into Mom and her horsey friends, then what?"

"We decided to study together at his house. While I was getting my books and keeping Grandma from jumping to conclusions, he played basketball with my brothers. I think that's when I decided I could bend the no-guy rule."

"Of course you did. Because as much as your brothers

drive you crazy, you have a super soft spot for them. What was Ethan's house like?"

I sipped my tea. "It's in that new neighborhood where all the homes look alike. It was pretty but kind of bland."

"Bland? Like no color?"

"More like a show home. I mean, the furniture was pretty and looked new and there were a few pictures hanging, but no real homey touches. Nothing personal. And there weren't any signs of a big move. No boxes."

"Maybe they're in the garage." She flapped her hand back and forth. "So, you were studying and…"

"Neither one of us could focus."

"Wooo. And…"

"We decided to watch a movie with his mom. Only she left and we were alone."

"E-e-e-e-e. We're getting to the good part."

"We kissed."

She flopped her head into the cushion and looked at the ceiling. "That's all you got? You kissed?"

"I'm not going to tell you all the details. It was a few kisses."

"But how was it?"

"Mind-blowing. Amazing. Wonderful. Then his dad called him downstairs and there was this family thing, so I left."

"Are you officially dating?"

I gripped my glass in both hands and worry began to snake its way into my mind. "I have no idea. He walked me to my truck, but he didn't say he'd call or anything."

"He kissed you. He'll call." She picked up the remote to the outdoor TV. "Want to binge some *Stranger Things*?"

"Sure."

We'd just finished episode two when Melanie Joy's mom joined us on the patio. "How are you girls today?"

Melanie Joy looked up at her mom. "We're good. How did the cake delivery slash check out the Smiths go?"

Mrs. Stapleton sat in a chair opposite us. "Odd."

"Odd how?" Melanie Joy turned off the TV.

"Well, they seem like perfectly nice people. But there's just something… off." She pressed a finger to her chin and stared into space for a few seconds. "I can't figure it out, but something was definitely off."

Melanie Joy said, "Jenna said there's some family drama happening."

"I did feel tension between them and then there was poor Mrs. Smith—she couldn't speak above a whisper."

I knew I should keep my thoughts to myself, but let's face it, that is not a skill I have. "Did you think the house seemed impersonal?"

"Oh yes, dear. It's been staged. We talked about it after we left. Mary Beth thinks they must be renting. Their things could be in storage."

"That makes sense." Relief that there was a plausible explanation blew through me.

Melanie Joy chimed in, "Of course. If they were in a hurry to get Ethan in school for the first day, they probably took the first thing they could find."

Mrs. Stapleton reached out to Melanie Joy. "Can I have a sip of your tea, baby?" She sipped from the glass and said, "You know, used to be we'd know all about the Smiths before they moved here. There's so many people moving to Hillside it's hard to keep up. I just don't like all those builder neighborhoods popping up."

Melanie Joy took back her glass. "Well, I do. We need new people at school. Most of us have known each other our whole lives. We're tired of each other."

"Meeting new people is what college is for. I'm afraid our sweet little town is getting too big."

Melanie Joy set her glass on the coffee table. "How was Mrs. Smith about having y'all in the house? I just can't imagine having anxiety like that."

"She was perfectly pleasant as far as I could tell. But the whole family was uncomfortable. Of course, Raeanne did embarrass everybody."

Melanie Joy cut her eyes to me and back to her mom. "What did she do?"

Mrs. Stapleton smiled. "She didn't mean to. She only mentioned that Ethan favors the boy who plays on *Morlich Castle*."

Melanie Joy nodded. "I can see that. He looks a little like Duncan Ross." She turned to me. "You didn't watch that show, did you?"

"Have you been to my house? I gave up trying to watch anything other than Grandma's crime dramas long ago."

Melanie Joy tipped her chin at my cell phone. "Look it up on IMDB."

I plucked my phone off the cushion next to me. "What's the name of the show?"

"Just type in Duncan Ross."

My insides squeezed as I waited for the site to load. But why was I so nervous? There were holes in Ethan Smith's story. Like the family drama happening. Like the visits to Scotland. Like the way his accent went wonky. Like the words he used. *Petrol*, anybody? But there was no way he was this Duncan Ross.

And then Ethan Smith's face popped up. Only it wasn't Ethan Smith. It was Frasier Anderson.

My heart pounded as I clicked on his biography.

Born January 13, 2002 in Alford, Scotland, UK. Parents Sarah and Gordon Anderson.

I was shocked and confused. Tears filled my eyes as I read on.

Frasier attended Alford Academy before being cast as Duncan Ross in the hit BBC drama Morlich Castle. Frasier was nominated for the British Academy Scotland Award for Best Actor in a Television Drama.

I couldn't read any more. My heart had cracked into a million pieces and one by one those pieces were splintering away.

Melanie Joy slipped my phone from my hand and scrolled through the article. "That explains a lot. But why is he in Hillside?"

I drew my knees up and wrapped my arms around them. If I could have folded into myself completely, I would have. Tears dripped silently from my eyes as I drew in long slow breaths. "He lied to me about everything. He used me." I managed the words without hiccups.

Mrs. Stapleton moved next to me and rubbed my back. "Oh, sweetie. I'm sorry."

I nodded and pressed my lips together to keep from sobbing.

Saint Melanie wrapped her arm around my waist. "There has to be a good reason. Don't jump to conclusions."

"A good reason for lying to me? A good reason for pretending he's somebody he isn't? A good reason for pretending he has feelings for me?" I wiped my cheeks, but that didn't stop the tears.

"I'll just get some tissues." Mrs. Stapleton hurried into the house.

Melanie Joy set my phone on the coffee table. "No. There's never a good reason for any of those things." Her face turned bright red. "I hate that he hurt you. I want to twist his 'nads until he squeals like the pig he is."

Not that the pain in my chest went away, but the thought of sweet Melanie Joy twisting 'nads made me laugh.

She stomped her foot. "It's not funny. How dare he come into our perfect little town and use us?"

"Us?" My eyes tracked her as she walked a little circle around the side chair—hands on hips, breathing like she'd just sprinted a hundred meters.

"Yes, us. The whole town." She waved her hand at me. "What he did was the worst, but his family lied to everybody. I'll bet his mom doesn't even *have* agoraphobia."

Mrs. Stapleton set the tissue box on the table. "Why would she fake something like that?" She folded her arms and shook her head. "Lordy, why would a family come to town and fabricate a life?"

Melanie Joy sat on one of the chairs, then stood. "You should confront them. I'll drive. We'll go over there and… you hold him down and I'll twist."

I couldn't help it. I burst out laughing again. She joined in and Mrs. Stapleton looked between us. "What? What are we twisting?"

"'Nads." Melanie Joy breathed.

Mrs. Stapleton didn't laugh. "As much as he deserves it, there will be no twisting of anything." She sat on the edge of the L part of the sofa. "I do think you need to confront him for what he did. But do it with advantage."

I wiped my face with a tissue. "What do you mean?"

"Honey, you need to arm yourself with a perfectly made-up face and the cutest outfit you can find. One that brings out all the confidence you try to hide on the inside. You are a strong and capable woman. You are going to graduate at the top of your class."

"Mom!"

Mrs. Stapleton flicked her glaze to Melanie Joy. "First or second, it's still the top." She turned back to me. "You are going to be a brilliant bioengineer. *You* will be changing lives, while that hack is reading lines, pretending to be someone else."

I felt better and giggles managed to make their way through the shock of my discovery.

Melanie Joy sat next to her mom. "True story. And in ten years, when you are changing lives, he'll be on his fifth wife. His kids will be drugged-out celebrity kids and—"

I stopped laughing. "Don't say that."

"What?" Melanie Joy cocked her head at me.

"Don't say drugged-out. I wouldn't wish that on anybody. Not even *Ethan Smith*." I air quoted his alias. "But you're right. I should never have let my guard down. I do not need Frasier Anderson. Ethan Smith. Duncan Ross. Or any other guy to complete me. I am freaking amazing Jenna Marie Wiley." I shrugged. "I'm not sure I want to waste my time confronting him. If I do that, he'll think I care. A few kisses do not mean I care. And I won't. I don't." I straightened my shoulders. "Joke's on him." I swiped my purse off the floor. "I'd better get home. I've got homework."

Melanie Joy stood too. "How are you going to handle Grandma?"

"I'm not. As far as they know, we were just friends. I just won't mention him."

"And you think that will work?" The truth and sarcasm in Melanie Joy's tone was irritating.

"Doesn't matter. It's what's going to happen. As of this moment, Ethan Smith doesn't exist. And you can take that literally."

I made a grand exit into the house and out the front door to my truck. It wasn't until I was buckled safely behind the wheel that I let the hurt wash through me. I didn't cry. I was too angry for that. But I wanted to hit something. The Smith family—or whoever they were—had played all of us. I could've driven to their house and called them out. But I knew this town and these people were nobody's fool. When the news got out, the people of Hillside would handle it their way.

Mrs. Stapleton was right. I needed the upper hand in Ethan/Frasier's deception. I decided the best way to get it was to do nothing. This way, I was in control. I could decide if I wanted to tell him I knew or let him twist in the wind wondering what had happened. He might not care for me as Frasier Anderson, but his character Ethan Smith would surely want to follow up on his seduction.

Hate burned in my belly and I didn't like the feeling. I didn't want Frasier to be worth the feeling.

My phone dinged. It was a text from *Ethan.* I ignored it, slammed the truck in Drive and headed for home. A few seconds later my phone rang and Ethan's name showed up on the screen. I hit Decline and shoved my phone in my purse.

I decline to acknowledge your existence, Ethan Smith.

15

Frasier

WE'D PACKED, straightened, and left the house in a couple of hours. Dad phoned Chief and explained we had a family emergency and were returning to Scotland, that we'd pay for a cleaning crew, and that he could do what he wanted with the leftovers in the larder.

I texted Jenna, but didn't get a reply, so I called her. It rang twice and went to voice mail. I left her a message to call me. An hour later, she hadn't called or texted. I kept trying to reach her as we raced down the interstate to the airport.

Dad phoned Dave Coleridge via Bluetooth. "Dave, we have a family emergency."

"I'm sorry to hear that."

"We're on our way to Aberdeen. Frasier is with us."

"Do you have any idea when he will return?"

Dad reached across the car and squeezed Mum's hand. "No."

"Does this mean he's pulling out of the movie?"

"No."

Mum whispered, "Tell him."

Dad nodded. "Frasier's sister is in hospital in Aberdeen."

"I didn't know you had a daughter. I'm sorry."

"Thank you. As soon as we know she's stable, we'll send Frasier back."

"I don't want to be unfeeling, but we have a schedule. We can adjust it some, but if he can't make it back in time, we'll have to find somebody else."

"I understand." Dad sounded all business, but his hands were almost white from the choke hold he had on the steering wheel.

"Do you understand that this could affect his career?" Dave's words were firm and unforgiving, but his tone softened the sting.

"Yes." Dad looked at me.

I spoke up. "My sister is critical. I just need to see her. Then I'll be back."

"Of course. I'll send an updated schedule. Please keep us in the loop. Prayers for your family."

"Thank you." I closed my eyes and took slow, deep breaths to calm the storm building inside.

As soon as the call ended, Dad said, "He's right. It doesn't matter why you breach your contract, it will destroy your career."

"I know." The thoughts swirling in my mind were horrible, but I couldn't stop them. I was angry with Fiona. She was lying in hospital unconscious and I was so angry with her I could hardly breathe. She'd done this to herself. Mum and Dad had tried everything to save her. They were still trying. I loved her and I hoped to God she recovered. But she'd not only messed up her life, she was totally screwing mine.

The wait in the airport and the flight to London Heathrow seemed to take forever. I made my bed as soon as we were at altitude, but still couldn't sleep. Anger at my sister had been replaced with guilt and I was terrified she'd never wake up. What if I never saw her again? When I tried to deviate from those thoughts, my mind went to Jenna. She hadn't answered my texts or calls. Something was terribly wrong.

I shouldn't have kissed her. But it wasn't like she was an unwilling participant. And she seemed happy that we were together. Had she gone back to her no-dating philosophy? If so, why wouldn't she tell me?

As soon as we landed, I texted Jenna. *Please call me. I have to talk to you.*

I started to tell her that my sister had been found but I just couldn't put it in a text. First, I wanted to explain who I was and why I had kept my identity a secret.

And speaking of secrets, when Dave called my dad with production updates, he told him that they were going ahead with the big reveal as planned. I wouldn't be there, but Charlotte Wray and Jack Ramsey were going to make an appearance. They were big names in US television so that should smooth some ruffled feathers.

The flight from Heathrow to Aberdeen was almost worse than the flight across the ocean. Thankfully it wasn't a long one. But it was a small plane with no real first class section. Not that I'm too good to sit with everybody else, but I'm fairly well known in the UK and several people on the flight recognized me. Typically, I don't mind talking to people and signing autographs. It's part of the job. But my mind was focused on getting to Fiona.

It was worse when we got off the plane. Most people were respectful. But as soon as the first person stopped us for a picture, others gathered.

The thing is, if I'd refused, I'd be considered a jerk. The tabloids were cruel. And I couldn't tell them my sister was in hospital. So, I plastered on the celebrity smile and endured the hugs, touches, and kisses from women of all ages.

Until, tired, worried, and stressed by all of the attention,

Mum shooed people away. "That's enough. Give him some space."

Avery met us in the public reception area. She hugged Mum and then held her hands. "I'm so sorry about all of this. I have a car waiting and I've booked a flat at the Marks."

Mum managed a tired smile. "I don't know how we'd manage without you."

Avery squeezed her hands. "It's my pleasure. Now, do you want to freshen up?"

"No, thanks. I think we'd all like to get to hospital as soon as possible."

Avery nodded. "Very well."

"Frasier!" A deep voice called out. I turned to find several mobile phones aimed at me.

Avery moved in front of me. "Not today."

Mum and Dad flanked me, with Dad's arm across my shoulder and Mum's wrapped around my waist. Together we followed Avery through the gathering crowd. Once in the car, I checked my phone a million times trying to make a text from Jenna appear. But nothing. Unless she'd lost her phone, something was definitely up.

Aberdeen isn't a huge city like Dallas or Austin, so it didn't take us long make our way to hospital. The driver let us off close to the main entrance.

Standing by the car, Avery hugged Mum again. "I'm staying at the Marks as well. If you need anything, you know to call me." To me she said, "I don't want you to worry about anything. Peggy is a brilliant agent. She'll take care of your contract and I'll take care of everything else."

"Thank you." *Does that include the mess I made with Jenna?*

Avery climbed back into the car and I followed my parents through the doors to reception. Anxiety buzzed through me as we followed directions to the Critical Care Unit. Double doors protected the critical patients from the world. Mum pushed a button and a voice came through a black box. "Can I help you?"

"We're the Anderson family. Here to see Fiona."

The doors clicked and swung open. A nurse greeted us on the other side. "I'm senior nurse Jennifer MacManus. Come with me."

We followed her to Fiona's room. She told us Fiona was in a medically induced coma and on a ventilator. Everything inside me squeezed and questions raced through my mind. *Will she survive? Will she be brain damaged? Was she brain damaged already?*

The nurse stopped outside her room. "It can be unsettling. There are loads of tubes and wires. When we go in, I'll explain everything to you. It's good if you talk to her. She won't react because of the medication, but she can hear you."

She opened the door and we followed her inside. Mum started crying as soon she entered the room, and that set off Dad and me.

Mum rushed to her side. "Fiona? Can you hear me? It's Mum. We love you." Her voice was shaking and full of false hope.

Dad stood on the other side of the bed. "Fiona. It's Dad. We're here for you."

I was stuck by the door. I wanted to move. But I couldn't. I wasn't prepared for what I saw.

The person in the bed did not look like my beautiful sister. This person was a skeleton covered with skin. Through the paper-thin hospital gown, I could see her ribs. Even her head looked more like a skull than a living human's head. Her hair was pulled into a bun, but it was a mess. Then there were the tubes. A line went into her chest, another in her upper arm. Wires seemed to come from everywhere. In between the whoosh of the machine breathing for her, a monitor beeped a steady cadence.

The nurse turned to me. "Are you all right, love?"

I didn't answer. I couldn't. I was still taking it all in. The wires. The tubes. The person in the bed. It all seemed unreal—like a movie set.

The nurse moved toward me. "Let's get you to a chair. You look a little pale."

Aye. Let's get me to a chair because… Black dots swirled in my vision. And then blackness and the world fell away.

I'd never fainted before. I'm pretty sure I hit face first. The impact of my cheek against the tile floor shook everything in my head. I don't know how Mum managed to get to me from Fiona's side so fast, but I think she was kneeling beside me before my head quit rattling.

The nurse grabbed a flannel and held it under my bleeding nose. I tried to sit up, but she wouldn't let me move.

Somebody, maybe Dad, must have alerted the other nurses that I'd fainted, because in the next few seconds the room was full of people.

I tried again to sit up. But Mum pressed down on my shoulder. "You listen to the nurse. You hit your head."

"It was just a wee fall. I'm fine."

The nurse replaced the flannel with an ice bag. "Well, that wee fall earned you a trip to A&E. We need to check out your head."

Mum said, "Can't you check him here?"

"Sorry. We need to get a picture of his head and we have to have him registered to do that." A man leaned over me and flashed a light in each of my eyes. "Judging by the edema in his cheek, I think we need to make sure nothing is fractured. He probably has a slight concussion, but I want to be sure there's no bleed there."

They loaded me onto a trolley and wheeled me out of the room. Mum walked next to me. This time when I tried to raise my head, it felt like a sledgehammer was banging on the inside. "Mum, go back to Fiona. I'm fine."

"Don't be ridiculous."

My head and face hurt too badly to argue. I lay back and closed my eyes. After much fussing about, it was determined that I had a badly bruised face and a slight concussion. I hadn't looked in a mirror, but I was sure it wasn't pretty. The whole right side of my face felt massive. I couldn't open my right eye and my nose was numb.

When we signed the release papers, the nurse offered to have someone escort us back to Fiona's room, if we could wait a few minutes. We'd already been away from her for a couple of hours, so I declined.

The nurse frowned. "Well, take it slow. If you feel dizzy at all, sit down and call someone."

Mum flashed a tight smile at the nurse. "Thank you. We'll be careful."

When we exited the A&E doors, I saw a small crowd gathered in the lobby, but it hadn't occurred to me who they were until the first camera clicked.

Somebody had recognized me. Somebody had called the press.

And the only way to the lifts was through the crowd. Mum walked on my right and I held on to her arm like a lost lad.

A group of girls held their up their mobile phones, apparently recording us.

If my head hadn't been throbbing, I would have managed to hurry to the lifts and away from the cameras. As it was, the best I could do was shield my face and keep my feet moving.

Mum pulled her arm from my hold and wrapped it around my shoulders. "Come on." She guided me toward the lift.

Fortunately, only one photographer followed us. He stood a couple of meters away and yelled, "What happened to your face, mate?"

"I fell."

"You don't have to answer." Mum spoke in a hushed tone ripe with anger.

"I'd like him report the truth." The doors opened and we stepped in.

The photographer was approached by security. As he walked away, he shouted, "Is it true your sister is in a coma from an overdose?"

The doors closed and everything inside me stilled. If that photographer knew, then the rest of the world wasn't far behind.

Mum stared wide-eyed at the doors as the lift sailed upwards. "It was bound to get out."

"Mum, I'm sorry."

She shifted her gaze to me. "You have nothing to be sorry for and we're not going to worry about this. Right now, our focus is on your sister. Nothing else matters at the moment."

The doors whooshed open and we made our way back to Fiona. One of the nurses stood up behind the desk. "Do you want some ice, Mr. Anderson?" The question would have been normal enough, if she hadn't finished it with a grin and a wink.

That wink made me want to refuse. But I really needed to put ice on my face. "That would be nice. Thank you."

"Right away." She hurried off and Mum and I made our way to Fiona's room.

Dad was still by Fiona's side holding her hand. He spoke to us without looking away from her. "How did you turn out?"

Mum answered. "Just a bad bruise and a bump on the head." She kept her arm around me and pulled me tightly against her side. "Are you okay? Are you ready to see her?"

"No." And I wasn't. I didn't want to see her this way. I couldn't imagine the hell she'd been through. But my feet moved toward her anyway. "She is so frail. She was starving, Mum."

Mum nodded and tears dripped from her eyes. "Aye. For a long time, I'm afraid."

Nurse Jennifer swept into the room with a chair in one hand and an ice bag in the other. She pushed the chair next to the bed. "This is to keep you off the floor." She handed me the ice bag. "And this is to ease the pain in your face. Now sit."

I did as I was told.

Jennifer stood at the end of the bed. "Now that we're here in one piece, I want to explain what you're seeing here." She moved around Mum to the head of the bed and pointed to the machine making rhythmic whooshing sounds. "This is the ventilator. Right now, it's doing the breathing for her. She is starting to breathe on her own, but not enough to remove it. We need for her to over-breathe the machine."

"So, she can breathe on her own. The machine won't stop her." The question was probably stupid, but asking questions was the only way I could make sense of this whole thing.

The nurse nodded. "That's right." She lifted a wire from Fiona's chest. "These wires are just monitoring her heartbeat." She pointed to a clip on her finger. "This measures the amount of oxygen in her blood. We want to keep it between ninety-eight and one hundred percent." She turned back to us. "Questions so far?"

We all shook our heads.

"Good." She scooted around to the other side of the bed. "I know all these tubes and wires look rather scary. When you get to know them and understand what they're for, it's not so bad."

She placed her hand on the top of a pump with a bag of what looked like a chocolate shake hanging from it. The tube went into Fiona's nose. "This is feeding Fiona. She is on a continuous feed." She shook her head. "Poor lass."

That was when Mum lost it and began to sob. "We've been looking for her for so long. And she was out there starving."

"Aye. But she's here now. And so are you. You can all focus on recovery."

Dad reached across the bed and took Mum's hand. "The nurse is right. This is our chance to put things right."

The nurse smiled. "Exactly. Shall I continue?"

Dad released Mum's hand and nodded. "Please."

She pointed to another pump, which was a little different from the feeding pump and had two lines running from it. "There are two IV lines." She ran her fingers along the tube. "This one goes into a what's called a PIC line in her upper arm." She pointed to a bandage on Fiona's chest and the tube sticking out from beneath it. "This is a subclavian line. As scary as they look, they're just the super version of a regular intravenous line." She moved away from the head of the bed. "Doctor will talk to you soon. In the meantime, do you have questions for me?"

Dad asked the question burning in all of our minds. "Will she survive this?" His voice was so weak the words came out almost a whisper.

The nurse's face grew serious and we all held our breaths. "All indications are that she will. As you know, there were a lot of drugs in her system. At this point she's detoxed, but addiction is a slippery road."

"But she'll live. That's something to hang on to." And we needed something to hang on to.

"Aye," Mum said, "it is. We can deal with the rest when she wakes up."

Jennifer nodded. "One step at a time." She started toward the door. "I'll bring in another couple of chairs."

She left the room and Mum brushed a hand across Fiona's forehead. "Come back to us, my sweet girl. We're all here."

I moved to Fiona's side and took her hand in mine. "You've been through so much. No wonder you're letting that machine do the work for you."

I squeezed her hand and prayed she'd squeeze back. But it was limp and heavy in mine, without even a twitch of movement.

The door opened and Jennifer stuck her head through. "Doctor would like to speak to you in the family room. If you'll follow me."

I didn't want to leave Fiona and as I followed the nurse down the hall I felt as if the tiny thread that bound us might snap and she'd be lost to us again. I wished I had someone to talk to. Someone like Jenna. But she was an ocean away and didn't know who or where I was.

The nurse led us to a large room, where there were recliners and chairs situated as if they'd been used to create cubicles of sorts. A large group had used chairs to cordon off an area on the far end of the room.

"This is the general waiting area for the Critical Care Unit. After the doctor speaks with you, you're welcome to come here. You can stay in the waiting room as long as you like. You're allowed to bring food in. There's a small galley in the back with tea, coffee, and a small fridge." She pointed to a sign with the visiting hours posted. "We're strict about visitation. The patients need their rest."

She led us to the door of a smaller room. "Doctor will talk to you in here. I know the tendency is to not want to leave the hospital. But I encourage you to take breaks. Get out and get something to eat before you return. We have your numbers and will call you if there are changes."

She opened the door and ushered us in. Chairs lined one side and a sofa the other. A box of tissue and a bottle of hand sanitizer sat on a coffee table. She said, "I'll tell doctor you're waiting."

Mum's eyes were heavy with tears, but she managed a smile. "Thank you."

Dad, Mum, and I sat in the row of chairs and held hands.

A petite woman wearing green scrubs and a white coat entered the room. The earpieces of a stethoscope stuck out of one of her pockets. She shook our hands as she introduced herself. "I'm Doctor MacLeod. I'm the intensivist caring for your daughter."

After she shook our hands, she squirted sanitizer into her palms and rubbed them together. I wondered if I should do the same.

The doctor sat next to Dad. "Your daughter is very sick." She paused to let the news sink in as if we weren't aware. "She is grossly malnourished. The drugs are out of her system, but this is just the beginning."

Dad said, "We're prepared to do whatever it takes. We'll get her the best rehab out there."

The doctor nodded. "That's good. But meanwhile, her body is weak and we need to treat that first. The opiate addiction compounds the situation."

Mum began to cry again. I jerked a tissue from the box and pressed it into her hand. Mum dabbed her eyes. "Will she wake up?"

The doctor nodded. "She's been heavily sedated. Tomorrow morning we're going to back off those drugs. She may try to fight the ventilator. I've ordered soft restraints to keep her from dislodging her tubes."

Mum nodded. "How long will it take for her to wake up?"

"We're slowly withdrawing the meds, but if all goes as planned, she should begin to arouse almost immediately."

Mum blew a sigh of relief. "Can we be there?"

"Yes. I think it would be good."

The doctor went on to explain what would happen after Fiona woke, but my mind was focused on the simple fact that she was going to wake up. How would she react when she saw us there? Would she be angry?

It didn't matter. We were there for her and we were going to keep trying until she accepted us back in her life.

The doctor shook our hands again and left.

Dad's mobile buzzed and he pulled it from his coat pocket. "Dave sent over the updated production schedule." He looked at me. "They want you back by the middle of next week."

I shook my head. "We can't leave her."

Mum pleaded, "Can you put him off for a bit? We need time to sort this."

"Aye."

I tried not to worry about how this was affecting my career. As I watched Dad drop his mobile back into his pocket, I said, "There were photographers at reception."

Dad brushed a hand through his hair. "Great. How did that happen?"

"Somebody told them." I glanced at Mum and back to him. "One asked about Fiona."

Dad's eyes widened. "Well, decision made. We have to talk about it." He stood and walked around the room. "The important thing is that we have the chance to get our Fiona back."

16

Jenna

I HAD BEEN IGNORING Frasier's texts and phone calls and voice messages… and then they quit coming.

I told myself I was glad he'd stopped trying. The truth was, I needed to know why he'd lied. Why he'd pretended I was someone special. But it wasn't a conversation I wanted to have over the phone.

Monday morning, I stood by his locker and mentally edited, refined, and rehearsed all the things I wanted to say to him until I had it perfect.

He never showed.

He wasn't in AP English either. In fact, he wasn't in school at all.

I was irritated that I hadn't been able to hurl my speech at him, but I also had an overwhelming sense that something wasn't right.

After school, I met the girls at my locker. Bree leaned against the door next to mine. "Have you talked to him?"

"No. I was going to do it face to face, but obviously that didn't happen."

"You could call." Melanie Joy shook her phone in the air.

Kenzie flicked her gaze from Melanie Joy's cell to me. "He doesn't know that you know, right?"

I nodded.

"Then he has to be freaking out that you haven't answered his texts." She cringe-shrugged. "Just sayin'."

I pulled my phone from my back pocket and held it up. "Sixteen texts and five voice messages. He's freaked about something."

"Well, what were his messages about?" Melanie Joy's face looked stricken, as though she couldn't believe I hadn't shared this information before.

"I don't know. I haven't listened to them." I shoved my phone back into my pocket.

You'd have thought that I'd revealed some deep dark secret by the shocked expressions passing between them.

"I know." I closed my eyes for a second. "I'll listen to them in my truck. I want to be alone in case—you know—" I cleared a throat that was suddenly rough. "I'm not going to study with y'all today. I just can't focus."

Bree rubbed my shoulder. "Okay. Call us after you listen. You know we've got you."

"I do. And I will."

My heart thudded against my sternum all the way to my truck. I buckled in, started the ignition, and turned off the Bluetooth connection. I didn't want his voice echoing through the truck cab—too easily overheard.

My sensory neurons must have been on high alert, because they'd sent *insides must quiver now* signals as I stared at the first voice message. Why was I so nervous? What was I afraid of? Judging by the litany of texts he'd sent asking me to call him, it wasn't likely that he was going to say, *You've been punked. I'm really Frasier Anderson.*

But I was nervous. I wanted so badly to believe that the boy who'd kissed me, who'd said he wanted to be with me, had meant it. But how could he when that boy wasn't real?

I took an extra sip of air and tapped the triangle beneath his name. His message started before I could jam my phone tight against my ear. Just the sound of his voice made my pulse jump and my heart ache.

"Jenna. Please call me. I have to talk to you." There was urgency in his tone and something else. Sadness? Fear?

I listened to the rest of the messages and managed to cry only a small river of tears. In each of his messages he sounded more desperate and less like Ethan Smith. The last message was in full-on Scottish accent.

A part of me had hoped that somehow Ethan Smith was a döppelganger. But after hearing that last message, I knew the truth. He really was Frasier Anderson. I wasn't sure how to wrap my head around that.

I really wanted to believe that the Scottish TV star was the same as his fake American version. I wanted to believe that he was sweet, and kind, and shy. I wanted to believe he liked me.

But why would he? I was nobody. I was the loudmouthed girl who spun her hair.

Tears rolled down my cheeks and off my chin and I realized I was spinning my hair right at this moment. And that made me angry. I had to stop. No more weird hair-spinning.

I called Mom. She answered on the first ring. "What is it, honey?"

"I need to talk to you." My voice hitched. "But I don't want anybody else around."

Mom sucked in a breath. "Are you okay?"

"Yes. I just need to talk to you without an audience."

"Okay. Where are you? I'll come to you."

"Can you meet me at the park?"

"I'm walking out of the house now." Then in a muffled voice, I heard her say. "Abby, tell Grandma I had to go out."

Abby's voice whined through the phone. "Where are you going?"

"I have to run some errands." I heard the door slam and then she was back. "I'm on my way."

When Mom pulled into the parking space next to me, I saw worry in her face. I got out of my truck and waited for her to join me. We walked together to a picnic table under a huge live oak tree. I brushed leaves and dirt off the bench and sat.

Mom did the same from the other side of the table. "What's this all about? Did something happen at school?"

"Yeah. It's about Ethan. Which is why I didn't want to be around snooping people."

Mom's face paled and she swallowed hard. "What about Ethan?"

"He's not Ethan Smith. That's a fake name. The whole family is fake."

"What do you mean?"

I pulled up the picture on my phone and handed it to her.

She stared at the picture of Frasier Anderson. "Are you saying Ethan Smith is really this Frasier Anderson?"

"That's exactly what I'm saying."

"But this boy is from Scotland."

"Yep. He lied about that too."

"Did you ask him about it?"

"I haven't had a chance." And then another thought occurred to me. "I don't even know if those were his real parents. They might have been actors too."

"But why come here and pretend you're somebody else? There has to be a logical explanation."

"He didn't show up at school today."

Mom shook her head. "That doesn't mean anything. He could be sick. You said his mom had laryngitis."

"He doesn't have laryngitis. He's left five voice messages

asking me to call him. In the last message, his accent is full-on Scottish." I pulled up the message and tapped Speaker.

Mom leaned closer to the phone as we listened. "That's certainly not an American accent." She sighed. "This is all very odd. I think you need to ask him point blank why the deception. He sounds pretty desperate to talk. Does he know you found out?"

"I don't think so. That's the other reason I wanted to talk to you. He's got some family thing he said he couldn't talk about. But he also told me his sister was a runaway drug addict."

"Oh, that's horrible."

"I know. I assumed the family thing was about her. But he could be lying about everything. He may not even have a sister." I was twisting my hair at hyper speed now. "For all I know he's in his twenties, married, with a couple of kids."

Mom sat back. "Okay, now you're letting your imagination take control. Put your mind at rest. Call him."

She was right. I pulled up his number and hit Call. My heart pounded while I waited for the phone to ring. But it went to straight to voice mail. The recording was Ethan Smith's voice, and I felt as if it were mocking me. "This is Ethan Smith. Leave a message." Ethan Smith. Yeah, right.

I texted: *I need to talk to Frasier Anderson.*

I showed Mom before I hit Send. "That should get his attention."

She smiled. "I would think so." Then she got serious. "I'm sorry this happened to you. I know you were friends."

I nodded and a few tears shook from my eyes. "He kissed me. I thought I was special." I wiped tears away. "I feel… used." *Just like with Travis.*

"You deserve an explanation, but don't do anything until you're ready. If you want to be mad, be mad. Don't let Ethan—"

"Frasier. Ethan was the nice guy."

"Frasier. Don't let Frasier dictate your reaction."

"What about forgiveness?"

"Forgiveness is important. But sometimes you need to be a little angry first. I can't imagine a single good reason why Frasier would lie to you. But we don't know his world. Maybe he was trying to keep the paparazzi away. But if he had feelings for you, he should have trusted you enough to tell you the truth."

I nodded and swiped at my face again. "Do you think he liked us… liked me?"

"He seemed to. I hope he did. I'd hate to think it was all an act." She swung her legs over the bench and stood. "How'd you figure this out, anyway?"

"Melanie Joy's mom, Raeanne Kennedy, and Mary Beth Nelson took them a welcome cake. Raeanne recognized him. When Mrs. Stapleton told us, we looked him up."

"What did they say when Raeanne called him out?"

"Apparently they played it off as a coincidence, but Mrs. Smith—" I air quoted *Smith*. "—choked on her cake."

"I bet she did. Are you ready to go home? I have to start dinner."

"I guess." I swung my feet around and stood. "Thanks for coming. I guess it was kind of silly for me to drag you here."

Mom put her arm around me. "I'm always here for you. So is everybody else, even if they don't always show it the way you want."

"I know." We walked to the parking lot together. "Can I get my hair cut?"

Mom stopped. "That's random."

"Not really. I've been thinking about it for a while. I want to go short. Like Ryan Quinn."

"Make the appointment. Just remember that it's going to take forever to grow back if it's not what you want."

"But that's the thing. It does grow back. I really want a change." *And to stop twirling my hair.*

"Okay." She opened the door to her car. "I'll meet you back at the house."

I nodded. "I might stop by Frasier's house. It's practically on the way."

"Just be home by six-thirty."

I was tempted to ask Melanie Joy if she wanted to come with me, but decided I really needed to talk to him by myself.

When I pulled up to the house, there was a white Fiat 500 parked in the drive. Green letters spelled out CARLA'S CLEANING CREW along the side, with a yellow daisy at the end of the name.

I parked in the street and walked up to the front door. When I pushed the doorbell, I felt my pulse surge. He hadn't answered my text. He didn't answer my calls. Was he paying me back for ignoring him?

I heard heavy footsteps before the door swung open.

"Chief?"

"Hi. You're one of the Wiley girls."

"Yes. I'm Jenna, the oldest. Is Fr—Ethan Smith here?"

He raised his brows and I wondered if he knew the truth. If he did, he didn't let on. "No. The Smiths left last night. Family emergency."

"Left? As in they're not coming back?"

"It seems that way."

My heart squeezed deep into my chest and I knew a flood of tears was on its way. I did not want to be standing in front of Chief when they hit. "Thank you."

I turned and ran to my truck. I barely made it before the tsunami hit.

I picked up my phone and stared at his texts. Was that why he was so urgent? Was he trying to tell me he was leaving? Why hadn't he told me while I was there?

Because he's a liar.

They were all liars. They'd snuck away as quietly as they had appeared. In a couple of weeks, people wouldn't remember the Smiths. They wouldn't even be a blip in our history.

Except I'd remember him. I'd remember the kind, shy version that was Ethan Smith. And maybe I could forget the other version. The one who'd taken my heart and twisted it until it cracked.

As soon as I could pull myself together enough to drive, I checked my face in the mirror. My cheeks were splotchy and my eyes were starting to swell from crying. No way was I going home looking like this. I headed for Bree's.

When she opened the door, she took one look at me and pulled me into the house. "Come on. Melanie Joy is upstairs."

When I entered Bree's room, Melanie Joy looked up from her books. "I thought you weren't coming. What happened?"

I didn't want to cry again. I didn't want to care, but as soon as she asked the question, the floodgates opened. Bree put her arm around me and guided me to sit on the edge of her bed. Melanie Joy grabbed a box of tissues from Bree's desk and sat on my other side.

I jerked tissues from the box and dabbed my eyes. "He's gone."

Melanie Joy balanced the box on her thighs. "What do you mean, gone?"

"I went by the house and Chief had a cleaning crew there. He said they left. They had a family emergency."

"Maybe he's coming back." Bree tried to sound hopeful.

I shook my head. "Chief said they aren't. Ethan—I mean Frasier—tried to text. He left messages, but I didn't answer any of them. Now he's not answering mine. I think he went back to Scotland." I inhaled deeply and let out a shuddering exhale. I sounded desperate, but at least the tears had stopped flowing. "This is why I didn't want to get involved in the first place."

And then something changed in me. I went from feeling helpless and abandoned to feeling *angry*.

I wiped my face and stood. "He *knew* grades were important to me and that I didn't want a relationship. He *knew* his time here was temporary. He didn't just use me, he manipulated me."

Melanie Joy pulled her hair behind her back. "You said it was a family emergency. It sounds like leaving wasn't his choice."

"But it was his choice to pretend he was someone he wasn't. It was his choice to chase me when he knew it was all a sham." I was hurting and I didn't want her to play devil's advocate. I wanted her to be mad along with me.

Bree looked at Melanie Joy. "She has a point." To me she said, "But you need to talk to him."

"Part of me wants to rip him a new one. The other part of me doesn't want him to know I care enough to even notice he's gone."

My phone signaled a text and my heart stalled. As much as I didn't want to care, I hoped it was from Frasier. I pulled it from my pocket. When I opened the screen, disappointment fell heavily into my gut. "It's from Mom. I guess I'd better get going. You know how my family is about dinner time." I put it away. "Do I have mascara under my eyes?"

Bree shook her head. "No. You cried it all off. Do you want to borrow some makeup?"

"Thank you. I don't want to face Grandma looking like this. You know what she's like."

Melanie Joy and Bree nodded. They knew.

On the way home, I listened to Frasier's last message over and over.

Jenna, please call me. It's important. I really need to talk to you.

The high and low inflections of his accent and the slight roll in the way he said *really* sang across the Bluetooth. Who was this person? There was not a single consonant or vowel in that short message that sounded like Ethan Smith. It was a stranger's voice. It could have been a wrong number. It kind of was, because by the time I rolled into the driveway, I'd decided that while Ethan Smith deserved to be heard, I didn't owe Frasier Anderson a single thing.

17

Frasier

MUM LEFT to get takeaway for us while Dad and I used the family room for a conference call with Dave. In the end, Dave said they could shuffle the schedule a bit more. His tone was sympathetic as we spoke, but I knew they couldn't hold off longer or they'd have to re-cast the role. That would end my career. Delays in production were costly. It didn't matter why they couldn't shoot, they still had to pay everyone involved in the production as if they were working.

I had to be there by next weekend.

We also decided I would release a statement about Fiona before the paparazzi twisted it into something ugly. The production company was going to follow it with well wishes. The reveal at school was to be the next school day instead of on Friday.

After the call, we moved to the larger waiting room. I scanned for a place that offered a little privacy. There was a large group in the back and a few small groups scattered throughout the room.

At the front, close to the double doors leading to the unit, was a small alcove. A plastic covered loveseat took up one side, a row of three straight back chairs the other. Two recliners closed off the square.

Once we settled, I pulled my laptop from my rucksack to work on a statement. "How much do I say?"

"I hate that you need to say anything, but it's better than what's going to get out there," Dad said. "Keep it simple but honest."

Prayers, positive thoughts, and privacy are appreciated while my family surrounds my sister with love and support.

I flipped my computer around for Dad to see.

"Nice. I think we should let Mum have the final vote of approval."

"There you are." We looked up to see Mum walking toward us. She held up two sacks. "The Co-op was closer, so I popped in and grabbed some sandwiches."

"Perfect." Dad took the bags from her. "We have things sorted with the production company."

Mum followed him to the corner of the room where we'd set up camp. "Good. When does Frasier have to be back?"

"They're trying to be flexible, but he needs to be back by the end of next week."

Mum sat on one of the straight chairs. "Okay. We'll make it work."

I sat next to Mum and emptied seven sandwiches and six bags of crisps on to the table. "Are you planning to feed the staff too?"

"I wasn't sure what anybody wanted, so I got one of each."

We all broke into laughter. It was a stupid thing to laugh about, and inappropriate considering where we were, but completely needed.

The laughter died away like a long, sad sigh. And an empty, hopeless feeling hung in the air as we ate in silence.

The worry was stamped on my parents' faces. They'd spent countless hours worrying about and looking for Fiona. She was back. For now. But what was left of her? How would this affect them? Anger at my sister burned deep, followed by guilt for feeling that way. I closed my eyes and pushed it aside.

I couldn't take away the pain Fiona had caused them, but I could do what I always did—make sure I didn't add to it. I didn't want to hurt anybody. And that brought my mind back to Jenna. What had happened? She'd been fine when she pulled away from the house in Hillside. What had I missed?

Mum patted my arm, dragging my thoughts back to the hospital. "I'm going to stay here tonight. I think you and Dad should go to the Marks and get some rest."

I shook my head. "I don't want to leave. What if something happens?"

"I'll be here. I'll call with any updates."

"Your mum is right." Dad wrapped his arm around her. "But *I'll* stay. I slept on the plane. You didn't sleep at all. You need to rest."

Mum set her chin. "I'm not going to leave my daughter."

"How about if we stay in shifts? Everything is stable now. Go with Frasier, get a few hours of sleep." Mum shook her head. Dad took her hand in his. "We need to be strong for the days to come. We can't do that if we're exhausted. Just for a few hours."

"Come on, Mum. You know Dad's right." I pushed.

Mum rubbed her face. "I am knackered. Okay. Give Avery a call."

Dad punched her number on his mobile.

Mum turned to me. "What are you working on?"

I handed her my laptop. "A statement. I thought I'd shoot it out on Twitter."

Mum nodded as she read it. "Perfect. That's all that needs to be said."

I tweeted the statement and tucked my laptop into my rucksack. "The media is going to do whatever they want, but at least I'll get a word in first."

THE THOUGHT of a bed and sleep only a few minutes away made the wait for the car seem like hours. Once Mum and I were settled in the backseat, I got a bonus shot of energy. But not the good kind. The overtired, fidgety kind. The kind that annoyed my overtired, overstressed mother.

"Friseal! Can you keep still for one second?"

"Sorry, Mum."

She scrubbed her hands across her face. "Sorry. That was uncalled for."

"No. It's fine."

"Have you spoken to your Jenna?"

"No. I've called and texted, but she hasn't returned any of them. To tell you the truth, I'm afraid she's found out who I am."

"If she has, that would explain why she hasn't replied."

I pressed my head into the seat back. "I know. She talks about honesty a lot. I doubt our friendship will recover from this."

Mum creased her forehead. "You do realize that now that we've left Hillside, we're never going back."

"Why? Why can't I have friends there?"

"Friseal. Our home is in Alford." She spoke to me like I was four, not seventeen.

"Aye. But the world isn't so big. I'm going to be in Texas filming for a few months. Austin isn't that far from Hillside. Would it really hurt for us to be friends?"

"We both know you can't leave it as friends. And how do you think this will play out once the film wraps?"

"I don't know. I didn't expect to meet someone like Jenna. I like her, Mum. And I wish I'd told her."

"You should have protected her."

"Protected her from me?"

"Aye. This was always temporary."

"Mum, if I were a normal lad, with a normal job, would you have approved?"

"Aye. I would have. And you can be that normal lad. You can walk away."

"Is that what you want me to do? Quit? Because it seems to be a running theme in our house." The words came out sharper and meaner than I'd intended, but I'd held them in for so long, they'd taken their own path out.

"No. I just don't ever want you to think it's not an option." Her voice wavered as she spoke and my insides tightened.

"I'm sorry, Mum."

She shook her head. "We're all tired. It's fine."

I stared at my hands. "I love what I do. I'm lucky I got to go to Hillside in the first place. It's just… What makes my life awesome also complicates it."

"I know. And I don't say it enough, but you handle things really well and I'm so proud of you."

"Thanks." I leaned on her shoulder and closed my eyes. My throat tightened as I tried to choke away tears. But they came anyway. "I need you, Mum," I managed to whisper.

"I need you too."

We didn't speak the rest of the way to the Marks and I think we both even dozed a bit.

When we arrived, we found Avery pacing around reception speaking to someone via earbuds. Trainers, running tights, sweatshirt, red face. She looked like she'd just come in from a run. But the red face could have been the conversation she was having. "But he has a solid contract."

When she spotted us, she held up a finger. "Could you hold

for a second?" She pulled the buds from her ears and hugged Mum. "How are things?"

"Looking up a little." Mum looked too tired to say more, so I stepped in.

"They going to try to remove the ventilator tomorrow."

"Grand! Your keys are at reception." She pointed to the desk behind us. "Get some rest. I'll talk to you later." She plugged her earbuds back in.

We were at the desk when Avery's half of the conversation drifted our way.

"I'm back. I'll get a commitment. You work on this ridiculous notion of Luke Bonham."

Everything inside me froze. Mum and I both turned from the reception desk. Avery had her back to us as she walked through the doors leading outside.

Mum's face was red and her lips were white. "Oh no. Not today. Get the keys, Frasier." She stalked across reception and though the doors.

The man behind the desk wore an anxious look as he slid the key cards across the counter toward me. I ignored them and followed Mum outside.

She had caught up with Avery at the bottom of the steps. "What do you mean, *notion of Luke Bonham?*"

"I'll call you back." Avery pulled on the wire connecting the earbuds and let them drape around her neck. "I'm handling it."

"What's there to handle?" Mum stepped closer to Avery. "Frasier has a contract. He's done everything the studio has asked him to do. Including duping an entire town."

"They're concerned that he might not be able to return to set."

"And shouldn't his agent be informed of that concern? The last time I paid your invoice, it said personal assistant, not film agent."

Avery stepped back as though Mum's words had pushed her. "Peggy contacted me. She knows what you and Gordon are going through."

Now Mum's face had gone from red to white. I'd never seen her so angry. "So the studio went behind our backs?"

"No. Just a discussion." Avery drew in a breath and I visibly saw her composure shift from defense to offense. "Sarah, I can't imagine what the last twenty-four hours have been like. Nothing is changing as yet. Get some rest and we can talk about the studio concerns in a couple of hours."

Mum fired a narrow gaze at Avery. "Are you *handling* me? Shall I remind you that until a few years ago, I was CFO of a major financial corporation? I didn't get there by being *handled*."

Avery's fortitude crumbled. "Okay, we can talk, but let's go somewhere private. We can meet in my flat."

"No. We'll meet in the flat we're letting."

Avery nodded. "Okay."

I stood at the top of the steps with my mouth gaping. I'd never seen Executive Mum before. I opened the door for them. They both marched through.

Mum turned to me. "Do you have the key cards?"

The receptionist held up the cards. "I have them and a copy of your receipt."

Mum took the cards and the papers and led us to the lifts.

The flat was crackin'. Modern with sleek furniture in the lounge. Nobody said a word until we were all seated.

Mum looked at Avery. "Don't think we don't appreciate everything you do for Frasier and for us. We could never have returned from the States so quickly without your help. But if there are contract issues, you refer them to me or Gordon."

"Or me." I was, after all, seventeen. But the crack in my voice when I spoke would argue that. Mum turned to me with arched eyebrows. "It's true. I've finished school and legally I'm of age. I should start learning this end of the business."

"Fair enough." Mum turned back to Avery. "Are we clear?"

"Yes. Of course. Look, when Peggy contacted me, I should have told you straight away."

"When did she contact you?" I was hurt and angry that Avery seemed to have gone beyond her duties, but for me, the timing was a key issue.

"While you were on your flight here. Mr. Coleridge's assistant had contacted her. They wanted to know if your sister's illness would affect your ability to return to set." She held up a hand. "Before you ask, she reminded them that you are a committed actor and would never shirk your contractual duties."

"Thank you."

Mum said, "But—"

Avery pulled up her phone. "Peggy said they had somebody in mind in case we were wrong."

"Luke Bonham." I said.

"Yes. And there's something else you need to know." She scrolled through her phone. "This came out about an hour ago."

She handed me her phone. Mum and I looked at the screen together and a mix of rage and despair hit me in the gut.

18

Jenna

I CHECKED my face in the mirror before getting out of the truck. My eyes were still a little red, but hopefully Grandma wouldn't notice.

I hesitated before walking into the house, took a deep breath, and forced my face into a bright smile. As I pushed through the door, the smell of frying chicken warmed my soul and eased the sadness that had taken root there. "Helloooo, I'm home." Yes, it was an enthusiastic greeting, but as they say, *go big or go home*—or in my case—go big *at* home.

"We don't carrre." Abby's voice sang back. Good. At least she wasn't aware of my emotional trauma.

Mom leaned around the doorway from the kitchen and gave me a questioning look.

I shrugged.

She nodded and disappeared back into the kitchen. "Abby, set the table. Lucy, tell the boys to wash up for dinner."

I hung my backpack on the hook by the door and walked into the kitchen. Grandma was mashing potatoes by hand. Mom was stirring cream gravy in the cast-iron skillet she'd fried the chicken in. Abby was practically throwing the placemats around the table.

I pulled silverware from the drawer to help her. "Where's Dad?"

"On his way. He should be here any min—" Her words were cut off as my dad came through the door to the garage.

He tossed his keys and billfold on the counter and kissed Mom on the neck. "Smells good in here. And the chicken ain't bad either."

Mom giggled and Grandma shook the potato masher at them in fake disgust. "You two stop it."

And I smiled. A real smile.

Ethan was right. My family was amazing. As much as I tried to escape the chaos in my house, I needed it. I needed to fall into the warmth and craziness that was my family.

I wondered what Frasier thought of them. And I wondered what his family was like—really like. What was true? Had those been his parents or actors? Did he even have a sister?

The whole *I have a sister who's a runaway drug addict* was probably made up. Hurt squeezed my chest. Why? Why had he said those things? Why had he told me I was special? Why had he kissed me?

"Are you okay?"

I looked across the table at Abby. "What?"

"You haven't moved from the first place you set."

"Dreaming about her boy—friend." Josh came into the kitchen.

"Shut up. He's not my boyfriend."

Lucy shook her curls. "He said he was."

"Well, he was wrong." I finished arranging the silverware while Abby set the plates on the table.

Grandma didn't say a word, but she narrowed her eyes. She knew something was up. It was only a matter of time before the inquisition. I decided to head her off at the pass.

Once we were seated and the food blessed, I heaped potatoes on my plate and passed the bowl to the left. "Before the Wiley family gossip starts, you should know Ethan Smith won't be coming back." I sounded casual and confident and braced myself for questions.

Andrew handed me the bowl of green beans. "We know."

I looked at Mom. "Know what?"

Mom looked as confused as I felt.

Josh groaned and dropped his hand on the table, rattling the dishes. "That he's not Ethan Smith. Duh."

Abby grinned. "Who cares about Ethan Smith? I want to know if *Frasier Anderson* is coming back."

"No." I said it with force and braced myself again for questions.

"Shame. Seemed like a nice kid." Dad bit into his chicken breast.

Seconds passed with nobody saying a word. This was not like my family. Mom had to have warned them. To tell you the truth, it was unsettling.

Grandma sipped from her sweet tea. "Did you hear the news in town?"

Here it was. Leave it to Grandma to butt in where she wasn't wanted. I prepared to defend my stance of not talking about boys.

Mom shook her head. "No."

Grandma chuckled. "Fred White and Nate Sturgeon nearly came to blows over the last piece of coconut cream pie down at the Early Bird."

Dad wiped his mouth. "I'd fight someone for the last piece of T-bone's coconut cream pie."

Grandma was still laughing. "Apparently, Sandy tried to convince them to split it, but they wouldn't agree. They began tuggin' on the plate and it ended up on the floor. Mary Beth Nelson said she thought both men were going to cry.

Fred even got down on all fours and swiped a taste off the top."

The whole table broke out in laughter. Okay, I had to admit it was a little funny. But everybody acted like it was hilarious. It was not hilarious.

When everybody quieted, Grandma continued, "T-bone was so mad, he came out of the kitchen with a dustpan and a roll of paper towels and told them they had to clean it up or be banned for life."

"For life!" Josh laughed. "I'd die if that happened to me."

Everybody went into a second laughing fit and I wondered what was up with my family. When Travis broke my heart, it was like he'd broken their hearts too. Granted, I hadn't known Ethan—Frasier—as long, but he'd spent time with them. Even Grandma didn't seem upset. Honestly, I was a little disappointed. I had all the things rehearsed in my head. Grandma would be angry on my behalf and I'd tell her it didn't matter because I didn't have time for dating. My brothers would lament losing a basketball buddy. My sisters would say they missed his extra attention. But none of that happened. They went on talking about everyday, mundane life.

My phone rang from the depths of my backpack and I started to get up. Mom pinned me in my seat with a look. "You know the rule."

Andrew recited it at rattle-the-windows level. "No cell phones at the table. Whoever needs to talk to you can wait until after family time."

I ignored my brother and met Mom's gaze. I pleaded with that look. She knew what was at stake.

Mom's gaze didn't waver. "Your brother is right. Whoever it is can wait a few minutes."

"Unless it's Frasier Anderson." Josh spoke in a sing-song voice.

Little brothers. Want one? You can have my two.

I ignored him and focused on my dinner. The last thing I wanted was to rush through it and make everyone suspicious. They had been amazingly normal about my announcement that Ethan/Frasier wouldn't be returning, but I didn't trust that would last. I needed to talk to Mom. I needed to find out what was going on.

After dinner I helped Grandma with the dishes. She never said a word about dating, boys, Ethan or Frasier, but I couldn't shake the sense that something was up. I wanted to ask her, but I didn't want to open a can of worms that didn't need opening, so I kept my mouth shut.

Grandma handed me a container to put the leftover mashed potatoes in. "How was your day?"

Right. Here it comes. "Good. How was yours?"

"The boys tell me that Ethan is an actor."

"Yes." I sighed the word and tightened my gut like a fighter about to receive a series of blows.

"Well, I think it's pretty clever of the movie people to put him in a normal school for research. He was a nice kid. I'm glad our family got to be a small part of it."

What? Why hadn't I thought of that? It made perfect sense. Still, he'd used me. "Do you really think he was nice?"

"Don't you? You hung out with him."

"He's an actor. I don't know *what's* real."

"Oh, I see. That's a fair point." She snapped a lid on the green bean container. "I'm sure he's a good actor, but his manners weren't scripted. He was awfully sweet with your sisters and brothers."

"So how can you judge him so quickly as nice and still be angry about Travis? He wasn't right for me, but he's still a nice guy."

She swatted the air. "I don't know. I suppose Travis is okay. I didn't trust his motives from the moment I met him. He always seemed a little skittish. He never paid much attention to anybody—including you. I think if a boy wants to date a girl, he ought to fawn all over her. Ethan fawned all over you."

"He was acting." I blinked back the stinging in my eyes.

"Maybe. But as I said, his manners were real. No reason to suspect his actions toward you were any less real."

"Well, it doesn't matter now. He's gone. Moved away." And then I couldn't hold the tears back. I ugly cried while Grandma wrapped me in a hug.

"I'm sorry. Sometimes life is pretty unfair."

I pulled away and snapped a few tissues from a box on the counter. "I wasn't going to cry."

"Crying is not a bad thing. Sometimes it's exactly what we need."

I nodded and blew my nose.

Dad wandered into the kitchen. "Everything okay?" He had that freaked-out *she's crying* look and edged to the refrigerator to refill his glass with water.

I nodded.

Grandma said, "Fine. Just a little girl talk."

Dad saluted us with his ice water and said, "I'll leave you to it, then." He skittered out of the kitchen as though he was afraid he'd get trapped in the conversation.

"I get that he could have been undercover and that he had to leave. But I don't understand why he didn't say good-bye." Guilt hung heavy in my heart. I was such a liar.

He'd tried. Sixteen texts. Five voicemails. He'd tried.

"Have you tried asking him?"

I nodded. "He hasn't answered."

"Give him time. You don't know what may be happening in his life."

"Thanks, Grandma. Do you need any more help?"

"No. Go on."

I fished my phone out of my backpack and headed for my room. Disappointment burrowed deep in my heart when I looked at the screen. The call hadn't been from Frasier. It was from Bree. She hadn't left a message, but she had texted.

My heart squeezed as I stared at the image on the screen. Frasier had his arm around a gorgeous redheaded girl. He was smiling, but she looked like she had just swallowed rotten raw fish. *Cara Gentry claims dating Frasier Anderson was six months in hell.* The date on the caption was a little over a year old.

Bree answered my call on the first ring. Not even hello. She started with, "Did you see it?"

"Where did you find that?"

"Google. There's more."

I sat in my desk chair and opened my laptop. "Is it all that bad?"

"Yes. But it's hard to tell if it's true."

I plugged in my earbuds and set my phone on my desk so I could do my own Google search while we talked.

Picture after picture of Frasier with Cara Gentry. "Who is she, anyway?" I typed *Cara Gentry* into the search bar.

The first thing that came up was her link to Frasier Anderson. "I found something in the *Scots Guardian*. It says Cara Gentry alleged that Frasier Anderson was mentally abusive during their six-month dating relationship."

"How did Frasier respond?"

"Apparently, he didn't."

I heard Bree's fingers clicking on the keyboard as she spoke. "That doesn't sound like Ethan Smith."

"True. But we don't know Frasier Anderson." I wasn't sure how to process all of this. Could Frasier have been mentally abusive? I didn't know him, but I wanted to think he was at least a little like Ethan Smith.

Bree said, "Wait. I found an article about Cara Gentry. It says she was an extra on the set of *Morlich Castle*. She was fired from the show and shortly after, she claimed Frasier Anderson was abusive."

"Okay that just sounds like she's nuts." I felt a little sorry for Frasier. If he was anything like Ethan, those allegations would kill him.

"Yeah. Frasier's parents threatened legal action if she didn't cease and desist."

I scrolled through pictures of him. "I can't wrap my brain around all of this."

"You were kissed by Frasier Anderson. Do you know how many girls would kill for a chance to be kissed by him?"

"No. I was kissed by Ethan Smith. That's what makes this so hard to take in. The guy I like doesn't exist."

I could almost see Bree nodding. "You have to talk to him. He owes you an explanation."

"I know, but I can't get hold of him."

"Maybe he went back to Scotland."

"Maybe. I don't understand what he was doing here anyway. Why did he pick *our* town? Why did he choose to play with *my* heart?" And then the hurt and tears came rushing back. "I feel like a joke."

"You are not a joke."

"He made me think he liked me. God, I was so stupid." *Travis 2.0.*

"No. He's an excellent actor. You had no way of knowing what he was up to."

I pulled up a picture of Frasier at the BAFTA Scotland awards wearing a kilt. *This* was the guy I'd kissed? *This* was the guy who at least pretended to like me? Why not Melanie Joy or Bree?

I slapped my laptop closed. "I'm so angry. What a total jerk."

Abby bounded into the room. "Mom said you have to help me with my homework."

"I've got to go. I'll see you tomorrow."

I ended the call and turned to my sister. "Okay, what do you have?"

"Algebra." She sat on the end of the bed and folded her arms across her chest. "I know he was hot and all, but you can do better. He wasn't smart enough for you."

That made me smile. "Thanks, sis. I don't need no stinkin' guy anyway."

"Exactly."

I stood. "Come on, math awaits."

19

Frasier

I COULDN'T BREATHE AS I looked at the image on Avery's phone. Mum squeezed my forearm and if I could have torn my gaze away, I was sure I would have seen tears rolling down her cheeks. I looked at the picture of my unconscious sister. Emaciated. Lying in the hospital bed—tubes, lines, and a machine breathing for her.

"How did they get a picture?" I croaked.

Avery answered my question with one of her own. "Did you see the caption?"

I shifted my gaze to the words above the picture. *Frasier Anderson's abandoned sister left to die on the streets of Aberdeen.*

My heart fell deep into my chest and my lungs folded over it and my gut clenched so tight it pulled my torso to my knees. Nothing was working. My heart. My lungs. My mind. All stalled.

And somewhere, anger ignited. Anger at my sister for running away, for refusing help, for nearly dying. We hadn't abandoned her. She had abandoned us.

Mum wrapped her arm across my back and sobbed. She wasn't comforting me, she was hanging on for dear life. I felt it.

If she let go of me, it was if she would lose what was left of her family.

Avery took her phone. "We have to respond. I've been getting calls since this hit social media."

Slowly, my lungs reactivated and drew in sips of air as realization came to me that this was all my fault. I sat up and stared at the glass topped table.

When I'd been cast in *Morlich Castle*, Fiona had been furious. She began to call me "Mum's golden boy." Eventually she'd shortened it to Goldie. I hated that nickname. When the show won its first BAFTA, she got high. After that, things spun out of control. But it was all because I'd chosen acting.

The tabloids had trashed Mum and Dad. Nobody would care if I hadn't been a celebrity. Fiona wouldn't have gone off the rails if I hadn't been a celebrity. And that made me angry too.

I'd chosen to be an actor. I knew the tabloids were brutal, but why was that part of the deal? Who wrote the rule that said the more you worked for success the more people would try to tear you down? My career had ignited this mess. Now I was going to fix it.

I pinned Avery with a determined look. "Have you talked to Dad?"

"Not yet."

I turned to Mum. "I'm going back to hospital. Avery is right. We need to respond, but first, I need to talk to Dad and I don't want to do it on the phone."

Mum brushed her palms across her cheeks. "I'll come with you."

"I know you want to be with Fiona, but you're knackered—"

"No." She drew in a deep breath. "You know what I am? I'm tired of being told what I need. I need to be with my daughter. Give me ten minutes to change and I'm going the hospital and I'm not leaving until she's awake."

I nodded. "I could really use a shower."

Avery fielded text messages and calls while we cleaned up. By the time we'd both showered and changed, ten minutes had turned into forty-five.

Avery drove. As we pulled into the car park, we saw a herd of paparazzi camped by the doors of the hospital. Two uniformed security people confronted the cameras. Avery said, "I'm sure there's another entrance, but I wouldn't know where."

"We'll go through the front. I'm not going to let them intimidate me." I looked at Mum for support.

She hesitated for half a breath, then said, "He's right. We're not hiding this."

We made it halfway up the walk before they recognized me. Cameras clicked around us as they shouted questions. I was determined to ignore them, but when I reached the doors, I turned toward the cameras. "I'll issue a statement later today."

I turned and went through the doors, where Mum and Avery waited at reception. I'm not sure who was more shocked —the paparazzi, Mum, Avery, or me.

When I joined them, Avery smiled. "Well done, you."

I'd texted Dad that we were on our way up. He met us in the waiting room. He quickly shook Avery's hand before wrapping Mum and me in a tight hug. When he released us, he said to Mum, "Visiting hours just started."

He'd barely finished speaking before Mum rushed to push the button by the doors leading to the unit.

I got that hair-raising feeling on the back of my neck and knew the people in the waiting area had recognized me. I looked around and sure enough, all eyes were on me. I smiled and nodded as I turned back to Dad.

Dad was looking over my shoulder. "We should talk in the family room."

"No." I pointed to the little corner we'd carved out for ourselves. "This will do. I have nothing to hide."

Dad raised his brows. "Okay."

We sat. Dad opened his mouth, but before he could speak, I rushed to start the conversation. "Dad. Avery. You know I couldn't survive in this industry without you. But this mess is mine to clean up."

Dad shook his head. "Son."

I put up a hand. "This is important to me."

He sat back and gestured for me to continue.

I asked Avery, "Has the studio been made aware of the photo?"

"They know. They agree that we should jump on this. The hospital administrator has also been contacted."

"Okay." I sat tall, with my palms over my knees. Anything to look more adult. "Let's craft a statement."

It didn't take us long to figure out what to say.

A tall, slender woman wearing a skirt suit stepped off the lift and walked toward us carrying a clipboard. "Are you the Anderson family?"

Dad nodded and stuck out his hand. "Gordon Anderson. This is my son Frasier. My wife is with our daughter."

The woman cut her gaze to Avery, who shook her hand. "I'm Avery Sutherland, Mr. Anderson's assistant."

The woman introduced herself as Karen MacPherson, a representative of the hospital, then directed her gaze to Dad. "First, let me say I'm very sorry about your daughter, but she's exactly where she needs to be and we will give her excellent care."

"Thank you," we all said.

Ms. MacPherson straightened her back. "Have you seen the social media post concerning your daughter?"

"Yes," Dad answered flatly.

"I'm very sorry. There has obviously been a breach of privacy. We take this very seriously. We will find who took the picture and he or she will be dealt with."

Dad nodded. "Thank you." The woman wiggled her shoulders as if she were trying to get comfortable with what she was going to say next. "Is there something else?" Dad asked.

She cut her gaze to me and I got a clear *wish you weren't in the room* vibe before she spoke, again to Dad. "Unfortunately, your son's celebrity status has caused quite a frenzy. Perhaps your assistant could help with the circus going on downstairs."

"She's the other Mr. Anderson's assistant." Dad turned to me. *It's all yours, son.*

I smiled. "We'll cooperate in any way necessary. I'd like to issue a statement in a few minutes."

Ms. MacPherson's gaze flitted between Dad and me. Finally, she settled on speaking to me. "That's a good idea. As hospital representative, I need to be there as well. We'll also follow with a statement on social media."

"Aye. Makes sense."

Ms. MacPherson pressed the clipboard to her chest. "Now. Do you have any questions for me about the care of your sister?"

I shook my head. "Dad?"

"The staff has been keeping us well informed."

She nodded. "Very well." She pulled a card from the clip and handed it to me. "If you need anything, call my mobile. I'm going to talk to the staff about this breach, but when you're ready to speak to the reporters I'll go with you."

She scooted out of our area to the doors leading to the unit. She held her badge close to the black box on the wall and the doors swung open.

Avery's mobile buzzed in her hand. She glanced at the screen and then at me. "It's Peggy." She got a freaked-out look on her face and turned to my dad. "The studio asked her to call me."

Dad nodded. "I know. Sarah called from the Marks and filled me in. Tell her he'll be there by the end of next week, as agreed. There's nothing more to discuss."

Avery smiled. "Okay." She stood and walked to an empty corner of the room to speak.

Dad looked at me. "Are you ready to face the pap?"

"I'd like to see Fiona first."

He looked at his watch. "Aye. We should go while we can."

We buzzed through the door and made our way past the sounds of beeps and whooshes coming from the other rooms.

Mum sat in a high-backed chair next to Fiona's bed with her head resting on the side of the mattress. When we walked in, she opened her eyes and sat up. "I must have dozed off."

"Mum, you need to rest."

"I know. But after three years of searching, I'm not going to leave her." She stretched her arms in front. "Did you sort things?"

I nodded. "I'm about to go down and talk to the paparazzi. It'll also go out on social media. The hospital will follow up."

Mum shifted her gaze to Dad. "Are you okay with this?"

"Aye. Frasier is taking the lead on this and I trust him."

My heart bloomed a wee bit and I hoped I wouldn't disappoint them. They'd had enough disappointment for a lifetime.

Then I looked my sister and guilt dug into my gut. I shouldn't have been angry with her. But I was. She'd caused so much pain for Mum, for Dad. For me.

Even now that we'd found her, she was putting them through hell. But she was also fighting for her life. And looking at her thin, frail, bruised body, I wondered what horrors she'd endured. The thought made my stomach churn and my insides hot. Confusing emotions swirled inside me. From love to hate, sorrow to anger, it was all there.

I couldn't deal with it. I had to get out. I had to escape that room. I jerked my gaze to Dad. "I'm ready. Let's get this over with."

He nodded and followed me out.

Once we were in the waiting area, I called Ms. MacPherson. She met us at reception near the entrance to the hospital. We reviewed what we were going to say and Ms. MacPherson briefed security on the plan.

As we came through the hospital doors, the click of the cameras sounded like some cyber bug invasion. Ms. MacPherson led us to the area where the reporters had been sequestered.

She stood in front of Dad and me. Avery hung behind us. "I am Karen MacPherson, a hospital representative. We regret that the privacy of one of our patients has been breached. The hospital is investigating this breach and the person responsible will be dealt with in the strongest possible terms. Mr. Anderson will issue a statement, and then we respectfully request that you allow this family the privacy they need and deserve."

She stepped aside.

I took a couple of breaths to calm my nerves and stepped forward. The first question was fired before I was even able to speak. "Is it true you refused to acknowledge your sister?"

"No. That's ridiculous. My sister—"

"In a recent interview you said you were an only child."

My face flared red-hot. I had said that. "As a family, we'd decided to keep our private lives private." But how could I untwist the implications of that statement?

"You mean that your family abandoned her."

"No."

The questions and accusations came faster after that. Each one was a stab to the heart. And all of a sudden, I was just a lad again. Not sure how to proceed. I looked at Dad for guidance.

He moved in front of me. Almost shielding me with his body. "I'll ask you to remember that Frasier is a seventeen-year-old lad. His mother and I decided not to broadcast our daughter's circumstances. We asked him to keep it private. Sadly, Fiona has a history of drug abuse and rehab. We have been searching for her for three years. Now that we've found her, our family is going to focus on recovery."

My mind screamed that I should say something. I should stand up for my family, but I was still reeling from the attack.

The reporters all talked at once. Dad slung his arm around me and ushered me toward the door. Before we got inside, one last question was hurled at me.

"Frasier, what's your status with the American girl, Jenna Wiley?"

I stopped. Everything inside me went cold. How did they know? Were they camped out in Hillside, Texas too? If they knew who she was, it was only a matter of time. She didn't deserve this. I'd chosen this life and other than bouts of cruelty from the tabloids, it was an amazing way to make a living. But Jenna hadn't and it wasn't fair. It wasn't right.

If I acknowledged the question, would it be worse for Jenna? If I ignored it, would they leave her alone? No. Facts aren't how they deal. If they don't get a story, they make one up. The one they concoct is always worse than the real one.

"Frasier? Jenna Wiley."

I turned to see a man so thin and so tall he looked like a living stick figure holding a camera just to the right of his eyes. "The world is waiting, mate."

Avery stood in front of the man. "You need to leave now."

The man didn't move. His straight line of a mouth turned up at the corners. "I think I have my answer."

"No!" I lunged forward. I wanted to smash that camera into his face.

My dad was faster and grabbed my shoulders. "Let it go, son."

"Jenna is a schoolmate and a friend."

"Are you dating her?"

Before I answered, Dad stepped in. "That's enough." He guided me toward the doors. "Avery, take care of this."

When we entered the hospital there was another crowd. Not paparazzi, but ordinary people—visitors, staff—with their mobiles held in record mode. I ignored them and let Dad guide me to the lifts. Once inside, I fell back against the wall and fought the urge to cry. "That was a bloody mess."

"We knew it would be rough."

"Aye. They're vicious." I wiped sweat from my forehead. "Dad, they could be in Hillside. Do we need warn the studio?"

"Aye. Avery can do that. You need to take a step back from the spotlight for a few days."

A step back. I'd like that. But now more than ever I needed to talk to Jenna. I checked my mobile. No Service. Fine. As soon as we were off the lift, I would find a quiet place to phone her. The lift dinged and the doors slipped open.

My mother stood just outside, dark circles around her eyes and tears streaming down her face.

20

Jenna

I'D TEXTED FRASIER after helping Abby with her homework, but the lack of reply had me convinced that either I was no longer a concern for Ethan/Frasier, or that he had returned to Scotland and left the phone with the Austin area code behind. I desperately wanted it to be option two.

When I drove to school the next morning, I saw the Channel Eight news truck parked in front. I guessed the word had gotten out about Ethan Smith—aka Frasier Anderson. Or was it Frasier Anderson—aka Ethan Smith? Anyway, I wasn't sure whether to be excited, angry, or depressed. Excitement that maybe he'd returned to reveal the truth swirled in me because it was a chance to put things right and see if the real person was anything like the one I'd kissed. But then, anger mixed with sadness swirled big. He hadn't answered my calls or texts. Had he used me? Was I just part of his good ol' American research?

I parked, turned off the ignition, and for the first time in my life, considered ditching classes. I couldn't face being rejected by him in public. As it was now, only a few people knew the full extent of what he'd done to me. If Frasier

Anderson treated me like an adoring fan, it would crush me. And then I'd be the joke of the school.

On the other hand, it was an opportunity to confront him. It was a chance to see who he was. Because the Ethan Smith I'd met would never treat me as less than a friend—I was sure of it. If Frasier treated me like a stranger, I'd call him out on it. Maybe Cara Gentry was telling the truth. Pretending to be somebody he wasn't, or pretending he liked me, wasn't abuse, but it was mean and I wasn't above expressing that opinion.

And then, the embers of anger that burned inside flared. I didn't want to be the victim of a prank or a publicity stunt or whatever had happened. I was going to go into that school, find Frasier Anderson, and tell him exactly what I thought of his deceit.

I nearly ran across the parking lot to the courtyard outside the cafeteria. Bree, Melanie Joy, and Kenzie stood in a group near the double doors—they wouldn't open for another five minutes. The girls started talking before I reached them.

Melanie Joy grabbed my arm and tugged me into the circle. "Did you hear?"

"What? Is Frasier here to reveal his identity?"

"I don't know about that, but Jack Ramsey and Charlotte Wray are here." Everybody squealed and a couple of weeks ago, I'd have joined in. At the moment, I didn't feel a bit giddy about Hollywood's hottest superheroes. Instead, I had a sick feeling in my gut.

Call it intuition, but I had a sense that the day was about to go from bad to epic tragedy.

When the bell rang signaling admittance into the school, everybody rushed to their lockers. The buzz was all about the news crew and the actors who were rumored to be visiting the school.

Melanie Joy practically sprinted to our lockers. "Do you think Frasier will be in class as Ethan?"

"Of course not. He's not a real student here."

"Oh yeah, sure. That makes sense. So, what do you think this is all about? I hear they're going to shoot a movie here."

"God help us if they do."

"You're cranky." Melanie Joy put up a hand as soon as I opened my mouth to speak. "And you have a right to be. But remember, you haven't heard his side of the story. I'm sure Frasier had a good reason for not telling you the truth."

"Yeah." That was all I said. Okay. Maybe the tone was flat or a little sarcastic, but it was one word. It certainly didn't deserve the look I got.

"Well, I'm not going to let your crankiness ruin my day. I choose to think the best about Frasier Anderson. Besides, this is sooo exciting."

When I entered the classroom, my gaze rolled to Ethan's seat. I knew it'd be empty, but my heart squeezed anyway. Once we settled in our seats, a tone signaled an announcement. Mr. Bledsoe's voice boomed overhead. "There will be an assembly in the gym. We will follow the pep-rally schedule."

That made my pulse kick up a notch. I was going to see him again. Probably for the last time. Would he speak to me? Would he acknowledge me?

Then my mind went into a weird series of daydreams where he either ignored me, thanked me for helping with research for the film, or worse, declared his feelings for me in front of the whole school. And why was that worse? Because A, it would never happen, and B, it would be mortifying. I couldn't do it. I couldn't go to the assembly. As much as I wanted to confront him, there were too many possible scenarios out there and none of them were good.

But when Mr. Shipley told us to line up, my feet fell in step with the rest. I hated myself for it but, there was a little flicker in my heart that hoped that he would tell me that the kiss had been real, and that his feelings for me were real.

I walked to the gym with Melanie Joy full of anger, hurt, and hope. She was full of excitement and like a sober person at a drunken party, I was annoyed.

"You do realize they are human. They are not real superheroes."

Melanie Joy flicked her hair. "Maybe. But this is the most exciting thing that has ever happened in Hillside."

I rolled my eyes and tried to ignore the mix of feelings rattling my nerves.

We met up with Bree and Kenzie and ended up sitting in the stands two rows from the floor. I wasn't sure if that was good or horribly bad.

The cheerleaders stood at one end of the gym. Bree smacked the back of her hand against my upper arm to get my attention. "How did they know to wear their uniforms? I swear they were in regular clothes this morning."

"Maybe they keep a spare in their lockers," I offered.

Kenzie shook her head. "Nope. I saw Monica Bayer this morning. She was in uniform."

"I guess this wasn't supposed to be a secret." I scanned for Frasier and my pulse picked up. If he meant even a tenth of what he'd said, shouldn't he be looking for me?

Melanie Joy laughed. "Haven't you learned yet? There are no secrets in a small town."

Mr. Bledsoe stood in the center of the gym floor with a wireless microphone. "Good morning." His voice was a little too cheery for me, but judging by the way everybody yelled the greeting back, I was in the minority.

Melanie Joy elbowed me and pointed to the double doors opening into the gym.

The news crew camera guy had his back to us, but the camera was poised as though he was filming. My heart wanted to believe that was why I hadn't seen or heard from Frasier. My pulse ramped up and everything inside me tensed.

Mr. Bledsoe raised his hand to quiet the crowd. "We have a little surprise this morning."

The crowd went wild again. We needed to get this over with. Now!

The cameraman moved to the side of the door leading into the gym and aimed his camera at Bledsoe.

"As many of you know, we welcomed a new senior student this year named Ethan Smith."

My heart literally stopped.

"Ethan was here doing research for a movie. His real name is Frasier Anderson. A bright young Scottish actor."

Bree, Kenzie, and Melanie Joy looked at me. I ignored them and kept my eyes focused on those doors leading into the gym.

"Unfortunately, Mr. Anderson couldn't be here today."

The crowd groaned and my heart dropped from my throat to my toes.

Bledsoe held up his hand again. "Now wait. We have a couple of superhero co-stars."

And cue the cheers.

"Let's give a big Hornet welcome to Jack Ramsey and Charlotte Wray."

Cue the jumping up and squealing.

I stood too, but I wasn't as enthusiastic as the rest of the school. A few weeks ago, I would have lost my mind. I'd seen every movie both Jack Ramsey and Charlotte Wray had been in. I'd obsessively gobbled up every interview on YouTube.

The disappointment that Frasier hadn't bothered to show up knocked any starstruck enthusiasm right out of me. I didn't cry. I didn't even come close. I was kind of impressed with myself over that. Maybe it was because I was reeling from the fact that not only had he lied to me, he hadn't bothered to say good-bye.

And then I got indignant.

He hadn't just abandoned me. He'd abandoned my friends. He'd abandoned the school. We had welcomed him with open arms. And in my case, open lips. Anger rose again. He'd done his stupid research and left. We'd all been conned. He'd used us to get what he wanted and snuck away in the middle of the night.

Bree grinned at me. "This is awesome! Way better than Frasier Anderson."

"They're fakes." I stood with my arms hanging by my sides.

"What?" She shook her head at me.

"They're actors. They're fakes. I'm not clapping for them."

Melanie Joy rolled her eyes. "Let it go, Ilsa. Enjoy the moment."

But I couldn't. I was hurt, angry, and feeling a little self-righteous.

"Wow. Need a Snickers?" Bree turned away from me.

I ignored them and watched Jack Ramsey and Charlotte Wray grin and wave to the crowd. Both held mics.

Jack dropped his already deep voice as he spoke into his. "Hell-low."

OMG you would have thought he'd just told the girls he would give each one of them a kiss. The decibel level of hundreds of girls squealing at their highest pitch could break your eardrums.

Charlotte shouted into her mic, "Hello, Hillside Hornets!"

Again, with the eardrum piercing.

Jack didn't wait for anybody to quiet before speaking again, which was probably good because I'm not sure it would have quieted. "Thank you for having us here today. We're sorry our friend Frasier couldn't be here. He had some things to take care of in Scotland."

Charlotte said, "Were you surprised that mild-mannered Ethan Smith was really a rugged Scot?"

Screams. More screams. You know the drill.

Jack spoke. "If we could get serious for just a second." The screams faded and one by one people sat down.

Jack pulled a piece of paper from his pocket. "I have a message to you from Frasier." Hushes circulated around the gym like a giant snake hissing. When everybody was quiet, he read, "Thank you for welcoming my family and me into your town, homes, and school. I'm sorry I had to leave on short notice, but I had a family emergency back home. I will return to the US in a few days and will thank you all personally then." The crowd started to clap, but Jack and Charlotte both held up their hands signaling there was more. "I want to give a special thanks to the guys on the soccer team and to Bree Davis, Kenzie Quinn, Melanie Joy Stapleton and my very special friend Jenna Wiley."

Everybody clapped and there were a few whoops, but nothing like before.

Jack looked around the gym. "If you're here, could you girls come down, please?"

We stood and all eyes turned to us. I'm not sure which one of us was redder, but I felt like my skin was going to combust before we got down the steps to the gym floor. My legs were shaking so hard it almost felt as if the ground was moving beneath me. The camera was aimed at us the whole way across the floor. And we were grinning like goons.

When we reached celebrity central, the camera moved close. Like inches away close. Both Jack Ramsey and Charlotte Wray shook our hands.

Jack said, "Frasier said you ladies kept him out of trouble."

Melanie Joy was the coolest under the spotlight—of course. "We were just showing him Hillside hospitality."

Charlotte spoke close to my ear. "Frasier wanted me to tell you, he's been trying to reach you. His sister has been found."

My gaze flicked up to hers as my blood froze in my veins. "What?" I barely breathed the word.

She pressed a piece of paper into my hand. "This is his private cell. He asked if you'd call him. He said it didn't matter the time."

I blinked away the sting in my eyes.

Charlotte continued, "He's a really private guy, so I'm guessing you're pretty special to hm. Just so you know, he's one of the nicest guys in Hollywood. Don't break his heart."

Wow. That just happened.

And the emotional turbulence I'd been experiencing took off again.

I shook Jack's hand like a robot. When we were finished, we were motioned out of the gym toward the reporter. I was on total autopilot. Vaguely aware of Jack and Charlotte speaking. The crowd cheering.

When we got to the reporter, another cameraman filmed us. A mic was stuck in front of our faces and the female reporter asked questions I neither heard nor answered.

I did manage to smile and nod—a lot.

Then the lady focused on me. "Charlotte Wray seemed to have a special message for you. Care to share?"

"Frasier spent time at my house. He played basketball with my little brothers. She was just thanking me on his behalf." I wasn't sure where I'd pulled that from but—go me.

"Were you surprised at his identity?"

"Of course. We all were. It's a nod to his acting ability."

"It sure is. This is Delaney Nance, Channel Eight News. Back to you, Chris."

I squeezed the paper in my fist so hard my arm ached. He was with his sister. He hadn't lied about her. And apparently those had been his real parents. So what did that mean about me?

Did he have feelings for me? He couldn't. Guys like him don't like girls like me. They like the Melanie Joys of the world. And who could blame them? She was beautiful, smart, and kind. I was just—me. Not so great hair, pimples on my forehead me.

"Are you okay?" Bree asked me.

I looked at my friends gathered in a circle around me. "I don't know. I think I'm in shock."

Melanie Joy nodded. "My knees are still shaking. Did anybody get a selfie?"

We all exchanged horrified looks. How had we not taken a selfie?

We turned back toward the gym as the actors were coming through the door.

"Excuse me!" Leave it to Melanie Joy to take care of business.

Jack Ramsey stopped and looked her over from head to toes and back, and grinned. "How can I help you?"

"Could we get a selfie?"

"Of course." Jack and Charlotte stood on either side of Melanie Joy while she held her camera out.

"Wait." I said. "I'll take the pic."

We all took turns with the celebs. Then we did a big group picture.

As soon as we were finished, a man who I assumed was some kind of handler stood between us and them. "Okay. You're set to sign autographs in the foyer by the front door."

He led them away and we all squealed. Yes. I squealed too. But not so much because I'd met Jack Ramsey and Charlotte Wray. I squealed because clasped in my tight little fist was my connection to Frasier. I couldn't wait to call him. But I would. I wanted to have time to talk, so I'd tuck that note away in a safe place until after school.

I was in a haze for the rest of the day. All day people asked me what Charlotte had said to me. I stuck to my story but my mind kept drifting to the kiss.

Frasier Anderson liked me.

When school was finally over, I rushed to my truck. Pulled the number from where I'd slipped it into my billfold. Carefully, I unfolded the paper… and my heart stopped.

"No. No. No."

I closed my eyes, then looked again.

Sweaty palms. Number written in ink. It was a blur.

I couldn't make out more than three of the long line of numbers.

21

Frasier

"WHAT'S HAPPENED?" Dad's voice held the same fear that kept me on the lift. I couldn't get off. The look on Mum's face, the tears. It couldn't be good news and if I stepped off the lift, that would make it real.

Mum broke into a wide smile. "I was coming to find you." As soon as we were off the lift, she wrapped us in a group hug. "Fiona opened her eyes."

"What?" I backed away. "That's amazing. Can we see her?"

"No. Doctor is with her now." A new set of tears dripped down Mum's cheeks. "I'm not sure she knew who I was."

I felt the eyes of the other people in the waiting room on us. "Can we go to our corner?"

Dad nodded and led the way with his arm wrapped around Mum as if they were hanging on to each other for dear life. We sat in the far corner of the little nook we'd claimed.

Mum grabbed a few tissues from the box on the table and dabbed her face. "The nurse said not to put much stock in her reaction to me. She said sometimes the mind is a little slower to wake up."

Dad nodded. "I'm sure she's right. Let's focus on the positive. She's awake. Have they talked about taking her off the ventilator?"

Mum shook her head. "No. Maybe we'll know more after doctor sees her." She breathed a deep sigh. "I have a feeling she's going to be okay. Maybe not our same girl, but okay."

"Aye, she will be." My words sounded hollow and useless. Mum must have thought so too. She sent a pseudo-patronizing smile my way. "How did it go with the beasties downstairs?"

I didn't want to give her anything else to worry about, but it had been horrible.

Dad answered for me. "About as you would expect. A total disregard for the truth."

Mum cocked her head at Dad. "You didn't leave Avery down there to deal with them alone, did you?"

"Aye, it's her job. Besides, hospital security is with her."

Mum shook her head. "It's tragic the way they're allowed to do and say whatever they please."

My mind went to Jenna. Would their lies reach all the way to Texas? Had Charlotte managed to get my message to Jenna? Would it make a difference?

Mum patted my hand. "What is it, Frasier?"

"They asked about Jenna."

Mum squeezed my hand before withdrawing hers. "Poor lass. She has no idea who you are. What if they go after her? It would be terrifying."

"By now, they've announced everything at school. She knows it all."

Mum raised her brows at me. "How do you think she'll feel?"

"Betrayed. Lied to. Angry." I propped my feet on the table for a millisecond before Mum swatted them off. "I need to talk to her."

Mum looked at her watch. "Aye. But it's half four in the morning there. She might not like it if you called her just yet."

"Aye. Mum, you look terrible. Can't you get some rest?"

"I'm fine. I could use some tea, though."

Dad sat up. "How about sandwiches? I can walk to the Co-op."

"I can go." I stood.

Mum shook her head. "Don't be ridiculous. You'll create a stir."

"I don't really care about the photographers right now. I'm going on with my life and if they want take pictures, fine. I don't have anything to hide. We—" I circled my arm in the air between us. "—don't have a thing to hide. We've done nothing wrong. They'll just be curious about us until the next celebrity catches their eye."

Dad reached for his wallet.

"I've got it, Dad." I stood. "I'll be back as quick as I can." I didn't wait for him to argue as I made my way to the lift.

Reception was fairly empty and nobody seemed to recognize me.

"Frasier." I stopped at the sound of Avery's voice. She sat nestled on a sofa with her laptop open and a cappuccino on the end table. I walked over and she moved her laptop to the coffee table.

"How's your sister?"

"Mum said she opened her eyes. Doctor is examining her now."

"That's good, yeah?"

I nodded, even though I wasn't sure if it was good or meant anything at all. "Were the beasties horrible after we left?"

"Nothing I couldn't handle. They've been ordered across the street."

"That's something, anyway."

"Where are you off to?"

"Co-op to get some sandwiches. I could use the walk."

"If you walk, you'll wind up right in the beasties' den."

I shrugged. "I'm tired of caring. I have to live my life. Maybe if they see how truly boring I am, they'll find someone else to harass."

"Not likely, but worth a shot. How about you test that theory when you're not running on zero sleep. I'll take you. There's a chippy not far away, if you'd like."

"Mum loves fish and chips. She'll kill me because she's trying to eat healthy, but I'm willing to risk it."

"Grand. Let's go."

When we drove past the area where the paparazzi were camped out, I was thrilled that only a few diehards were left. "See? They're already getting bored with me."

"Let's hope so."

At the chip shop, two girls stood behind me and I could tell by their whispering giggles they were trying to decide if I was who they thought I was. I never knew what to do in these instances. Turn and tell them I was Frasier Anderson? Then I'd just sound like a prick. Pretend I hadn't heard my name whispered between them?

I turned toward them and smiled. Maybe that would get them to ask or shut up.

A ginger girl smiled back. "Are you Duncan Ross?"

"Aye. I'm the actor who played him." I smiled big, ready for them to ask for a selfie.

The dark-haired girl with her said, "We heard about your sister. I hope she gets better."

"Thank you. She's already on the mend."

"And we don't believe those horrible things they said about your family abandoning her," Ginger added.

"Thank you. That means a lot. Really it does."

The lady in front of me took her order and started for the

door. She stopped and turned. Dread flowed over me. The look on her face said she was about to disagree with the girls.

She narrowed her gaze and said, "I think it's tragic the way they they're allowed to write whatever they want. Anybody with half a brain would know it's rubbish."

"Thank you."

The woman turned and hurried through the door.

The girls passed a look between themselves. Ginger said, "Could—could we have a selfie with you?"

Avery stepped forward. "He's had a long day."

"It's okay. I'm happy to do it."

She looked at me. "Are you sure?"

"Yes." Avery took pictures while I posed with the girls and the four-person staff of the fish and chip shop. I got duplicate pictures with my phone and tweeted.

Thanks, guys! It's easy to forget that most people are kind when you're surrounded by cameras, insults, and false accusations. #Donniesfishandchips

I hashtagged the shop and the girls. When it was my turn to order, the woman behind the counter blushed and said, "I couldn't buy the kind of advertising that hashtag will bring us. It's on the house."

"Oh, no. I couldn't do that. Instead, I'll get these two girls' orders as well."

"Very well. Tell your parents we're all praying for your sister."

"Aye. I will. Thank you." The support of these strangers lightened my heart.

Two men with cameras came into the shop as I was gathering my order. The woman behind the counter said, "Not in my shop, lads."

One of the men said, "I just want to order a basket."

"Then you'll leave your camera elsewhere."

The man swore and they left the shop.

I knew he'd be on the other side of the door, but it made me smile that she was so protective of my privacy. I thanked her again, said good-bye to the girls, and followed Avery through the door to the car.

Charged with the positive energy from the shop, I smiled for the cameraman.

"How's your sister, mate?"

"Improving." I ducked into the car.

Avery put the car in reverse. "What just happened in there probably did more to counter their rubbish than any statement we could make."

"How so?"

"Those few people in the shop will post on social media how nice you are and it'll spread." She pulled into the lane. "I'm proud of how you've handled this whole situation. Not all seventeen-year-olds would have handled the pressure."

"Thank you. I'm not sure how well I'm handling it. I made a mess with a girl in Texas."

Avery kept her eyes focused on the road, but her brows arched into her hairline. "Texas? The girl the paparazzi mentioned?"

"Aye. Jenna Wiley. Until today, she didn't know who I am. Worse. We left so fast I didn't get a chance to tell her."

"You didn't call her?"

"I tried. I called. Texted. Left messages. She didn't return any of my attempts. Which is odd. The last I saw her, we were good. Better than good."

"I think it's very likely she found out who you are before the reveal."

"How? Nobody knows me in the States—" Wait. The women who'd brought us cake. "Never mind. I know what happened. Some women brought us cake. One of the ladies said I looked like Duncan Ross from *Morlich Castle*. It wouldn't have been difficult to confirm her suspicions."

Avery glanced at me. "I'm sorry. Sounds like you need to make a call to America."

"Aye. Jenna will be up in a couple of hours. I'll try to catch her before school."

Avery and I each carried a sack with takeaway containers stacked inside. The smell of the fried food filled the space in the lift and my stomach went into a series of feed-me-now growls.

Avery gave me a mum-worthy look. "You need to feed that thing."

"Sorry. It's been a wee while since I've eaten." The doors slid open and she stepped off. "Let's get some food into you."

"Aye." But when I rounded the corner into the family room, everything inside me stopped. Mum and Dad were standing in our alcove with the doctor. Silently I pleaded that she was telling them good news.

Mum's gaze caught mine. "Excuse me, Doctor, our son has just arrived."

I hurried to them and set my bag on the coffee table.

Mum waved Avery over, but she shook her head and backed away. "I'll just have a seat over here until you've finished."

Mum smiled. "Thank you."

I looked between Mum and Dad. "What did I miss?"

The doctor smiled. "I was just telling your parents that Fiona is tracking movements with her eyes, but we're not sure how aware she is of what's going on. I'm changing some of her medications. At this point we want to stimulate her mind. We don't want to keep her room dark and quiet. Lights are on, the television is on. When you're in her room, talk to her, read to her. Typically, as these patients wake up, they'll try to pull the tube from their throat. We have her hands covered in soft mitts and tied down to keep her from pulling out the tube. We'd rather not have restraints. To do that, we'd need someone with her at all times."

"We can do that. We can take turns." Mum's voice was full of hope.

The doctor smiled. "That would be good." Her smile faded and my insides prepared for bad news. "We won't know how she is cognitively until she's off the ventilator and can talk to us. With her history of drug abuse, there may be some drastic changes."

Mum tucked her lips and nodded.

Dad said, "We just want our girl back."

The doctor nodded and looked at the sack on the table. "Donnie's Fish and Chips. My favorite. You don't want to let it get cold. By the time you finish, the nurses should have finished adjusting her meds and such."

"Doctor, would you like some fish and chips?" I offered. "We have more than enough."

She stared longingly at the sack. "As much as I would love to take you up on that, my husband is waiting for me to join him for tea."

She left and we called Avery over. The four of us huddled around the coffee table devouring the food.

Mum sipped from a bottle of water and smiled. "Thank you for getting this. I was really dreading another sandwich. This is just what we needed. Did you have any trouble with the cameras?"

Avery shook her head. "No. There were a few fans at the shop, but they were sweet."

I pulled up my tweet and handed the phone to Mum. "There are a lot of people sending prayers and thoughts."

Mum nodded as she scrolled through the responses. "Your tweet was perfect."

Dad leaned over Mum's shoulder. "And Donnie's will probably be very busy for the next few days."

We tucked in and ate without a word uttered between us until Avery closed the lid over her takeaway and sat back. "I can't eat another bite. I hate to bring this up now, but we need to think about who is going to return to America with Frasier. You can assign a guardian. I just need to know who so I can prepare the paperwork."

Mum looked at Dad. "We have no idea what lies ahead for Fiona. I can't leave her. I think you're the obvious choice."

Dad nodded. "We can fly back here whenever he has a few days between filming."

"I turn eighteen in December," I said to Avery. "Would they make an exception so my parents can stay with Fiona?"

Avery shook her head. "It's the US law."

I nodded. "Then Dad and I will be back on set, on time."

"Aye. I'll let them know." Avery stood. "Unless you need me, I'm flying back to London early in the morning. I hope you use that nice flat you're paying for. You need a break from the hospital."

"Thank you." Mum stood and hugged her. Dad and I walked her to the lift.

Just before the doors closed, she said, "Don't forget you have a call to make."

When she was gone Dad looked at me. "What call?"

"I need to sort things with Jenna."

His shoulders dropped as he released an exaggerated sigh. "You need to warn her about the paparazzi. But what needs to be sorted?"

"I think she found out who I was before we left. I've left her messages and she hasn't returned any of them. I asked Charlotte Wray to give her my personal mobile number yesterday. And I haven't heard anything."

He leaned against the wall and folded his arms across his chest. "What do you expect to gain out of this?"

"Gain? I don't know. She may hate me forever, but I have to explain. She has a right to know why I was there and why I couldn't talk about it."

"She's knows why you were there. She's a bright girl—I'm sure she's figured out why you couldn't tell her the truth."

"But she deserves an apology. Dad, I really like this girl."

He rubbed his hand across his mouth. "Just how serious were you two?"

"We kissed."

Dad looked at the ceiling as though imploring it for help. "Friseal."

"It's not like we hooked up. I'm seventeen. It's not a crime to have a girlfriend."

"No. But did you consider that she lives in a wee town in a country across an ocean?"

"Aye. Okay, no. But it shouldn't matter. If we really care for each other, we'll figure it out."

He narrowed his gaze. "And do you? Do you know if she cares one whit for Frasier Anderson? Because I'm pretty sure the lad she kissed was Ethan Smith."

"That's why I need to talk to her." I shook my head. "Just don't tell Mum. She has enough to worry about without thinking I'm about to go down the Cara Gentry road again."

Mum spoke from behind me and made us both jump. "I think you should call her. Tell her everything you told your dad. We're not doing secrets anymore. If you like that girl, you tell her."

I checked the time on my watch. Six in the morning in Hillside. She might still be asleep, but a bigger part of me couldn't wait.

I pulled up her number on the screen. "Wish me luck." I tapped the green Call circle.

22

Jenna

I TRIED to decipher the number. But there was no way. It was a black smear. I couldn't contact him. Couldn't apologize for ignoring his texts and calls.

But Mr. Bledsoe was bound to have information.

I ran back into school and didn't stop until I was in the office. I leaned on the reception counter, panting. "I have to talk to Mr. Bledsoe."

The office lady jumped from her chair and rushed to me. "What's happened?"

I shook my head and gulped some air. "I just need to talk to him."

"I'll see if he's available." She scooted behind the counter and picked up the phone. In a low voice she said, "Are you available? Jenna Wiley is here to see you." She hung up and motioned me behind the desk. "Right this way."

I followed her to Mr. Bledsoe's office. The door was open and he was typing something on his computer. When he saw me, he moved away from the computer and sat back in his chair. "Come in, Ms. Wiley. What can I do for you?"

I waited until the office lady left. "I'm sorry to bother you."

I showed him the slip of smeared numbers. "Charlotte Wray gave me this. It's Frasier Anderson's number. He had a family emergency and had to return to Scotland, but he wants me to call him and I can't read the numbers." The words rushed out in one long continuous sentence and when I finished, I was as out of breath as when I'd run into the school.

Mr. Bledsoe squinted at the note. "I'm sorry, I can't read this either." He handed it back to me. "Is there something else you needed?"

I sat on the edge of one of the chairs positioned in front of his desk. "I thought you might know how I could contact him."

Mr. Bledsoe's face reminded me of one of those morph gifs. It went from pity to amusement to indifference.

"I promise I'm telling the truth. He asked me to call him." Why else would I have his blurry number?

His face stopped moving. "I'm sure that's true, but I can't help you. I signed a confidentiality agreement."

My heart squeezed. "Can you give me the studio contact? Maybe they can help me."

"I'm sorry. If it's that important to him, I'm sure he'll call you." He leaned back in his chair. "Is there anything else I can do for you?"

"No." I left his office feeling like a complete loser. I'm sure he thought I was some fangirl trying to weasel Frasier's number out of him.

I waited until I was safely buckled in my truck to react. I tossed the paper in my cup holder and pounded the steering wheel. I. Was. Not. A. Fangirl.

Mr. Bledsoe had said that if Frasier wanted to talk to me, he'd call. In a normal world he would, but I'd refused his calls and texts. What if he thought I hadn't called because I didn't want to speak to him? Which, let's be honest, was true. But that was then. Would he call again or give up?

I grabbed my phone and searched on Twitter.

My heart stalled when I read his most recent tweet. What had happened to his sister? There were hundreds of messages of people sending out prayers and positive thoughts.

I typed into Google, *What happened to Frasier Anderson's sister?*

A picture of a girl in a hospital bed came up, looking like she was at death's door. I read the article beneath it and my stomach squeezed into a ball. This was so wrong. His family hadn't abandoned her. They'd been looking for her.

My heart sagged in my chest. Poor Frasier. I had to contact him. I clicked back to Twitter. If I Direct Messaged him, would he even see it? At least it was proactive.

I'm so sorry about your sister. I'm praying for you and your family. I lost your number. Please call me.

I sent it with a hope and a prayer. Now there was nothing to do but wait and focus on not crying. Because at that moment, my heart was so heavy in my chest, all I wanted to do was curl up in a ball and release the tears that had remained locked, loaded, and ready to spill since Frasier had made his escape from Hillside.

But I didn't. I was stronger than disappointment.

I put my truck in gear and drove over to Bree's house. The urge to check my phone every second for a reply to my DM made my right hand twitch. At a red light I picked it up, looked around, and noticed a cop to my right. I didn't even open the screen. I dropped my phone in my purse.

I'd barely come to a stop in Bree's driveway when she and Melanie Joy came barreling through the front door. They'd reached my truck by the time I turned off the ignition.

Bree swung my door open. "Did you call him?"

I shook my head.

Melanie Joy took a step back. "What happened?"

I handed her the note that I'd tossed in my cup holder.

"Oh, Jenna. What are you going to do?"

I pressed my head into the back of the seat. "I sent a DM on Twitter, but who knows if he'll see it."

"Oh man. He probably gets hundreds of those a day." Bree opened my door wider. "Come on. Let's get a snack."

Melanie Joy handed back the paper. I crumpled it and dropped it in the change tray, then grabbed my backpack and purse and trudged into the house behind them.

It took a lot of strength to resist looking at my phone, but I managed to wait until we had our sweet tea and were settled around Bree's huge dining table.

I pulled my phone from my purse and opened Twitter. There was no little blue circle over the envelope symbol in the lower right corner, but I opened it anyway. Nada. Nothing.

Melanie Joy and Bree looked hopeful—until I slapped my phone down on the table.

Bree said, "Maybe it's the time difference. What time is it there?"

I looked on my World Clock. "Ten. They're six hours ahead."

"See?" Melanie Joy pulled her books from her backpack. "Don't give up hope yet. It's just going to take longer to connect."

"I hate sitting around waiting for him to answer. We don't even know if he reads his tweets, much less his DMs. Don't they have people who do that for them? A woman of action would figure out a way to get in touch with him."

Bree nodded. "Let's think this through, then. We're smart." She held up her index finger. "Mr. Bledsoe—"

I slumped back in the chair. "Tried that. He said he'd signed a confidentiality agreement."

"Obviously Charlotte Wray has his number, I say we figure out how to get ahold of her." Melanie Joy opened her laptop.

"Does anybody know the name of the movie they're shooting?"

Bree and I shook our heads.

She typed on her keyboard. "Let's see what Google says."

I sipped my tea as casually as if it my heart wasn't running around in my chest screaming *Hurry UP!*

Melanie Joy looked up. "I went to Charlotte Wray's IMDB page. The movie is called *Hashtag Cowboy* but it's in preproduction in Austin. Does that mean they're not filming yet?"

"I don't know. Is that a good thing or a bad thing?" I set my glass down and opened my Physics book. "But you know what? It doesn't matter. There's no way my parents would let me drive to Austin. Even if they did, there's no way I'd be able to get on set or talk to Charlotte anyway."

"What happened to 'we'll figure it out?'" Melanie Joy closed her laptop.

"I'm not saying I'm giving up. It hasn't even been an hour since I sent the DM. I'm going to be patient. Go on with life. Do my homework. Tonight. Tomorrow. Maybe in five minutes I'll freak out. Right now, my focus is Physics."

Bree got up from the table. "Well, that was inspiring. Homemade Chex mix, anybody? Mom made a new batch last night."

"Are you trying to kill me?" Melanie Joy's tone was threatening, but she was already in the kitchen digging in the cupboard for a bowl. "You know I can't stop once I've had the first bite."

I turned to my homework and pretended I really was strong enough to focus on the assignment. The truth was, my mind had already drifted to the *what ifs*. What if he flew all the way from Scotland to see me? What if he had some man wearing a dark suit and sunglasses deliver a plane ticket for me to go to Scotland? The more I tried to study, the more ridiculous my thoughts became.

Melanie Joy set the bowl on the table and grabbed a handful of Chex. "You okay?"

I dragged my thoughts from the comfort of daydreams. "Of course."

"Well, whatever you think you're writing in that notebook is a little scary."

I looked down at my spiral. It wasn't that bad, but apparently while my mind had been taking me on a romantic vacation, my hand was doing some sort of cross between writing and doodling. I looked up and flashed a fake grin. "Busted."

Bree said, "Play the last message again—on speaker. We want to hear that accent."

I pulled up the message and let it play.

Jenna, please call me. It's important. I really need to talk to you.

Bree sighed. "I love the way he says 'important.' The little roll of the *r* and the way he chops the rest of the word off."

Melanie Joy smiled. "I like the whole thing. Imagine listening to that voice for the rest of your life."

I nodded. "I've listened to it a thousand times at least. I just hope if—when I see him again—that Frasier is as nice as Ethan."

Melanie Joy shook her head. "Why wouldn't he be?"

"Why *would* he be? He's an actor."

Bree cradled a palmful of Chex mix. "True. But he could have left without trying to contact you. And that message sounded desperate."

I ducked as if lightning were about to strike. "Is it horrible that I hope he was desperate?"

"No." Bree and Melanie Joy harmonized the response.

Melanie Joy eyed me. "You know, if he turns out to be a jerk—"

"Which he won't," Bree interrupted.

"Right, but if he does, the worse that will happen is that you'll be able to tell your kids you kissed a movie star."

The worse that would happen is that I'd tell my kids my heart had been broken by a Scottish lad pretending to be American, but I didn't say that. "True." I looked down at my book. "For real, I have to study. You know that once I get home, all bets are off."

And I did study. I can't say I was focused, but I managed to get my homework done. By the time I left, I felt better too. I still hadn't heard from Frasier, but it was late in Scotland and he was probably spending time with his sister. He hadn't seen her for three years. I could wait a little longer to hear from him.

I kept telling myself he had my number. He would call.

He would.

I parked on the street because my brothers were in full basketball mode in the driveway. It reminded me of when I'd dropped off Ethan to play with them. It had been kind of a mean thing to do. At the time, I'd thought I was making some grandstand. I was all about school.

I *was* all about school, but that didn't have to be mutually exclusive with having someone special in my life. I just wish I'd realized that before I got angry with Frasier. I think the day he got to know my family while I was at Bree's was when I really started liking him. My family didn't faze him. Not even Grandma.

He could have been playing a role, but I when I looked back, I was sure he hadn't been. He'd been genuine with my family. Ethan or Frasier, he was the same guy. And if he had been playing a role with me, why would he have told me about his sister? He hadn't told anybody before. Why would he have told Charlotte Wray to give me his private number? I looked at my phone and sighed. Why hadn't he DM'd me?

I closed my eyes and in my most demanding voice said, "Frasier Anderson, call me now."

I held my breath.

Nothing.

I opened one eye and glared at my screen. Nothing.

Both eyes open, I unbuckled and opened my door. I stepped down from the cab, reached across the seat, and jerked my phone from the cup holder. *Jerked* being the operative word. Somehow, it shot out of my hand like a seed at a watermelon spitting contest, over my opened door and into the street.

Things kind of happened in slow motion after that.

As I turned to watch it slide across the road, I slammed my truck door. Only I didn't quite get my hand out of the way before it closed. All four fingers of my right hand were caught between the door and the truck frame. I'm not sure if the scream that ripped from my throat was from the pain in my hand or the pain in my heart as I watched my dad's right front tire crunch to a stop on my phone.

Dad jumped out of the car. I yanked opened the door with my good hand and fell to my knees cradling my injured one. The boys were by my side before Dad. I couldn't stop screaming. The pain was unbelievable.

Josh and Andrew squatted in front of me. Andrew was shouting, "Let me see your hand."

I couldn't move. The pain went from my fingertips all the way up my arm to my shoulder. But I managed to go from screams to breath-holding and long exhales.

Dad took Josh's place. "Andrew, go tell Mom what happened and get some ice.

I tried to walk with Dad to the house. I really did. But my legs were like noodles and my knees kept buckling. He scooped me up and carried me into the kitchen.

Mom was making an ice bag. "What happened?"

Andrew answered, "She slammed her hand in her truck door."

"How?" Mom pulled my hand away from where I held it against my chest and positioned the ice bag on it.

"I don't know." I sobbed. "I was trying to get my phone."

Josh came through the door and set my phone on the table. The glass was broken and it had an unusual bend in the center.

Abby leaned over the table. "Do you think it still works?"

Mom shook her head. "I'm not worried about her phone right now." She lifted the sandwich bag full of ice off my hand to inspect it. "Can you move your fingers?"

They looked like four purple sausages. I had some movement, but just that little bit sent a new wave of pain through me.

Mom looked at my Dad. "That's it. We're getting this checked out."

Grandma spoke up from somewhere in the kitchen. "I'll feed the kids. You and Rick take Jenna."

I walked to Dad's car with Mom's arm around my shoulders. It was warm outside, but I was shivering. Mom said I was in shock. I thought about what I'd learned in Science. Was it the body's autonomic reaction to trauma? I couldn't remember, but trying to work out the physiology of what was happening to me kept my mind from focusing on the throbbing in my hand.

At the Emergency Room, I got into triage right away, but then was sent back to the waiting room. It was forever before I got called in. The nurse who took us helped me on to the stretcher and placed a pillow across my lap. "Do you go to Hillside High?"

"Yes, sir."

Carefully, he removed the ice from my hand. "Amazingly, as bad as it looks, often these kinds of injuries don't break bones." He examined my fingers gently. "My son, Justin, graduated from Hillside last year."

"You're Justin's dad?" I sucked in a quick breath as he touched my knuckles. "I'm friends with his girlfriend's sister."

"Which one? Kelsey or Kenzie?"

"Kenzie."

He nodded. "They're nice girls." He laid my arm across the pillow in my lap and placed the ice on my fingers. "We'll get an X-ray to be sure nothing is broken." He looked at my parents. "I don't like the looks of the fourth and fifth fingers. I'm going to have Dr. Jules pop in before we send her to radiology."

As it turned out. My ring and pinky fingers had a hairline fracture. They splinted them and sent me on my way.

My phone, however, was terminal.

While Mom heated up our dinner, I sat at the table with ice on my hand and stared at the corpse of my phone and sighed.

Dad sat across from me. "How did this happen, again?"

I went through the story, but it seemed ridiculous. If I didn't have throbbing fingers, I wouldn't have believed it. "When can I get a new phone?"

He picked it up and examined it. "Saturday."

"Saturday? But that's four days away."

"Sorry. I have to work. You'll have to survive the old-fashioned way until then."

I looked at Mom. "Can't you take me after school?"

She shook her head. "No. I have a full week. And don't forget, you have a hair appointment tomorrow after school."

I wouldn't forget. I was so ready for a change. But… but…

Dad set the phone back on the table. And as if it were begging to be revived, it rang.

At first, I thought it was something Dad had done. But then I realized it was really ringing. An actual call coming in. I didn't recognize the number but it was long and my heart filled with hope as I tapped on the green Accept circle.

Only it didn't accept. I pressed again and again. Each touch of my fingertip was like a knife jabbing into the hope that I was about to speak to Frasier. I kept tapping, more and more frantic, until the green and red circles disappeared. In fact, I was so focused on that stupid green circle, I hadn't memorized the number.

23

Frasier

I TUCKED my mobile in my jacket pocket and leaned back in the recliner. Another day had passed and I still hadn't heard from Jenna. It was four in the morning. The waiting room was quiet. Dad was in with Fiona. Mum was resting in the chair next to me. I thought she'd finally managed a little sleep until she patted my arm. "Still not answering?"

"No. I understand that she's angry, but I'm not getting why she won't let me explain or at least apologize. I even asked Charlotte to give her my private number. I get that it was wrong to lie, but I didn't set out to deceive her."

"Have you tried her friends?"

I rubbed my eyes. "When we turned in our phones, the only number I transferred was hers."

"Well then, you have two choices. Either you wait it out and let time soothe her anger, or you get creative."

"Creative how?"

"She's bound to be on social media. Twitter. Instagram. Facebook. Have you tried to reach her that way?"

"*You* are suggesting social media? Brilliant idea." I'd shied away from social media since the whole Cara Gentry circus.

Avery had tweeted for me if it was related to my career. To be honest, I hadn't missed it. But now it was time to step back into the ring.

I pulled my mobile from my coat pocket and opened Twitter.

Six hundred DMs.

I was astounded by the messages of hope and prayer. People told their stories of substance abuse and recovery. My throat knotted as I fought back tears. "Mum. Look at this."

She scrolled down the messages. Tears rolled down her cheeks. "These are lovely. Such an outpouring of support." She focused in on my screen. "You need to see this one."

I took my phone and read the message she'd pulled up. I don't know if it was the knowledge that so many people cared about my sister, or exhaustion, or relief at what I'd read. But as soon as I read Jenna's message, emotions poured out of me.

I cried like a little kid. I mean heaving, hiccupping, shoulder shaking, noisemaking, totally unmanly crying. And once the dam broke, I couldn't stop.

I levered the recliner into a sitting position and grabbed a handful of tissues from the coffee table.

I heard Mum straighten her chair and the next thing I knew, she'd wiggled into my seat and taken me into her arms. I might have been seventeen, making more money than most adults, but in that moment, I needed my mum. I needed her hugs. I needed to feel her arms around me.

So many emotions churned in me. Anger at what Cara had done. Anger at what Fiona had done. Anger at what I had done. And for the first time in a long time, I didn't feel I had to be responsible or mature or aware of my public image. I felt safe just to be a lad who needed his mum.

I cried until I was exhausted. When the emotions settled, I let Mum hold me for a little longer. When I felt like I could breathe again, I slowly pulled away. "I'm better. I guess I needed that." I stared at the nearly empty box of tissue. "I've never cried over a lass before."

"I don't think you were just crying over Jenna. Frasier, you've had so much pressure on you for the past five years. You've handled the spotlight better than most adults. I'll be honest, there were times it worried me that you were so calm. It had to come out somewhere."

I nodded. "It came out, all right."

"Do you feel better?" She moved to her chair.

"Aye." But my insides were still full of worry. "Mum?"

"Hmm?"

"What if Fiona refuses to get help? What if she runs away again?"

"We've never given up on her. We won't start now. We'll keep trying." She swiped tears from her eyes. "Earlier today, when I was with her, I sang 'Coorie Doon' to her. Her eyes focused on me and I think she knew I was there. It didn't last long, just a few seconds."

"That's something to hang on to." That was Mum's go-to lullaby. Scarped knee, Mum sang it. Fiona's first broken heart, Mum sang it. *Your daddy's howkin' coal, my darlin'* probably wasn't the usual theme of a lullaby, but it was comforting for us.

She stood. "I think it's my turn to switch out with Dad."

She walked toward the double doors and I hit reply on the message Jenna had sent. I typed in my number and added:

I'm sorry. I'm so sorry I lied.

I got a reply almost immediately.

My phone is toast. I'm on my laptop. It's okay. But we still need to talk.

Yes! Can you Skype?

Yes!

I moved to the far corner of our area and pulled up Skype.

As soon as I saw her face pop up my screen, everything inside me lightened. You know those cartoon movies where the birds start singing and the woodland animals gather around? That was what it was like.

"Hiya," I said.

"Hi yourself." She was beautiful and grinning. And then that grin turned to concern. "What happened to your face?"

"Oh, I fainted." I touched the bruise. "I don't get on well with hospitals."

"Are you okay?"

"Aye. It's just a wee bruise." She smiled back and I felt everything inside me brighten.

"You cut your hair!" It was short and sexy.

"Yeah."

"I love it."

"Really?" She touched her hair and winced at the action and I winced at the sight of her hand.

"What happened to you? Your hand—"

"I smashed it in the door of the truck. It's fine." Then she laughed. "We're a mess."

I laughed too. "That we are." Then I got serious. "Jenna. It gutted me not to tell you who I really was, but I was contractually obligated not to. When we got the message that Fiona had been found, we left on the next flight. I tried to call you."

"I should have called you back. I should have answered your texts. I'm sorry I didn't give you a chance to explain. I was just having such a hard time wrapping my head around the whole thing. I wasn't sure if the person I met was the real you."

"The things I said, the way I feel about you, is me. Not Ethan Smith."

There were a few seconds of silence as we just looked at each other through the screen.

She took a deep breath. "How's your sister?"

"She's still in a coma."

Jenna's eyes filled with tears. "I'm sorry. I didn't know."

"I know. She's malnourished. She was beat up pretty bad. But she's started opening her eyes—so we're hopeful."

"Ethan—I mean Frasier. I'm sorry. I wish there was something I could do."

"She's back with us. Hopefully, we can heal."

She nodded and looked down.

I had to ask the question that had been burning inside me since we'd left. "Do you still want to see me, now that you know who I am?"

Her gaze jerked to the camera. "Yes."

"Thank God." The words whooshed from me. "I don't know exactly when I'll be back. As soon as I know, you'll know."

"Okay. I won't have a phone until the weekend, though."

She smiled. I smiled. But the whole thing was awkward, like we were strangers. I had to figure out a way to get us back to Ethan and Jenna.

I heard the doors to the unit open and turned to see my dad come through. "I have to go, but I'll DM you. Let's plan another time to chat."

"I'd like that."

"Cheers." I clicked off and turned to Dad. "How is she?"

"She's looking around. Nurse said you could come back. If you'd like. I'll watch our things."

I set my computer aside. "Of course."

I made my way through the doors to Fiona's room. Mum sat facing her with her back to the door. She was reading aloud.

I took a seat on the other side of the bed. "*The Secret Garden*. You must have read that book to us a dozen times."

Fiona opened her eyes when I spoke. I stood and wrapped my hand around hers. "Hey, Fi."

It was light, but I felt her fingers move beneath my hand. I squeezed and tried to think of something to say. The only thought that screamed through my mind was, *Why did you do this to yourself?* Instead, I smiled and said, "I've missed you."

Her eyes focused on me. Her hand moved beneath my palm, and at first, I thought she was withdrawing it, but then she turned it over and, palm to palm, squeezed.

Tears flooded my eyes. I was afraid to look away. I was afraid to move. I didn't want anything to break the connection between us. I leaned closer and my tears fell on her bedsheets. "I've missed you so much."

A tear slid from her right eye down her cheek.

"Are you hurting?"

She shook her head.

Mum spoke from the other side. "Fiona. My sweet Fiona."

My sister released my hand at the sound of Mum's voice and rolled her head to look at her. Mum leaned over the bed rail and Fiona raised her arms.

Mum folded over the bed and laid her head next to my sister's. To me, she said, "Get the nurse and Dad."

Fiona turned her head toward me.

"I'll be right back, I promise."

Outside the room, I grabbed the first nurse I saw. "My sister's awake. I'm getting my Dad."

I didn't wait for her response. I ran to the waiting room. As soon as the doors opened, I yelled, "Dad! She's awake."

He bounded to me. Together we jogged back to Fiona.

The nurse was checking the ventilator. The side rail had been lowered and Mum was perched on the edge of the mattress holding Fiona's hands. "Sorry, darling, you have to keep that tube in your throat a little longer."

Fiona wrinkled her forehead and shook her head.

The nurse backed away from the machine. "She's over-breathing the ventilator, which is good. But if she wants that tube out of her throat, she needs to fight for it."

Dad stood behind Mum. "Hello, Sunshine. It's so good to see those beautiful blue eyes."

More tears slid down Fiona's cheeks. She shifted her gaze to where I stood on the other side of the bed.

The nurse said, "Now is a good time to tell her where she is."

I spoke before Mum and Dad had a chance. "Do you know where you are?"

Her head turned back and forth in slow motion.

Mum said, "You're in hospital in Aberdeen. They're taking very good care of you. And we're all here."

She nodded and closed her eyes.

Mum looked around the room with desperate, tear-filled eyes. The nurse was quick to come to her side. "She's resting. It's okay."

Mum started to stand, but Fiona squeezed her hands as if she were asking her to stay by her side. Mum settled a little more onto the mattress. "I'm not going anywhere, darling."

The nurse smiled at Dad and me. "She needs her rest."

Mum looked over her shoulder at us. "Go on.."

Dad and I filed back to the waiting room. We'd left our stuff strewn all over our little corner. My computer was on the coffee table for the taking. I scanned the waiting room. There were a few people either sleeping in the recliners or huddled together in the little spaces they had created for themselves. They all had the same worried and worn look we had. Survival mode. Not willing to leave in case their loved one's condition changed. Too tired and worried to think about eating.

The café was closed. The vending machines offered sweets, but that was about it.

I took the recliner next to Dad.

He rubbed his face. "I'd almost kill for an apple."

I nodded. "Dad, we've been looking for a charity. I think I know what I want to do."

"Something with the hospital?"

"Aye. Something with the waiting room. The patient care is excellent. These recliners are horrendous. The whole arrangement of the room is cold. Why not have something like the pods in first class?"

Dad raised his brows. "That's an expensive prospect."

I nodded. "It's just a thought, but I'd like to explore the idea." I looked around. "At least there ought to be a better tea station."

Dad stifled a yawn. "I'm proud of you. I think giving to the hospital is perfect. We just have to find the right people to talk to." He couldn't stifle the next yawn. "Try to get some rest. Your turn to sit with Fiona is just a few hours away. We'll talk more about your idea tomorrow."

For the first time since this nightmare started, I felt hopeful. Fiona knew we were there. She was going to be okay—at least physically. I didn't want to think about the possibility that she could leave us again. That she could return to drugs and whatever else.

I had to get back to set. I had a contract to honor. I was excited about the part. I loved the script. But it seemed so unimportant compared to being with Fiona.

But, getting back to the movie also meant getting back to the States, to Texas, and to Jenna. I couldn't wait to see her, to kiss her, to know for sure we were okay.

WHEN MY PHONE alarm chimed a couple of hours later, it took a second to figure out where I was. When I did, dread and worry replaced the hope I'd felt before.

Dad looked crunched in the recliner, but he was asleep. I

popped forward and stood. Maybe today was the day Fiona would get the tube out.

The sun was almost fully up by the time I made my way to her room. The unit was buzzing with shift change. There was an alarm screaming down the hall from the direction of Fiona's room. My heart ramped up as I increased my pace.

Just outside her room, I heard Mum's voice. "Where is everybody? Help!"

I raced into the room. Fiona had sat straight up, but was falling to the right. Mum had her leg braced against Fiona's side to keep her from falling out of bed. The tube that went from Fiona's throat to the machine had come undone. Mum was trying to reconnect it. Fiona was grabbing at the tube taped to the side of her mouth with her free hand.

I ran back into the hall and grabbed the first uniformed person I could find. "Help us!"

24

Jenna

IT TOOK me forever to go to sleep after my Skype call with Frasier. He looked horrible. The deep, dark circles under his eyes highlighted the black eye and the bruise on his cheek. His hair obviously hadn't seen shampoo in a while, nor had his face seen a razor. Still, those eyes were the same. The way they consumed me was the same. And the accent he no longer hid made me smile.

I couldn't wrap my brain around it all. Frasier Anderson, actor, who could have any girl he wanted, wanted me. And then doubt crept in.

Why did he want me? How long would he want me? Was this a movie thing? Hook up with the local girl until shooting was over, and then move on? And then the big question. The one that had no easy answer.

If we did decide to take this thing to dating level, how would we manage the impossible? He lived in Scotland. I lived in Texas. He was famous. I was not.

Then I thought about the kiss we'd shared and it seemed a little more possible. Or at least worth fighting for.

The first thing I did when I woke up was check my

computer for a message from him. I tried not to be disappointed that he hadn't messaged. But disappointment still snuck in there. I had to remind myself that he'd taken the time to make a Skype call to me in the midst of a family crisis. It was petty of me to expect him to have messaged too.

I'd seen his face! Every part of me filled with sunshine at the thought. I wasn't even annoyed that Abby took forever in the bathroom. I sang in the shower. I took my time with my makeup. Walking down the hall from my bedroom to the kitchen, I smelled bacon and my stomach rejoiced. Today was going to be a good day.

Josh called out from the den, "Jenna, come see this."

The entire family was crowded around the TV watching the local morning show.

Charlotte Wray and Jack Ramsey were perched on director's chairs being interviewed. The host held index cards with the studio logo on the back. "So, you're in Austin shooting a movie with British actor Frasier Anderson."

"Scottish!" Andrew shouted at the TV.

Mom shushed him. "It's the same thing."

"No, it isn't." I corrected Mom.

Jack Ramsey answered the woman. "Yes. It's sort of a Cyrano de Bergerac tale set in the high school rodeo world—without the nose. Frasier is the Cyrano character. He and I are team ropers and I convince him to help me win Charlotte's affection. Of course, he gets the girl."

The host looked into the camera. "Unfortunately, Frasier couldn't join us today. He had a family emergency." She turned back to her guests. "Now, Charlotte, I understand you've worked with Frasier before."

"Yes. I did two episodes on *Morlich Castle* when I was fourteen." A picture of a younger Frasier and Charlotte popped up on the screen.

The camera returned to the studio. The host continued, "Frasier is playing a Texan. How's his accent?"

Andrew shouted. "Perfect!"

We all shushed him this time.

Charlotte answered the question. "He fooled a whole high school. He fooled a whole *town.*"

"Tell us a little about that."

Jack smiled. "Michael Ramos, the executive producer, thought it would be a good idea to give Frasier a taste of American high school."

"I understand he posed as an American transfer student for a whole week."

Jack and Charlotte both nodded.

"Do you think he fooled them?"

Charlotte nodded enthusiastically. "He did."

Jack threw in a chuckle and said, "Just ask Jenna Wiley."

And a lead ball fell into the bottom of my gut. *Just ask Jenna Wiley?* His words alone stung, but the ridicule dripping from them was like acid to my heart. It burned through my insides, screaming, "You're a joke, Jenna Wiley! You're a joke, just like you were with Travis!"

Without skipping a beat, the reporter looked into the camera. "Coming up. We were there the exact moment the students found out about their special transfer student. We'll be right back after these messages."

I sat on the coffee table and waited for the cereal boxes on the screen to stop singing. *Just ask Jenna Wiley.*

Charlotte Wray and Jack Ramsey thought I was a joke.

And now so did all of Texas.

The commercial ended and the host popped up on the screen. "We're here with Charlotte Wray and Jack Ramsey, talking about their upcoming movie, *Hashtag Cowboy.*" She turned to the actors. "For folks who just tuned in, tell us about your appearance at Hillside High in Hillside, Texas."

Charlotte took the lead. "Well, Frasier Anderson—"

"Your co-star," the host interrupted.

"Yes. Frasier grew up in Scotland and got most of his education with tutors on the set of *Morlich Castle*. This was a chance for him to experience high school in America."

"And he spoke with an American accent for an entire week," the reporter said.

Charlotte and Jack nodded.

The host turned to the camera. "We were there the moment the students discovered their transfer student was really Scotland's hottest young actor. Watch as four young ladies get a very special surprise."

The screen flashed to Mr. Bledsoe announcing Charlotte and Jack. Everybody was screaming like it was a pep rally. The cheerleaders did flip-flops across the gym floor. Then it cut to the four of us being called down from the stands.

When it ended, the host leaned toward Charlotte. "I see you handing something to one special lady. Can you share with us what that was about?"

Charlotte smiled. "Frasier asked me to give her a note."

"Have either of you spoken with Frasier?"

Jack shook his head. "Charlotte has."

Charlotte nodded. "He said he appreciates the outpouring of love and concern for his family."

The reporter looked into the camera. "We'd hoped to have Frasier join us by phone this morning, but he had to cancel. Frasier, our prayers are with you and your family in this difficult time." She turned to Jack. "Now, Jack. You play the part of Frasier's best friend and team roping partner. What can you tell us about your character?"

He nodded. "I play Chance Rogers. He's dated every rodeo queen since he was fifteen. Barrel racer Lacey Little is next in line. He realizes it's going to take more than good looks and charm, so he turns to his best friend and cowboy poet, Tanner

Givens. It's a fun movie, with lots of rodeo action. I'm really looking forward to the shoot."

"Well, we are looking forward to its release. Thank you both for joining us today."

When she ended the interview and signed off, I couldn't move. *Just ask Jenna Wiley.*

To Frasier I wasn't a joke, but to his co-stars, I certainly was. And now the whole school would be in on it. The whole town. The whole state.

Abby looked at me. "What difficult time?"

I shook the image of everybody laughing at me out of my head. "Frasier's sister is very sick, but last night he said she was improving."

Abby cocked her head. "Will we see him again?"

I nodded. "I'm sure of it. As soon as he comes back."

Mom called from the kitchen, "Jenna, come get your breakfast. You'll be late for school."

"I just have to check one thing." I ran to my room and opened my laptop. No messages. Was that good or bad? I mean, it could be that he had nothing new to report. It could also mean that something bad had happened and he was too upset to talk. I sent him a quick DM.

The news did a report about your movie. Talk tonight?

I swooshed it into cyberspace and ran to the kitchen.

Mom had poured a bowl of cereal for me. "Hurry up. You don't want to be late."

I dug my spoon into the bowl. "Do I really have to wait until Saturday to get a new phone? I'm having to communicate by DM on my computer. Do you know how slow that is?"

Mom put her hand to her forehead. "Oh, the horror of it all."

"It's not funny." But I did kind of laugh.

Mom cradled her coffee between her hands. "Sorry, kiddo. But Dad got the first appointment at the Apple Store on Saturday."

Grandma chimed in. "You're getting a new phone. I wouldn't complain too much."

"I know." I shoved my spoon into my bowl. "Still, this is going to be the longest week ever."

Mom shook her head. "It'll go faster than you think. How's the hand?"

"Sore. I took some Ibuprofen."

Mom nodded. "Good. Now finish your breakfast before you're late."

I grabbed a piece of bacon and headed toward my room. I checked my computer before I brushed my teeth and again before I left for school. Scotland was six hours ahead. It wasn't like it was the middle of the night. Not that I expected him to answer my message right away, but he would get it on his phone. And the fact that at least twenty minutes had passed without a reply made me worry that something had happened.

Something bad.

25

Frasier

BY THE TIME the nurse and I got into the room, Mum had the machine reconnected and was holding Fiona's hands down. The lady I'd dragged into the room, silenced the alarm. "What's happened?"

Mum continued to hold Fiona's struggling hands. "All of a sudden she sat up and tried to get the tube out of her throat."

The woman nodded. "I'm Doctor Clarke. I'm standing in for Doctor MacLeod today. Let's have a look at the madam here." She leaned over Fiona. "Fiona? We're going to see about getting that hose out of your throat. Would you fancy that?"

Fiona nodded.

"Okay. I need you to relax while I check things out. Can you do that for me?"

She nodded and stopped struggling against Mum.

The doctor pressed the call light and turned to us. "I want to do a quick check before we extubate her."

A nurse came through the door. "Can I help you?"

Dr. Clarke said, "I think this young madam is ready to breathe on her own."

The nurse smiled. "Excellent." She moved next to Mum.

"It's going to take a few minutes. If you want to have some tea, we'll call you back in when it's done."

Mum said gently to Fiona, "We'll be back as soon as they finish. Okay?"

Fiona nodded and closed her eyes.

Mum ran to Dad as soon as we were through the waiting room doors. "They're going to take her off the ventilator."

"That's grand!" He stood and hugged her long and hard. "Now the healing begins."

Mum pulled away from Dad and wiped her eyes. "Aye. We have her back."

It wasn't long before the nurse came through the doors for us. "We're ready for you. Doctor has some more tests she wants to do, so you can't stay long."

"Thank you," Mum said.

We followed the nurse back to Fiona's room. She was sitting up cross-legged in her bed sipping water. A nurse was helping her drink.

When she saw us, she pushed the drink away and held out her arms. Mum was the first to reach her. She leaned over the side rail and wrapped her arms around Fiona. When my sister's arms came around Mum's neck, they were so frail and thin they looked like a child's.

After we'd hugged and cried, the doctor returned to the room. "I'm going to have Occupational Therapy run some tests this afternoon. I'd like to have a dietician consult, and we have some other issues to think about. I think we can transfer her to a regular room."

Mum smiled. "Thank you, Doctor."

The nurse said, "It's going to take a while to get her settled." She asked Fiona, "Would you fancy a shower?"

Fiona nodded and I wondered how much she could speak.

The nurse turned back to Mum. "This would be a good time for your family to get away from hospital."

Dad leaned close to Fiona. “Okay, sweetie. We’re going to leave, but we’ll be back.”

My stomach churned at Dad’s tone. It was like he was speaking to a four-year-old, not a twenty-four-year-old. I hugged her. “Get better so we can have chili con carne at the Alford Bistro.”

Fiona gave me an extra squeeze and I almost lost it. She wasn’t rejecting us—me.

When we were in the waiting room, Mum said, “After all this time away from her, I don’t want to leave. What if something happens while I’m gone?”

Dad put his arm around her. “She’s awake. The nurses are with her. You are exhausted. Let’s go to the flat. Get cleaned up and we’ll come straight back.”

I looked at Mum’s worried face. “I could stay.”

“No. Your dad’s right. We need to get away from this place. I could use a long, hot shower.”

We were exhausted as we left hospital, but also energized by the hope of Fiona’s recovery. I fell into bed while Mum and Dad cleaned up. The plan was to take a wee nap, but when I woke, the flat was quiet. I crawled from bed to find my parents. Instead, I found a note by the coffee pot.

We tried to wake you, but you were sound asleep. There’s food in the fridge.

Love Mum and Dad

It was half twelve. I’d slept for three hours and it felt so good. I stretched, popped a pod in the coffee maker, and opened the fridge. A croissant and chopped fruit weren’t going to satisfy the hunger storm brewing in my gut, but it was a start.

I checked my phone to find a message from Jenna. I clicked

the link and then watched the interview while I shoved the croissant down.

Just ask Jenna Wiley? What was Jack thinking?

I didn't know Jack Ramsey. I hadn't even met him. I really hoped he didn't turn out to be a jerk. Charlotte and I had got along brilliantly on the set of *Morlich Castle*. She'd played the spoiled daughter of a rich American. Nothing like the real person. Most kids have a guardian on set, but like me, her parents had taken turns with that duty. We'd bonded over our lack of freedom and had remained friends since. I texted Charlotte.

Thanks for giving Jenna my number.

No worries. How's your sister?

Much better.

Coming to work soon?

Yes. What's Jack like?

¯_(ツ)_/¯ *Seems okay.*

I almost asked her about the remark Jack had made, but decided to let it drop. I'd find out soon enough what he was like. Besides, I needed to get back to hospital. I texted Mum that I was on my way. She texted back Fiona's new room number.

The taxi driver was full of questions as he drove me to hospital. What was it like to be famous? Had I met the queen? The answer is no, by the way. Was I going to move to America? And then, Who was the American girl the tabloids had mentioned?

The girl the tabloids had mentioned.

My insides shrank a little as worry filled their place. What kind of mention?

As soon as we arrived at hospital, I picked up a copy of the *Scotland Globe*. On the front page was a picture of Jenna shaking hands with Jack Ramsey. Above the picture a bold headline asked, WHO IS FRASIER ANDERSON'S MYSTERY AMERICAN?

When I paid for the paper, the clerk smiled and said, "She's very pretty."

I nodded and muttered thanks before hurrying to the lifts. The article speculated that I'd hooked up with Jenna while in Hillside. Bad, but not horrible. Horrible was the last paragraph.

> *Reports are that Anderson's former partner, Cara Gentry, tried to contact Jenna to warn her about him. But Ms. Wiley would not accept her calls.*

Totally fabricated. At least, I hoped so. I'd talk to Jenna later—after I'd seen Fiona.

I made my way her new room. As I entered, Fiona gave me a weak smile. "Hello, you." Her voice was thready and wavered a bit and that made my gut clench.

I walked to the side of her bed and bent to kiss her on the cheek. "Hello, Fi."

She wrapped her frail arms around me and hung on. I pressed my cheek against hers.

She whispered, "I'm sorry." And her hold tightened.

"It's okay. Just don't leave us again." Her arms felt like bones and they shook as if she didn't have the strength to maintain the hold.

I carefully lifted her arms off my neck and kept her hands in mine. "Save your strength."

"You look like hell. What happened to your face?" Her voice was still weak, but there was a hint of the sister I had once known.

"I fainted."

She raised her brows. "Damn, Fraze."

Mum spoke from across the room. “Fiona ate a great lunch today.” Her tone was all nervous and not Mum at all.

Fiona nodded. “I tried. The food is horrible. You owe me chili con carne.”

I smiled from deep in my gut. “I can’t wait.”

Dad stood next to Mum and rubbed her back. “Let’s get some tea and let the kids have a moment.” Mum nodded and let Dad lead her out of the room.

Fiona squeezed my hands and tears rolled down her cheeks. “I’m going to disappoint them, aren’t I?”

“No. You’re not. You’re going to let them help you.” I squeezed back and tried to squelch the anger that had again begun to simmer inside.

“What if I’m not strong enough? I don’t want to die.”

“All you have to be is strong enough to accept help.” She looked away and let the tears flow. “Fiona. They’ve never stopped looking for you. They’ll never stop. You have to try.”

She turned back to me. “And you? Did you stop looking?”

I shook my head. “No. Not even after your last message.”

She squeezed my hands again and closed her eyes.

“Fi. It’s all in the past. Don’t even think about it. Focus on getting stronger, on recovery. Please.”

But this time she pulled her hands from mine and rolled on her side with her back to me. Her rejection brought tears to my eyes, but I would not let them fall. I backed away from her bed. “Dammit, Fi—don’t you dare break their hearts again.”

I flopped in a chair tucked in the far corner of her room. This was the way it was with her. One step forward and ten back.

Mum texted that she and Dad had decided to get something outside hospital and asked if I wanted anything. I declined and spent the next hour scrolling through the hundreds of messages on Twitter and tried to feel the same goodwill toward my sister as the rest of the world.

At last she rolled on to her back and opened her eyes. "Why are you still here?"

"Why wouldn't I be? Fi, we never abandoned you. We never will. You left us." My tone was full of barely controlled anger. I hated it too. I didn't want to be angry with her, but she was so mired in self-pity it was difficult.

She nodded. "I know. You can go. I'll be fine." She reached for the water on her bedside table, but was too weak to lift the jug.

I moved to her bedside and held the jug while she managed to get the straw to her lips. "Well, this proves that I can't leave."

She pulled away from the straw and gave it a thump, flicking water in my direction. "Don't be so cheeky, little brother."

I smiled and some of the anger cooled. "Ah, but I'm the one who can hold the water, so you be nice."

She gave a weak laugh and then turned serious. "I do want to get better. I'm scared. I'm so scared. I don't want to break their hearts. I've done that enough."

And my eyes spilled tears. "Hearing that you're afraid is really good news. Be afraid, be determined. And for God's sake, let us help you."

She cried and nodded. And then for some bizarre reason, we both wiped our eyes and laughed. She said, "Do you think you can get some cards?"

"Are you feeling strong enough to lose at Hearts?"

"I'm feeling strong enough to beat you at Hearts." She pressed the call light.

A nurse came bounding into the room as if she'd been standing outside. She skidded to a stop when she saw me perched on the edge of Fiona's bed. Her face turned bright red. "Can I help you?"

Fiona said, "Ah. One of your fans."

I shushed my sister and smiled at the nurse. "Do you happen to have a deck of cards?"

She winced. "I'm sorry, I don't. I'm about to go on break. I could pop down to the gift shop if you'd like."

"Thank you, but I can go down when my parents get back."

The nurse blushed redder. "I don't mind."

Fiona smiled. "That would be lovely. I'm not sure when my parents will return, and I don't want to be alone."

The nurse smiled. "It's settled, then."

I pulled a ten-pound note from my billfold. "It's very kind of you. My sister is already getting bored."

She giggled in a nervous reaction to my comment. "All right, I'll be back before you know it."

When she left, I turned to Fiona. "I can't believe you sent that poor girl on a mission for cards."

Fi grinned. "I've never used your celebrity status to get a favor before. This could be fun."

"Oh no. It's against the rules."

"What rules?" Some of the dullness had left her eyes and her skin even had a little color.

"My rules. I've grown up." I held out the water for her. "Drink this."

She took another long draw on the straw, and afterwards had to catch her breath. "I know. I've watched you."

"You have? Wow. Thank you." I grinned and tried to hide my astonishment at how exhausted she was after merely sipping from a straw. I stood. "I'm no Mum, but do you want me to brush your hair or something?"

She looked at me. "My famous brother brushing my hair? Sure. Actually, I'd love to get out of this bed and sit in a chair."

"Can we wait for the nurse to come back? As weak as you are, I don't feel good about doing it on my own."

"Fine. Then help me sit up so you can untangle this mess."

She took a few deep breaths. "There's a brush in the cupboard."

It took a bit of doing but I managed to situate Fiona so that I could brush her hair. It felt good to do something for her. After a minute, though, she sighed. "I need to lean back."

Her eyes closed as soon as her head lay on the pillow. I don't know what I'd expected, but it wasn't for my sister to be too weak to carry out basic tasks.

I had just about settled into my chair when my mobile rang. I had a Facetime call. I prayed it was Jenna when I hit Accept on my screen.

My heart nearly burst when I saw Jenna's face.

"Hello." I grinned into the phone.

"Hi." Jenna smiled back, but there was worry in that smile and in those eyes.

"What's the matter?"

She tucked her lips. "Well, the tabloids have found me."

I ran a hand over my face. "Oh God, Jenna. I'm sorry. What happened?"

"I was heading out for a run. I'd made it all the way to the end of the driveway before I heard the sound of the camera click. The guy was hiding behind his car. When I heard the camera, I didn't know what it was. I just froze."

"Jenna—" She didn't deserve this.

"With all the active shooter drills we do, my first thought was that it was a gun. Then the questions started."

My throat went dry. "What questions?"

"Were you abusive? Had I talked to Cara Gentry? Had we had sex yet?"

"Oh, God." Everything inside me squeezed. "I'm so sorry."

"I didn't know what to say. I just stood there. Then Josh nailed the guy with his basketball."

"I hope it knocked his camera out of his hands."

"No. But he yelled at Josh. Started calling him names. I lost it. I started yelling back and the whole time the guy took pictures. Andrew and Josh pulled me away and walked me back inside. I'm pretty sure Andrew flipped him off."

"I hope he did. That was horrible. They usually leave me alone."

"Welcome to America. I thought the British paparazzi were supposed to be the bad ones." Tears filled her eyes and my heart squeezed. I needed to be there. I needed to be with her.

"Listen. I have a personal assistant. She's called Avery. I'll give her Melanie Joy's number. She can help you with this until I get back. I'm so sorry."

"You have a personal assistant?" Her voice shook and she flitted her eyes away as though she didn't want to look at me. "Of course you do."

"I'm sorry. Please. Just hang on. I'll be there on Monday and we'll sort it."

She nodded and swiped tears from her cheeks. "I guess until then, I'll depend on your PA."

Panic surged through me at her tone. "No. Oh God. I've messed this up. Please."

"I've got to go. Tell your sister I'm praying for her."

The call ended and my heart stopped beating.

My sister's voice traveled from across the room. "That your girlfriend?"

"I hope so."

She opened her eyes. "I wouldn't mention your PA again."

I rubbed my hands over my eyes. "I figured that."

"She's American?"

"Yeah. Jenna Wiley."

"Nice name. You should go to her now. Why are you waiting?"

"Dad has to go with me."

She opened her eyes a little wider. "Oh, you're making a movie with her? In America?"

"Not with her. But I am making a movie. It's complicated."

She patted the side of her bed. "I'm not going anywhere. Entertain me while we wait for Nurse Bright-eyes to come back with the cards."

I called Avery and filled her in on what had happened to Jenna. I gave her Melanie Joy's number and hoped she really could sort it.

When I ended the call, my sister shook her head at me. "Impressive. You really have grown up."

"Shut up." I pulled my chair close to her bed. "Before you get too impressed, let me tell you about how messed up my love life is."

I'd just finished my story when the nurse came in with the cards and my ten quid. "The gift shop didn't charge." She blushed as she handed me the cards.

I looked at them and laughed. *"Morlich Castle."*

"I liked the irony." She worried her hands and looked like there was more she wanted to say.

"Is there something else?"

Her face turned bright red. "Not really. Just that nobody believes the rubbish they're putting out there."

"Thank you." I held up the cards so Fi could see them. "Wanna see which card I got?"

"I'm sure it's the joker." Fiona looked at the nurse. "I'm actually getting hungry."

"Good. I'll see what we have."

She left the room and Fiona sighed. "How do you put up with all that fawning?"

"You get used to it. People just want to be kind." I opened the pack of cards. We never got around to playing because we were laughing too hard at the images on the back. The cards had apparently been made after the second season, because every image of me was when I was at that awkward stage.

There was one picture of me climbing the banks of a burn.

My feet looked twice as big as the rest of me and that sent Fiona into a laughing/coughing fit. Which was about the time Mum and Dad rushed into the room.

Mum practically flew to Fiona. "Are you all right?"

"No." Fiona managed to catch her breath. "Golden Boy here is killing me with that deck of cards."

Mum relaxed as soon as she saw that Fiona was teasing. "What cards?"

I spread them on the bedside table. We all had a good laugh.

Until Mum went from laughing to crying.

Fi shot me a look. "See what you've done with your wee cards?"

Mum released a few chuckles through her tears. "It's just… I love seeing you two together like this."

Fiona grabbed my hand. "Me too. But Mum, Frasier needs to get back to America."

Dad flashed a tight smile. "We've got things in order."

Fiona rolled her eyes. "Sit down. I need to say something."

I stayed perched on her mattress. Mum and Dad sat on the little sofa centered under the window.

Fiona took a sip of water—on her own, I might add. "I know I've been a huge disappointment. I know you're worried. I'm scared. I'm terrified. But I want to get better. I want to come home."

Mum started to get up, but Dad pulled her against his side. "Let her finish."

Fiona continued, "I've wanted to come home for so long. But I wasn't strong enough to leave Ben. When I finally got the nerve to leave, he found me and did this."

The color in Dad's face passed red and went to white. "We'll have him arrested."

Fi looked at me. "That would wreck your career."

I shook my head. "No, it won't. And even if it did, I don't care."

"Are you sure? Because I haven't been a saint, but I think the police will be interested in more than what he did to me."

"Of course I'm sure." I squeezed her hand tight. "He doesn't get to get away with this."

She nodded and a few tears splashed onto her cheeks. "Then I want to talk to the police. I want to tell them everything."

"Okay." Mum's voice was dry and she had a distant stare.

Fiona released my hand. "Mum? Are you okay?"

Mum stood. "I wish we'd gotten to you sooner."

Fiona shook her head. "It doesn't matter. I'm here now. I'm going to get better." She raised an eyebrow at me. "Now Dad, get Frasier back to America before he drives me insane."

26

Jenna

I HANDED the phone to Melanie Joy and looked across the back patio. "I can't do this."

"Don't say that." She propped her feet on the coffee table. "Frasier said it wouldn't last."

"What if it does? What if I'm a joke? Did you hear the way Jack Ramsey said, 'Just ask Jenna Wiley'?"

"Yeah. But he doesn't know what you and Frasier have." She lowered her feet and turned toward me. "Look, Jenna. I've known you since you moved here. You are one of the strongest women I know. You're also one of the nicest."

"Me? Melanie Joy, we all take our cues from you."

She shook her head. "Don't be ridiculous. You have no idea what thoughts swirl in my head. Anyway, the point is, Frasier deserves a chance with you. You do still like him, right?"

"Yes." I nestled a little deeper into the corner of the L-shaped sofa. "I really do. As much as I preached about not needing a guy, I like him so much."

"There's a difference between need and want. Clearly, you

don't need a guy. But there's nothing wrong with wanting to be with Frasier."

"I wish I knew what to expect."

Melanie Joy's phone rang. "It's an unknown number from the United Kingdom."

"I'll pay for the charge."

She handed me the phone. "Don't be silly. Just tell me everything."

I answered. "Hello. This is Jenna Wiley."

"Hello, Jenna. I'm Avery Sutherland. Mr. Anderson's personal assistant." Her accent was clipped but pleasant.

"Hi." And that's when the epinephrine must have been released into my body, because everything trembled, including my voice.

"Frasier said the pap have been giving you a bit of trouble."

I nodded as if she could see me. Then answered, "Yes."

"Horrible creatures. Unfortunately, there are almost no laws to protect you, but there are ways to deal with them."

"Okay."

"First, know that as soon as Frasier gets back on set, they'll likely leave you alone. He really leads an unremarkable life compared to other celebs. Until then, it's best to be aware that they're there, but to ignore them. Remember, they're in it for the money shot. They can't sell your photo unless they get a clean shot of your face. Have you engaged with them?"

"Engaged?" I knew what she meant, but for some reason my brain was not allowing me to speak intelligently.

"Talked to them in any way?"

"Yes. I, um, yelled at one." I told her about the incident.

"That's unfortunate. If he took a picture of you shouting, that's a money shot. But it's not a disaster. Are you on Twitter, darling?"

"Twitter? Yes."

"I suggest you get ahead of the photo. Post something cheeky about the pap invading your privacy. Make a joke of it. The public love that. Can you do that?"

"Yes. I think so."

"Brilliant. Now give this number to your parents. I'm sure they have questions. I'm just a phone call away."

"Okay. Thank you."

"Darling?"

"Yes?"

"I'm sure you're asking yourself whether Frasier is worth all this. Trust me, he is. Call me any time. And don't forget to give your parents my number."

We hung up and I flopped down on the sofa cushion. "She was all darling this and darling that and all I could say was okay."

"It wasn't that bad."

"It was. She's probably wondering what Frasier is doing with me."

"Stop it." Melanie Joy's tone was serious and harsh. "What did I hear about Twitter?"

"I'm supposed to come up with something cheeky about the incident at my house." I signed on to my account through Melanie Joy's phone and together we came up with:

> *For some reason the paparazzi have decided to follow this small-town Texan. I kind of lost it when they went after my brothers. #dontmesswithTexans*

When we finished, Melanie Joy stood. "Come on, I'll take you home. You can give your parents her number."

I sat up. "Thanks for picking me up in the first place. I don't think I could have driven."

"I just want to hear what your grandma had to say to the

camera guy." Melanie Joy laughed. "I bet he hightailed it out of town after she finished with him."

"I hope so." I crawled off the sofa. "Come on."

My hopes that Grandma had run the paparazzi out of town were crushed when we pulled up to the house. Three more had joined the first one.

Melanie Joy pulled into the drive. "I guess it's going to be a while before this all blows over."

I took a deep breath. "Will you walk to the house with me?"

"Sure." She started to open her car door, but I stopped her.

"Avery said that they can't sell a picture unless they get a clear shot of our faces."

Melanie Joy smiled. "I have just the thing." She dug in her back seat and pulled out a floppy sun hat. "Here. Wear this."

"What about you?"

"They're not interested in me."

"Not yet. When they see your face, that's going to change."

Melanie Joy rolled her eyes. "That's not true, but if it'll make you feel better, I'll wear my ball cap." She pulled her cap from the backseat and shoved it low on her head. "Ready?"

We jetted from her car like it was about to explode. It would have been really cool if the front door had been unlocked. We could have slipped right in. But it wasn't. I nearly crashed face first into the wood. I frantically rang the doorbell.

Voices of the pap—as Avery called them—assaulted me.

"Who's your friend?"

"Give us a picture."

"Why won't you talk to Cara Gentry?"

"Any word from Frasier?"

When Mom finally opened the door, we practically fell inside. Mom shook her head at the cameras aimed at our house and closed the door. "Why didn't you use your key?"

"I left my purse here. When did those guys show up?"

"About twenty minutes ago. We need to do something about this." She looked out the front window. "Dad called the police, but there's nothing they can do unless they come on our property."

I looked at Melanie Joy and back at Mom. "Frasier's PA called on Melanie Joy's phone. She said to give you her number. She wants to talk to you and Dad."

Mom raised her brows. "Personal assistant? Okay. Sure. We want to talk to her too. Where's the number?"

Melanie Joy held up her cell.

"Come on." Mom led us into the kitchen.

Dad and Grandma were at the table both drinking a beer. Dad looked up. "Here's our little celebrity now." His tone was sarcastic, without a hint of humor.

"Don't call me that. This is a nightmare."

Grandma shook her head. "Poor Frasier. I can't imagine being followed like that."

"Poor Frasier?" Mom's voice rose an octave. "He chose this. Jenna did not."

"No. But I choose Frasier." All eyes snapped to me. It was a bold statement. Even Melanie Joy looked shocked.

My dad's face lost some of its angry color. "What exactly does that mean?"

I tried to look a little taller, a little more mature. "It means that I really like him and I'm willing to see where this goes despite the paparazzi. He said that they'll tire of us and go away. I'm going to trust him."

"What about the rest of the family? What about your brothers? They can't even play basketball out there." Mom's voice was tight with anger.

"If they want to play, I'll go somewhere and take those leeches with me."

Mom shook her head. "I wouldn't ask you to do that. I just wish there was something we could do."

"Frasier won't be here until Monday. Surely by then they'll get bored with us and leave."

But they didn't get bored with us and they didn't leave. The more we tried to ignore them, the more aggressive they got. By Saturday, we were practically prisoners in our own home.

Josh tossed a football across the den to Andrew. "Come on, Mom. We don't care if they take pictures of us. Just let us out of the house."

Melanie Joy and Bree had come over to keep me company and we were trying to watch a movie, but with everybody in the same room it was impossible. I clicked off the TV. "I think by ignoring them we're making it worse."

Dad stood and snatched the football out of the air before Josh could catch Andrew's return. "Have you talked to Frasier?"

"Yes. But what can he do all the way from Scotland?" I was frustrated too, but it wasn't his fault. It wasn't anybody's fault. Except the tabloids.

Dad's phone dinged and he looked at the screen. "It's from Chief. It says, *Look out the window.*"

Melanie Joy and Bree exchanged a look and smiled. Melanie Joy tapped her fingertips together like an evil genius. "And so it begins."

Ten people rushed to the window. A black truck had stopped in front of the house. I recognized one of the three guys in the back as Cody Biggs. He lifted a trash can and shuffled the contents out of it as the truck rolled slowly by.

Josh said, "Is that *manure?*"

Grandma patted him on the shoulder. "No, son. That's shit."

Dad scrubbed his hand across his face. "That's not going to help." He went for the door and we all followed.

It wasn't until I saw the paparazzi shaking out their clothes that I realized the manure had hit more than their cars.

The camera guy who'd yelled at my brother shouted, "The rental car company will have something to say about this."

One of the other boys kicked the empty can out of the truck. "We're so sorry, sir. We can't control it if it falls out while we're driving down the street."

One of the camera guys held up his phone. "Let's see what the police say." But before his finger touched the screen, we all turned to the clip-clop sound coming down the street.

Kenzie and Ryan Quinn were on horseback, heading toward the paparazzi. And behind them was a third rider. He wore a cowboy hat and dark sunglasses, but I'd know the contour of those neck muscles anywhere.

My blood didn't know whether to drop to my feet or rush to my head—so it just swirled inside me like a tornado, leaving me breathless.

Josh looked up at the girls. "Did you ride all the way?"

Kenzie shook her head. "No, we parked our trailer in front of Chief's house."

The girls nudged their horses closer to the men. "You want a story?" Kelsey called. "Write about how two girls on horse-back ran the rats out of town."

The guy with the phone said, "That's it. This is harass-ment. I'm calling the cops."

Except the cops were coming down the street. Okay, one cop car, but that's all we had.

The car stopped behind the black truck. Officer Jimmy Davis stepped out of the driver's side of the car and the chief the other. "Something going on here?"

That's when I noticed a figure in the back of the truck filming the scene with his phone. Chris Gomez tapped it off and held it up. "It's a shame about the manure. I didn't catch that on the video. Just you shouting."

I turned back to Frasier. I wanted to run to him. I wanted him to run to me. But this had to play out first.

Frasier lifted a lasso from his saddle horn. "Officer, do you want me to help you contain these men?"

Two of the men with cameras were snapping pictures, but the others were putting their equipment away. The loud-mouthed one shouted, "You can't do this!"

Officer Davis shook his head. "These young people haven't broken any laws that I can see. You haven't been touched. There's no ordinance that people can't ride their horses in residential areas."

"What about this horseshit?"

"Well sir, that's an unfortunate accident. I suggest if you want to avoid stepping in it in the future, that you move on down the road. Austin has loads more interesting people to take your little pictures of."

I expected the men to argue, but they didn't. They loaded their cameras into their rental cars and slung a little gravel as they left.

Frasier handed the reins to Kenzie and swung down from the horse. He hadn't taken two steps before I ran to him and threw my arms around him. He hugged me tight and buried his face in my neck. "I missed you."

I wanted to the hug to last forever. No. I wanted the hug to turn into a kiss that would last forever.

He pulled away and took my hands. And then his gaze met mine and tingles spread through me. I almost didn't hear the words that came out of his beautiful mouth. "I wanted to come straight here, but Melanie Joy convinced me to have a little fun with these jerks first."

That cooled those tingles. "Melanie Joy?"

My entire family snapped their gazes to her.

She curtseyed. "I'm pretty proud of myself."

Frasier nodded. "I called her to tell you I was coming—since you don't have a phone. She cooked this whole thing up."

I looked up at Frasier. "That's probably going to be all over social media."

He grinned. "Chris live-streamed it. They won't be able to sell their photos to a grocery store supplement."

He looked at my family staring at us and leaned close to my ear. "I really want to kiss you."

I grabbed him around the waist. "Me too. But I'd prefer not to have an audience."

He nodded. "I can wait."

Then without warning, the loop of a lasso fell over our shoulders and ensnared us. It wasn't a pleasant experience having the stiff rope slap around me. Or when Kenzie pulled on the long end, tightening the nose. We had to wrap our arms around each other to keep from falling.

Whoops sounded around us. Kenzie said, "I've been practicing."

I looked up at Frasier. "This is like a Hollywood ending."

He smiled back. "No. This is like a real-life beginning." And audience or not, he tipped his head and lowered his mouth to mine.

Epilogue

FRASIER

THE LIMO STOPPED and I turned to my date. "Are you nervous?"

"Aye. Yes. I shouldn't be here."

"Aye. You should. I'm so proud of you." I was on the verge of getting choked up again. Fiona had worked hard at recovery and was now living with Mum and Dad. When she'd stepped off the plane with Mum, I couldn't believe the change. I had my beautiful sister back.

Fiona smiled at me. "For what? Being a normal person?"

"Exactly."

"What about Jenna? Are you sure she's okay with me taking her place?"

"She's happy to be with Mum and Dad. You're *my* red-carpet date."

Fiona smiled. "I'm proud of you, little brother. So proud."

The door opened and I got out and reached for Fiona's hand. The cameras went crazy as she stepped from the car. One of the paparazzi called out, "Who's the new girl?"

I turned to the man and smiled. "My sister, Fiona. My girlfriend is with my parents."

Clicks went crazy after that.

Fiona held tight to me. "They're going twist this."

"No. It's already on social media. He was just trying to get a reaction out of me." I tucked her arm close. "Enjoy this, Fi. Enjoy the bright side of the industry."

She smiled. "I'll try."

During the movie's L.A. premiere, Jenna sat to my left while Fiona was on my right. I held Jenna's hand and practically squeezed the blood out of it when the movie started. I was relieved that the crowd genuinely seemed to like it. Spirits were high at the afterparty. Everybody was laughing and talking about the best scenes. All I wanted to do was get Jenna alone.

We'd spent as much free time together as we could during the filming. As soon as I turned eighteen, it became easier. Dad flew back to be with Mum and I was at last free. But after the film wrapped and leading up to the premiere, we'd had almost no time together. I'd barely made it to her graduation. Then I had press. She had University to prepare for.

The good news was that I had a contract for another movie, to be filmed in Atlanta. So at least we would be in the same country. I was to leave in three weeks. Jenna was to leave for University in two. We were going to spend every second of that time together.

She sipped from her fizzy water. "Are you okay?"

"Aye." I took in her body-hugging emerald dress and managed to resist pulling her against me and kissing her until we were both breathless. "I just want some time with you."

She put her drink on a table and wrapped her arms around my waist. "Then let's go somewhere."

"How does Scotland sound?" I held my breath.

"I do have a passport. I'm dying to see your country. I want to see where you grew up. Meet your friends. Hear all the embarrassing stories."

I pulled her closer. "How soon can you leave?"

"I have to get back to Hillside to get my passport and clothes. So it all depends on how fast Avery can book the flight."

"Going somewhere?" Fiona's voice broke into our conversation.

"Home." Frasier smiled at his sister. "Want to come?"

She shook her head. "No. I'll come back with Mum and Dad. I'm going to enjoy the sunny side of your job." She winked at us. "Go. I'll tell Mum and Dad."

I grabbed Jenna's hand and we headed for the long line of limos. I had no idea which one was ours, but fortunately the driver called to us. Before I crawled into the back seat, I said, "We're ready to go to our hotel, but could you wait for us? As soon as we change, we have a flight to catch."

Once we were in the backseat, I raised the privacy window. While Jenna called her mom, I texted Avery. Jenna had planned to visit Scotland, but I was afraid her parents wouldn't fancy the idea of a departure this sudden.

Jenna gave me a wide-eyed look and held up crossed fingers as she spoke into the phone. "Of course his parents will be there."

"In three days," I whispered.

She shushed me with her expression. "I'll call you with our flight information as soon as we get it. You don't have to pick us up at the airport. It'll be late....Okay. I promise."

She ended the call and tucked the phone into her sparkly evening bag. "I can't believe they didn't put up more of an argument. Mom said they trust you."

"Oh they do, do they?" I pulled the ends of my bow tie and let them dangle around my neck as I unbuttoned the top two buttons of my shirt and untucked it from my trousers.

"Yes." She giggled, grabbed the ends of the tie and pulled me to her.

We kissed until the driver pulled up at our hotel.

When the car stopped, we didn't wait for the bellman. We rushed from the car and into the lobby. We kissed in the elevator and all the way to her room.

When the door of the room closed behind us, Jenna wrapped her arms around my neck and smiled that soul-stealing smile of hers. "I feel like my heart is about to explode."

"Mine too." I nestled her against my body. "Jenna, sweet Jenna. You are my everything. I promise you, we'll make this work. I'll be in College Station as much as possible. And you know—I'll fly you to wherever I am during school holidays."

"I don't want to leave you. Part of me wants to leave college behind. But my parents are right."

"If we're meant to be, we'll still be meant to be when you finish school." I quoted the line we'd heard ad nauseum over the past months.

We laughed and then just stared at each other. It wasn't awkward or weird. It was my soul reaching out to hers, or maybe her soul reaching out to mine, or maybe both meeting in the middle. Whatever *it* was, it filled me with joy and warmth and happiness.

"Jenna Wiley. You do not need a man to be successful, but I need you. I need you every day, with every beat of my heart." I pressed my lips against her neck and whispered. "I love you."

Jenna pulled away and her gaze dug into my soul. "I love you, Ethan Smith. I'm so glad you're the real Frasier Anderson." She raised her mouth to mine and kissed me.

This kiss was better than the other kisses we'd shared. This kiss was full of love, and promises, and hope for the future.

And the odds were very much in our favor.

THE END

Afterword

I got the idea for this book after talking to one of the producers of a superhero movie in which they embedded a young English actor in a New York school to get a "high school experience." I have wanted to bring a little bit of Scotland to Hillside for a long time. After hearing that story, I just knew I'd found my next Hickville hero. I hope you think so too.

No book comes together without help and support from friends and family. This book is no exception. I would like to send my heartfelt thanks to Solveig MacCallum and her mum, Carola, for helping keep the Scottish bits real. To my sweet friend, Aileen Latcham, thank you for sharing the inside world of movies and production schedules. Thank you to my awesome editor Shelley Bates for making sure all the *p*'s and *q*'s and commas are in the right places.

And to you, dear reader, thank you for continuing on this journey through Hickville. I invite you to come along on the next journey—a romantic comedy series set in Scotland. I can't think of a better place to find love than while hiking the many trails in the Scottish Highlands. There will be culture, a wee bit of history, and probably a Gaelic phrase or two. And there will definitely be Scottish heroes and Texas heroines. See you there!

Meanwhile, be sure to visit my website at marykarlik.com to sign up for my newsletter, where you'll hear about my upcoming books (and maybe even a little gossip from Hickville).

Mar Sin Leat,

Mary Karlik

Also by Mary Karlik

Hickville High series

Welcome to Hickville High

Hickville Confessions

Hickville Redemption

Hickville Confidential

Hickville Crossroads

Fairy Trafficking series

Magic Harvest

Magic Heist

About the Author

Mary Karlik has always been a dreamer. When she was a teen, she read *The Lion, The Witch and the Wardrobe*, and then sat in every wardrobe in her Nanna's home, trying to open the door to Narnia. She didn't find it, but she did discover her voice as an author—one filled with her young-adult self, and grounded in her roots as a Texan and her Scottish heritage, nourished by obscure Scottish folklore.

You can find her Texas roots in her *Hickville* series of YA contemporary romance, which has been described as "100% solid storytelling," and begins with *Welcome to Hickville High*, a "lovely story about growing up." She digs deep into her Scottish roots—there is magic there, she just knows it—for her new *Fairy Trafficking* series, YA epic fantasy, beginning with *Magic Harvest.*

Mary recently moved from the beautiful Sangre de Cristo mountains of Northern New Mexico, where she was a certified professional ski instructor, to Texas. She is currently studying Scottish Gaelic at the Sabhal Mòr Ostaig in Skye. Mary also earned her MFA in Writing Popular Fiction from Seton Hill University, has a B.S. degree from Texas A&M University, and is a Registered Nurse.

Mary loves to connect with her readers. Please join her mailing list for giveaways and updates about her upcoming books. Visit her website at www.marykarlik.com, or send an email to her at mary@marykarlik.com.

Made in USA - North Chelmsford, MA
1109957_9780996155694
05.19.2020 1445